AF522123

THE MYTH OF THE HOLY COW

D.N. JHA

navayana

The Myth of the Holy Cow

First published by Navayana Publishing Pvt Ltd, 2009
Eleventh reprint, February 2025
ISBN: 978-8189059163

Navayana Publishing Pvt Ltd
155 2nd Floor
Shahpur Jat, New Delhi 110049
www.navayana.org

Printed by Sanjiv Palliwal at Param Offset, New Delhi
Subscribe to updates at navayana.org/subscribe

'. . . gāṃ ālabhate[2]; yajño vai gauḥ;
yajñaṃ evā labhate; atho annaṃ vai gauḥ;
annaṃ evāvarundhe. . . .'

Taittirīya Brāhmaṇa, III. 9.8.2-3 (Ānandāśrama-sanskritgranthāvaliḥ 37, vol. III, 3rd.edn., Poona, 1979).

'(At the horse-sacrifice) he (the Adhvaryu) seizes (binds) the cow (i.e. cows). The cow is the sacrifice. (Consequently) it is the sacrifice he (the Sacrificer) thus obtains. And the cow certainly is food. (Consequently) it is food he thus obtains.'

English translation by Paul-Emile Dumont, *Proceedings of the American Philosophical Society*, 92.6 (December 1948), p. 485.

'. . . Silver foil or "varak" used for decorating sweets has more than just a pleasing look to it. It is made by placing thin metal strips between steaming intestines of freshly slaughtered animals. The metal is then pounded between ox-gut and the sheets are carefully transferred in special paper for marketing. . . .'

Bindu Jacob, 'More to it all than meets the Eye', *The Hindu*, 5 June 2001 (A news item based on a publication of the Animal Welfare Board of India under the Ministry of Social Justice and Empowerment, Government of India).

In memoriam
BHUVAN SINHA

Contents

About the Author

Dwijendra Narayan Jha is a former Professor of History at the University of Delhi. He was a National Lecturer in History (1984–85) and General President, Indian History Congress (2005). His publications include *Revenue System in Post-Maurya and Gupta Times* (1967), *Ancient India* (1977), *Studies in Early Indian Economic History* (1980), *Economy and Society in Early India: Issues and Paradigms* (1993), *Early India: A Concise History* (2004) and *Rethinking Hindu Identity* (forthcoming). He has to his credit several edited works including *Feudal Social Formation in Early India* (1987), *Society and Ideology in India: Essays in Honour of R.S. Sharma* (1996), *The Feudal Order: State, Society and Ideology in Early Medieval India* (2000) and *Mind over Matter: Essays on Mentalities in Medieval India* (forthcoming), the last one jointly edited with Eugenia Vanina. Most of Jha's writings have been translated into several Indian languages and some into foreign languages as well.

Preface to the Navayana Edition

For more than a century the sanctity of the Indian cow has been not only a matter of academic debate—communalist Hindus and their fundamentalist organizations have even tried to hijack it into the political arena. Oddly, and despite historical evidence to the contrary, they have clung to the idea that this animal has always been sacrosanct and inviolable and that their ancestors, especially the Vedic Indians, did not eat its flesh. They have also associated beef-eating in India with the coming of Islam and have treated it as the identifying mark of the Muslim community. The present work, however, argues that the 'holiness' of the cow is a myth and its flesh was very much a part of the early Indian non-vegetarian food regimen and dietary traditions, though attitudinal divergences to beef consumption are also reflected in Indian religious and secular texts spread over a long period. It underlines the fact that beef-eating was not Islam's 'baneful bequeathal' to India. Nor can abstention from it be a mark of 'Hindu' identity, notwithstanding the averments of Hindutva forces who have tried to foster the false consciousness of the 'otherness' of the followers of Islam.

The present study is based mainly on Hindu, Buddhist and Jaina religious scriptures. The earliest textual evidence of flesh eating generally and beef eating in particular comes from the oldest Indian texts – the Vedas and their auxiliaries – which are religious and ritualistic in nature and range in date from 1500 BC to about 600 BC. It is from them that most normative works like the Dharmasūtras, Gṛhyasūtras, Smṛtis, the didactic portions of the epics (*Mahābhārata* and *Rāmāyaṇa*) and Purāṇas, commentaries and religious digests and much of the Brāhmaṇical rituals derive their sanction, at least in theory. Buddhist canonical works in Pāli as well as exegetical and narrative literature in Pāli and Sanskrit provide information relating to the dietary culture of the adherents of Buddhism and abound in references to their non-vegetarian food habits. The composition of the Buddhist canon was more or less complete before the Christian era though non-canonical works continued to be written till very late. References to flesh eating in Jaina literature are fewer in number than in the Hindu and Buddhist texts, but they are there and have been taken into account as far as possible. The sacred texts of the Jainas were codified in Prākrit, perhaps not earlier than the fifth century, though a vast corpus of their commentarial and narrative literature in Prākrit and Sanskrit was written subsequently. Early Indian medical texts and classical Sanskrit secular literature generally corroborate the evidence drawn from texts having distinct religious affiliations. The language of the texts, which form the basis of our study, varies greatly, from the archaic Vedic Sanskrit to the much more developed and complicated Sanskrit of later periods as well as to Pāli and Prākrit. Extensive citations from these varied Indian sources have necessitated the profuse use of diacritic marks though the reader may find them irritating at times.

A few words are necessary to explain the vicissitudes the present book has had to face on account of the increasing weight of Hindu fundamentalism in India. Its original publisher suddenly discovered excessive *sang-de-boeuf* in the manuscript in the final stages of printing and recanted from his professional commitment under pressure. Shortly afterwards, I began to get threats from unidentified callers asking me not to go ahead with the publication. Undeterred by all this Matrix Books, a new enterprising publishing house based in Delhi, mustered enough courage to publish the book promptly in the first week of August 2001. But some right-wing politicians and groups of religious fanatics, without reading a single page, termed it 'blasphemous', demanded my arrest and succeeded in obtaining a court order restraining the circulation of the book, and a self-appointed custodian of 'Hinduism' even sentenced me to death. The book was therefore published abroad by Verso (London) at the initiative of Tariq Ali to whom I am deeply beholden for defending my right to academic freedom and defeating attempts at censorship. The book was thus made available to readers in the West where, by and large, it has been well received.

During the last eight years since the first publication of the book I have come across considerable new material, bearing on the social dimension of beef taboo, its linkage with the growth of untouchability as well as the larger question of Hindu identity politics in contemporary India. But integrating the new material into the present book and developing fresh arguments on its basis would amount to rewriting it, a task I found daunting on account of my other academic commitments. All that I could do for this Indian edition was to add as an appendix a longish extract from the classic work of Dr B.R. Ambedkar, whose writings on the origin of untouchability, despite the great strides Indian historical scholarship has taken after him, remain a landmark in the study of social marginality in India. Moreover, I found it difficult to disregard the eagerness and social commitment of S. Anand of Navayana but for whose insistence I would not have probably thought of a second Indian edition of the book.

The inspiration to write this book originally came from Professor R.S. Sharma, but I have received much help from a number of scholars. Professor Shingo Einoo, Institute of Oriental Culture, University of Tokyo, made it possible for me to access many Sanskrit sources as well as relevant German and French works. Professor Michael Witzel, Harvard University, was kind enough to send me a copy of his unpublished paper on the sacredness of the cow, and Professor Michelguglielmo Torri, University of Turin, provided me photocopies of articles from libraries in Rome. Tiziana Lorenzetti, Toshie Awaya and Ryosuke Furui helped in myriad ways. At home, many friends and colleagues, notably Professors K.M. Shrimali, T.K. Venkatsubramanian, B.P. Sahu, Nayanjot Lahiri and Shri B.N. Varma supported my endeavour. Dr Ranjana Bhattacharya, Dr Vishwa Mohan Jha, Dr Shalini Shah, Ratan Lal, Shankar Kumar, Ajit Kumar, Gopal, Amar and Manoj assisted me in various ways. I am grateful to all of them. But I always run short of words when it comes to expressing gratitude to my wife, Rajrani, who has silently suffered me all these years. Bhuvan Sinha, who always stood by me in times of stress, is no more with us and I dedicate this edition of the book to his memory.

Abbreviations

AgniP	*Agni Purāṇa*
AitB	*Aitareya Brāhmaṇa*
Āṅgīrasa	*Āṅgīrasasmṛti*
ĀpDS	*Āpastamba Dharmasūtra*
ĀpGS	*Āpastamba Gṛhyasūtra*
AŚ	*Arthaśāstra*
ĀśGS	*Āśvalāyana Gṛhyasūtra*
Atri	*Atrismṛti*
AV	*Atharvaveda*
BaudhDS	*Baudhāyana Dharmasūtra*
BaudhGS	*Baudhāyana Gṛhyasūtra*
BhāradvājaSS	*Bhāradvāja Śrautasūtra*
BhaviṣyaP	*Bhaviṣya Purāṇa*
BṛhaddharmaP	*Bṛhaddharma Purāṇa*
Br. Up.	*Bṛhadāraṇyaka Upaniṣad*

BSOAS	*Bulletin of the School of Oriental and African Studies*
Caraka	*Caraka Saṃhitā*
Ch.Up.	*Chāndogya Upaniṣad*
Cikitsā	*Cikitsāsthānam*
Devala	*Devalasmṛti*
EI	*Epigraphia Indica*
GautDS	*Gautama Dharmasūtra*
GB	*Gopatha Brāhmaṇa*
GobhGS	*Gobhila Gṛhyasūtra*
HirGS	*Hiraṇyakeśī Gṛhyasūtra*
HiraṇyakeśīSS	*Hiraṇyakeśī Śrautasūtra*
J	*Jātaka*
JAOS	*Journal of the American Oriental Society*
JB	*Jaiminīya Brāhmaṇa*
KB	*Kauṣītaki Brāhmaṇa*
KālikāP	*Kālikā Purāṇa*
KauśGS	*Kauśitaka Gṛhyasūtra*
KauśS	*Kauśikasūtra*
KāṭhGS	*Kāṭhaka Gṛhyasūtra*
KātyāyanaSS	*Kātyāyana Srautasūtra*
KhādiraGS	*Khādira Gṛhyasūtra*
KūrmaP	*Kūrma Purāṇa*
MārkaṇḍeyaP	*Markaṇḍeya Purāṇa*
MatsyaP	*Matsya Purāṇa*
Mbh	*Mahābhārata*
MS	*Maitrāyaṇī Saṃhitā*

Nārada	*Nāradasmṛti*
Pārāsara	*Pārāsarasmṛti*
PāraskaraGS	*Pāraskara Gṛhyasūtra*
ṚV	*Ṛgveda*
Śarīra	*Śarīrasthānam*
ŚB	*Śatapatha Brāhmaṇa*
SBE	*Sacred Books of the East*
Saṃvartta	*Saṃvarttasmṛti*
Śaṅkha	*Śaṅkhasmṛti*
ŚāṅkhGS	*Śāṅkhyāyana Gṛhyasūtra*
SkandaP	*Skanda Purāṇa*
SII	*South Indian Inscriptions*
Sūtra	*Sūtrasthāna*
TB	*Taittirīya Brāhmaṇa*
TS	*Taittirīya Saṃhitā*
VaikhGS	*Vaikhānasa Gṛhyasūtra*
VasiṣṭhaDS	*Vasiṣṭha Dharmasūtra*
Vimāna	*Vimānasthānam*
ViṣṇuP	*Viṣṇu Purāṇa*
ViṣṇuDS	*Viṣṇu Dharmasūtra*
ViṣṇudharmottaraP	*Viṣṇudharmottara Purāṇa*
Yāj	*Yājñavalkyasmṛti*
Yama	*Yamasmṛti*

Note on Transliterations

अ	a	ए	e	क	k	च	c
आ	ā	ऐ	ai	ख	kh	छ	ch
इ	i	ओ	o	ग	g	ज	j
ई	ī	औ	au	घ	gh	झ	jh
उ	u	ऋ	ṛ	ङ	ṅ	ञ्	ñ
ऊ	ū						
ट्	ṭ	त	t	प	p	य्	y
ठ्	ṭh	थ	th	फ्	ph	र्	r
ड्	ḍ	द	d	ब्	b	ल्	l
ढ्	ḍh	ध	dh	भ्	bh	व्	v
ण	ṇ	न्	n	म्	m	श्	ś
ष्	ṣ	Anusvāra (.) ṃ					
स्	s	Visarga (:) ḥ					
ह्	h						

Introduction

> Mother cow is in many ways better than the mother who gave us birth. Our mother gives us milk for a couple of years and then expects us to serve her when we grow up. Mother cow expects from us nothing but grass and grain. Our mother often falls ill and expects service from us. Mother cow rarely falls ill. Our mother when she dies means expenses of burial or cremation. Mother cow is as useful dead as when alive.[1]

These are the words of Mahatma Gandhi explaining the importance of the cow. His explanation, devoid of religious rigmarole, is quite simple: the cow is important because of its resource value in an agrarian society whose members derive a substantial part of their sustenance from its milk and other dairy products. But Gandhi contradicts himself and says elsewhere, 'The central fact of Hinduism is cow protection. . . . The cow protection ideal set up by Hinduism is essentially different from and transcends the dairy ideal of the West. The latter is based on economic values, the former . . . lays stress on the spiritual aspect, viz., the idea of penance and self sacrifice for the martyred innocence which it embodies. . . .'[2] This statement of Gandhi is significantly different from the former, in that it lays stress on his religious commitment to protect the cow.

Most Hindus today are guided by a religious concern for cow protection. Therefore an average Indian, rooted in what appears to him as his traditional Hindu religious heritage, carries the load of the misconception that his ancestors, especially the Vedic Aryans, attached great importance to the cow on account of its inherent sacredness. The 'sacred' cow has come to be considered a symbol of community identity of the Hindus whose cultural tradition is often imagined as threatened by Muslims, who are thought of as beef eaters. The sanctity of the cow has, therefore, been announced with the flourish of trumpets and has been wrongly traced back to the Vedas, which are supposedly of divine origin and the fountainhead of all knowledge and wisdom. In other words, some sections of Indian society trace the concept of sacred cow to the very period when it was sacrificed and its flesh was eaten.

More importantly, the cow has tended to become a political instrument in the hands of rulers over time. The Mughal emperors Babar, Akbar, Jahangir and Aurangzeb are said to have imposed a restricted ban on cow slaughter to accommodate Jaina or Brāhmaṇical sensibilities and veneration of the cow.[3] Similarly Shivaji, sometimes viewed as an incarnation of God who descended on earth for the deliverance of the cow and the brāhmaṇa, is said to have proclaimed: 'We are Hindus and the rightful lords of the realm. It is not proper for us to witness cow slaughter and the oppression of brāhmaṇas.'[4] But the cow became a tool of mass political mobilization when the organized Hindu cow-protection movement, beginning with the Sikh Kuka (or Namdhari) sect in the Punjab around 1870 and later strengthened by the foundation of the first Gorakshini Sabha in 1882 by Dayanananda Sarasvati, made this animal a symbol of the unity of a wide ranging people, challenged the Muslim practice of its slaughter and provoked a series of serious communal riots in the 1880s and 1890s. Although attitudes to cow killing had hardened even earlier,[5] there was undoubtedly a 'dramatic intensification' of the cow protection movement when in 1888 the North-Western Provinces High Court decreed that a cow was not a sacred object.[6] Not surprisingly, cow slaughter very often became the pretext of Hindu-Muslim riots, especially those in Azamgarh district in the year 1893 when more than a hundred people were killed in different parts of the country. Similarly in 1912-13 violence rocked Ayodhya and a few years later, in 1917, Shahabad witnessed a disastrous communal conflagration.[7]

The killing of cattle seems to have emerged again and again as a troublesome issue on the Indian political scene even in independent India despite legislation by several states prohibiting cow slaughter and the Directive Principles of State Policy of the Constitution, which directs the Indian state to '. . . to take steps for . . . prohibiting the slaughter of cows and calves and other milch and draught cattle'. For instance, in 1966, nearly two decades after Independence, almost all communal political parties and organizations joined hands to mastermind a massive demonstration by several hundred thousand people in favour of a national ban on cow slaughter. This culminated in a violent rioting in front of the Indian Parliament and the death of at least eight persons and injury to many more. In April 1979, Acharya Vinoba Bhave, often called the spiritual heir to Mahatma Gandhi, went on a hunger strike to pressurize the central government to prohibit cow slaughter throughout the country and ended it after five days when he succeeded in getting the Prime Minister Morarji Desai's vague assurance that his government would expedite anti-slaughter legislation. After that the cow ceased to remain much of an issue in the Indian political arena for many years, though the management of cattle resources has been a matter of academic debate among sociologists, anthropologists, economists and different categories of policy framers.[8]

The veneration of the cow has been converted into a symbol of communal identity of the Hindus and obscurantist and fundamentalist forces obdurately refuse to appreciate that the cow was not always all that sacred in the Vedic and subsequent Brāhmaṇical and non-Brāhmaṇical traditions—or that its flesh, along with other varieties of meat, was quite often a part of *haute cuisine* in early India. Although the Shin, Muslims of Dardistan in Pakistan, look on the cow as other Muslims do the pig, avoid direct contact with cows, refuse to drink cow's milk or use cowdung as fuel and reject beef as food,[9] self-styled custodians of non-existent 'monolithic' Hinduism assert that the eating of beef was first introduced in India by the followers of Islam who came from outside and are foreigners in this country, little realizing that their Vedic ancestors were also foreigners who ate the flesh of the cow and various other animals. Fanaticism getting precedence over fact, it is not surprising that the Rashtriya Swayamsevak Sangh, the Vishwa Hindu Parishad, the Bajrang Dal and their numerous outfits have a national ban on cow slaughter on their agenda. The Chief Minister of Gujarat (Keshubhai Patel) announced some time ago, as a pre-election gimmick, the setting up of a separate department to preserve cow breeds and manage Hindu temples,[10] and recently a Bajrang Dal leader has even threatened to enrol 30 lakh activists in the anti-cow slaughter movement during the Bakrid of 2002.[11] So high-geared has been the propaganda about abstention from beef eating as a characteristic trait of 'Hinduism' that when the RSS tried to claim that Sikhs were Hindus, there was vehement opposition from them and a Sikh youth leader proposed, 'Why not slaughter a cow and serve beef in a gurudwara *langar*?'[12]

The communalists who have been raising a hullabaloo over the cow in the political arena do not realize that beef eating remained a fairly common practice for a long time in India and that the arguments for its prevalence are based on the evidence drawn from our own scriptures and religious texts. The response of historical scholarship to the communal perception of Indian food culture, therefore, has been sober and scholars have drawn attention to the textual evidence on the subject which, in fact, begins to be available in the oldest Indian religious text *Ṛgveda*, supposedly of divine origin. H.H. Wilson, writing in the first half of the nineteenth century, had asserted that 'the sacrifice of the horse or of the cow, the *gomedha* or *aśvamedha*, appears to have been common in the earliest periods of the Hindu ritual'.

The view that the practice of cow sacrifice and eating beef prevailed among the Indo-Aryans was, however, put forth most convincingly by Rajendra Lal Mitra in an article which first appeared in the *Journal of the Asiatic Society of Bengal* and subsequently formed a chapter of his book *The Indo-Aryans* published in 1891. In 1894 William Crooke, a British civil servant, collected an impressive amount of ethnographic data on popular religious beliefs and practices and devoted an entire chapter to the respect shown to animals including the cow.[13] Later, in 1912, he published an informative piece on the sanctity of the cow in India, but he also drew attention to the old practice of eating beef, and its survival in his own times.[14] In 1927, L.L. Sundara Ram made a strong case for cow protection for which he sought justification from the scriptures of different religions including Hinduism. While he did not deny that the Vedic people ate beef,[15] he blamed the Muslims for cow slaughter.

In the early 1940s P.V. Kane in his monumental five-volume *History of Dharmaśāstra* referred to some Vedic and early Dharmaśāstric passages that speak of cow slaughter and beef eating. H.D. Sankalia drew attention to literary as well as archaeological evidence of eating cattle flesh in ancient India.[16] Similarly, Laxman Shastri Joshi, a Sanskritist of unquestionable scholarship, drew attention to the Dharmaśāstra works that unequivocally support the prevalence of meat eating, including beef eating, in early India.[17]

Needless to say, the scholarship of all of authorities mentioned above was unimpeachable, and none of them seems to have anything to do with any anti-Hindu ideology. Nor can they be described as Marxists, whom the Sangh Parivar and the saffronized journalists and publicists have charged of distorting history. H.H. Wilson, for example, was the first occupant of the Chair of Sanskrit at Oxford in 1832 and was not as avowedly anti-Indian as many other imperialist scholars. Rajendra Lal Mitra, a product of the Bengal renaissance and a close associate of Rabindranath's elder brother Jyotindranath Tagore, made significant contribution to India's intellectual life, and was described by Max Mueller as the 'best living Indologist' of his time and by Rabindranath Tagore as 'the most beloved child of the muse'.[18] William Crooke was a well-known colonial ethnograher who wrote extensively on peasant life and popular religion without any marked prejudice against Hinduism.[19] L.L. Sundara Ram, despite his somewhat anti-Muslim feeling, was inspired by humanitarian considerations. Mahāmahopādhyāya P.V. Kane was a conservative Maharashtrian brāhmaṇa and the only Sanskritist to be honoured with the title of *Bharatratna*. H.D. Sankalia combined his unrivalled archaeological activity with a profound knowledge of Sanskrit. Besides these scholars several other Indian Sanskritists and Indologists, not to mention a number of western scholars, have repeatedly drawn our attention to the textual evidence of beef and other types of animal flesh in early Indian diet. Curious though it may seem, the Sangh Parivar, which carries a heavy burden of 'civilisational illiteracy', has never turned its guns on them but against historians who have mostly relied on the research of the above-mentioned distinguished scholars.

While the contribution of the scholars mentioned above cannot be minimized, the limitation of their work lies in the fact that they have referred to isolated bits of information on beef, concentrating mainly on the Vedic texts without treating those as part of a flesh-eating tradition prevalent in India. Thus in the present book textual evidence spread over a long period is surveyed so as to show that even when eating of cow's flesh was forbidden by brāhmaṇas they retained the memory of the ancient practice. The chapters that follow will familiarize the lay reader with the types of textual evidence bearing on early Indian non-vegetarian dietary culture of which beef eating remained an integral part for a considerable length of time at least in the upper strata of society.

NOTES

1. *Harijan*, 15 September 1940. It was suggested by Marvin Harris that cow protection 'was a major political weapon in Gandhi's campaign against both British and Moslems' ('The Cultural Ecology of India's Sacred Cattle', *Current Anthropology*, 7 (1966), p. 58) but that was immediately contested by N.K. Bose who asserted that 'cow protection was as much a part of Gandhi's "constructive programme" as, say, the removal of untouchability' (ibid., p. 60).

2. M.K. Gandhi, *How to Serve the Cow,* Navajivan, Ahmedabad, 1954, pp. 85-6.
3. L.L. Sundara Ram, *Cow Protection in India,* The South Indian Humanitarian League, Madras, 1927, pp. 122-3, 179-90.
4. *Śiva Digvijaya* quoted in Sundara Ram, *Cow Protection,* p. 191.
5. This is evident from the facts that much before the inception of the cow protection movement, Raja Rammohun Roy (1772-1833), who denounced India's religious divisions and superstitions, wrote a tract in defense of beef eating. It was entitled 'Hindu Authorities in Favour of Slaying the Cow and Eating its Flesh'. See R.K. Dasgupta, 'Spirit of India—I', *Statesman,* 15 March 2001.
6. Sandria B. Freitag, 'Contesting in Public: Colonial Legacies and Contemporary Communalism', in David Ludden, ed., *Making India Hindu,* Oxford University Press, Delhi, 1996, p. 217.
7. Sandria Freitag, *Collective Action and Community: Public Arena and the Emergence of Communalism in North India,* Oxford University Press, Delhi, 1990, Chap. 6; Gyan Pandey, 'Rallying round the Cow', in Ranajit Guha, ed., *Subaltern Studies,* vol. II, Oxford University Press, Delhi, 1983, pp. 60-129.
8. Several scholars have participated in the discussion on the sacred cow complex and the management of cattle in India. An idea of the nature of debate in the late 1960s and 1970s can be had from Marvin Harris, 'The Cultural Ecology of India's Sacred Cattle', *Current Anthropology,* 7 (1966), pp. 51-66; Alan Heston, 'An Approach to the Sacred Cow of India', *Current Anthropology,* 12 (1971), pp. 191-209; John W. Bennett, 'Comment on: An Approach to the Sacred Cow of India by Alan Heston', ibid., p. 197; Corry Azzi, 'More on India's Sacred Cattle', *Current Anthropology,* 15 (1974), pp. 317-24; V.M. Dandekar, 'Cow Dung Models', *Economic and Political Weekly,* 4 (1969), pp. 1267-9, 1271; idem, 'India's Sacred Cattle and Cultural Ecology', ibid., pp. 1559-67; idem, 'Sacred Cattle and More Sacred Production Functions', ibid., 5 (1970), pp. 527, 529-31; K.N. Raj, 'India's Sacred Cattle: Theories and Empirical Findings', ibid., 6 (1971), pp. 717-22; *Seminar,* no. 93 (May 1967), issue on the cow.
9. Frederic Drew, *The Jummoo and Kashmir Territories: A Geographical Account,* Edward Stanford, London, 1875, p. 428; J. Biddulph, *Tribes of the Hindoo Koosh,* Calcutta, 1880, pp. 37, 112-13; *Imperial Gazetteer of India, Provincial Series: Kashmir and Jammu,* Calcutta,

1909, p. 108. For a discussion and further references see Frederick J. Simoons, 'Questions in the Sacred-Cow Controversy', *Current Anthropology*, 20 (1979), p. 468.

10. *The Times of India*, 28 May 1999, p. 12.
11. *Frontline*, 13 April 2001, p. 97.
12. Rajesh Ramachandran, 'A Crisis of Identity', *The Hindustan Times*, 7 May 2000.
13. W. Crooke, *The Popular Religion and Folklore of Northern India*, 2 vols., 4th rpt., Munshiram Manoharlal, Delhi, 1978.
14. W. Crooke, 'The Veneration of the Cow in India', *Folklore*, XXIII (1912), pp. 275-306.
15. Sundara Ram, op. cit., p. 8.
16. H.D. Sankalia, '(The Cow) In History', *Seminar*, 93 (1967).
17. 'Was the Cow Killed in Ancient India?' *Quest*, 75 (1972), pp. 83-7. This is a review article on a book entitled *Beef in Ancient India*, authored by one Mr. Dalmia and published by Gita Press, Gorakhpur. No date.
18. For details see *Rajendralal Mitra: 150th Anniversary Lectures*, The Asiatic Society, Calcutta, 1978.
19. For a brief note on the activities of William Crooke see Editor's Introduction in William Crooke, *A Glossary of North Indian Peasant Life*, ed. Shahid Amin, rpt., Oxford University Press, Delhi, 1989.

1

'Animals are verily food' but Yājñavalkya Favours Beef

The Indo-European Background

Analysis of the social and economic organization of the Indo-Europeans has attracted much scholarly attention. There is an impressive bulk of literature[1] in which is revealed a consensus that their eastern branch, the Indo-Aryans or Vedic Aryans, migrated to India around the middle of the second millennium BC. They brought along with them several such traits of the Indo-European life as nomadic pastoralism, incipient agriculture and religious beliefs and practices including the practice of animal/cattle sacrifice, all of which conditioned their dietary practices in India.[2]

That the early Aryans came to India as a semi-nomadic people with a dominantly pastoral economy, in which cattle rearing played an important role and agriculture occupied a secondary place, may be inferred from a comparative view of the *Avesta*[3] and the corpus of Vedic literature. The term *gau,* meaning cow, in different declensions occurs 176 times in the Family Books of the *Ṛgveda*[4] and, the total number of occurrences of cattle related terms in the text could be around 700.[5] Cattle were the most valued possession and the chief form of the wealth of the early Aryans; a wealthy person was called *gomat*[6] and the tribal chief was called the *gopa* or *gopati.* The *Rgveda* contains many prayers for the increase of cattle, which were often the cause for inter-tribal wars. Therefore such terms for battle as *gaviṣṭi,*[7] *gavyu*[8] and *gaveṣaṇa*[9] occurring in this text are all derived from cattle. Some kinship terms were also borrowed from the pastoral nomenclature and the daughter was therefore called *duhitṛ* (= *duhitā* = one who milks). In the world of divinity we hear of a category of gods born of cows (*gojāta*).[10] All this reveals the pastoral basis of the economy inherited by the Aryans from their Indo-European past. This showed up prominently in religious practices, especially in animal sacrifice and dietary habits.

Like pastoralism, they brought from outside the practice of animal or cattle sacrifice, widely prevalent among the early Aryans. It has been suggested on the basis of linguistic and archaeological evidence that the practice of cattle sacrifice of the Vedic period, called *paśubandha,* can be traced in the earlier steppe cultures of Eastern Europe.[11] Nearer home, in ancient Iran, through which the eastern branch of Indo-Europeans migrated to India, the *Avesta* bears ample testimony to animal sacrifice and the Vedic term *yajña* (= sacrifice) occurs as *yasna* in the *Avesta*. The *Avesta* speaks of the sacrifice of 100 oxen and 1,000 small cattle, in addition to that of 100 horses, 10,000 sheep or goats and 1,000 camels[12] just as the Vedic texts frequently refer to the sacrifice of cattle, horses, sheep, goats and pigs.

Some Indo-Iranian gods also seem to have migrated with the early Aryans, though they may have somewhat changed their character and attributes in transit. Among the important ones, mention may be made of Indra, Agni and Soma.[13] Most of them seem to have been fond of the meat of sacrificed animals, especially of cattle, which were the most prized possession of Aryan pastoralists who delighted in sharing the leavings of the gods. For what was offered to the deity was what they themselves liked to eat as can be inferred from the materials used in the Vedic rituals and sacrifices

Divine Dietary Preferences

The *Ṛgveda* frequently refers to the cooking of the flesh of the ox for offering to gods, especially Indra, the greatest of the Vedic gods who was strong-armed, colossal, and a destroyer of enemy strongholds. At one place Indra states, 'they cook for me fifteen plus twenty oxen'.[14] At other places he is said to have eaten the flesh of bulls,[15] of one[16] or of a hundred buffaloes[17] or 300 buffaloes roasted by Agni[18] or a thousand buffaloes.[19] Second in importance to Indra is Agni to whom there are some 200 hymns in the *Ṛgveda*.[20] Born of the mythic parents Dyaus and Pṛthivī, the god Agni is described in many forms, most importantly as an intermediary between heaven and earth conveying the sacrificial offerings to the gods and bringing them to the sacrifice.[21] Unlike the licentious Indra, he drank Soma moderately, his main food being *ghee*. Protector of all men, he is, nevertheless, described in the *Ṛgveda* as 'one whose food is the ox and the barren cow'.[22] There is indeed nothing in the text to indicate his aversion to the flesh of the cattle and other animals. On the contrary, horses (*aśva*), bulls (*ṛṣabha*), oxen (*ukṣan*),[23] barren (?) cows (*vaśā*)[24] and rams (*meṣa*) were sacrificed for him.[25] In a passage dealing with the disposal of the dead, clear reference is made 'to the burning of a goat which is the share of Agni, and to the use of the flesh of the cow to protect the body against the flame'.[26] Third in order of importance was Soma, whose name is derived from a plant which was the source of a heady drink.[27] It has been suggested that 'the fundamental and typical Vedic sacrifices are those of Soma'[28] in which the killing of animals including cattle played a crucial role.[29] There was not much variation in the menu for the Ṛgvedic gods. Milk, butter, barley, oxen, goats and sheep were their usual food, though some of them had apparently their preferences. Indra, for example, had a special liking for bulls and the guardian of the roads, Pūṣan, devoid of teeth, ate mush.[30]

Sacrifice and Sustenance

The Ṛgvedic practice of killing animals continued. The later Vedic texts provide detailed descriptions of sacrifices and frequently refer to ritual cattle slaughter and the *Gopatha Brāhmaṇa* alone mentions twenty-one *yajñas*,[31] though all of them may not have involved animal killing. A bull (*vṛṣabha*) was sacrificed to Indra, a dappled cow to the Maruts and a copper-coloured cow to the Aśvins. A cow was also sacrificed to Mitra and Varuṇa.[32] In most public sacrifices (the *aśvamedha*, *rājasūya* and *vājapeya*) flesh of various types of animals, especially that of the cow/ox/bull was required. The *agnyādheya*, which was a preparatory rite preceding all public sacrifices, required a cow to be killed[33] and the *adhvaryu* priest is said to have 'put apart . . . on the red hide of a bull . . . four dishfuls of rice'.[34] In the *aśvamedha* (horse sacrifice), the most important of the Vedic public sacrifices, first referred to in the *Ṛgveda*[35] and discussed in the Brāhmaṇas, more than 600 animals (including wild boars) and birds were killed and its *finalé* was marked by the sacrifice of 21 sterile cows,[36] though the *Taittirīya Saṃhitā* (V.6.11-20) enumerates 180 animals including horses, bulls, cows, goats, deer, *nilgai* to be killed.[37] The *gosava* (cow sacrifice) was an important component of the *rājasūya* and *vājapeya* sacrifices.[38] In the latter, the *Śatapatha Brāhmaṇa* tells us, a sterile spotted cow was offered to Maruts.[39] Similarly, in the *agniṣṭoma* a sterile cow was sacrificed.[40] According to the *Taittirīya Brāhmaṇa* an important element in the *pañcaśāradīyasava* (*darśapūrṇamāsa*) was the 'immolation' of seventeen 'dwarf heifers under three'[41] and on the day preceding the sacrifice, the sacrificer himself was required to eat the forest plants or fruits.[42] The killing of animals including cattle (*paśu*)[43] figures in several other *yajñas* including *cāturmāsya,*[44] *sautrāmaṇi,*[45] and independent animal sacrifice called *paśubandha* or *nirudhapaśubandha,*[46] which was also an important component of many sacrifices.

That the killing of the kine in sacrifice was of great importance is evident from numerous references in the early and later Vedic texts. The *Taittirīya Brāhmaṇa* unambiguously refers to the sacrificial killing of the cow which 'is verily food' (*atho annaṃ vai gauḥ*),[47] and praises Agastya for his sacrifice of a hundred bulls.[48] The *Aitareya Brāhmaṇa* states that the man, horse, ox, goat and ram are sacrificial animals and that the flesh of the *kiṃpuruṣa,*[49] *gauramṛga, gavaya,* camel and *śarabha* (young elephant),[50] which were not meant for sacrifice, should not be eaten,[51] though it is extremely doubtful if such prohibitions were effective in real life especially in view of the fact that out of 250 animals mentioned in the Vedas 50 were considered fit for sacrifice and hence for eating.[52]

In this context it is necessary to bear in mind that in the predominantly nomadic pastoral society of the Vedic Aryans it was natural to eat the food produced by the kill, though it is stated at some places that the flesh of animals like dogs was thrown to demons.[53]

That the sacrificial victim was generally meant for human consumption is abundantly clear from a passage of the *Taittirīya Saṃhitā*,[54] which tells us about the mode of cutting up the immolated animal and thus gives an idea of the distribution of its flesh.[55] More explicit is the *Gopatha Brāhmaṇa* of the *Atharvaveda*, according to which the carcass was to be divided into thirty-six shares by the *samitāra* who killed the victim by strangulation.[56] There is thus evidence to show that the flesh of sacrificed cattle was consumed by various categories of people. Notwithstanding the view that 'when the deities to whom offerings are made are terrible . . . the offering should be regarded as not suitable for human consumption', the fact remains that the animals sacrificed to gods represented 'all food'. This is evident from several Vedic texts including the *Śatapatha Brāhmaṇa*,[57] which declares that meat is the best kind of food.[58] In fact, the Vedic texts regarded the sacrifice not only as the original source of all being and 'the locus of the origin of all food', but as food itself.[59]

Animals were killed not only in public sacrifices but also in ordinary and domestic rites of daily life. The later Vedic and post-Vedic texts mention many rites and rituals associated with agricultural and other activities and, in at least some of them the killing of animals including cattle was *de rigueur*. Among the rites related to agriculture, mention may be made of the *śūlagava* (sacrifice of 'the ox on the spit') referred to by several Gṛhyasūtras.[60] In this sacrifice a spit-ox was killed for Rudra; its tail and skin were thrown into the fire, and its blood was poured out on *kuśa* or *darbha* grass for the snakes.[61] The emergence of settled field agriculture led to growth of fixed settlements which provided the context for detailed and often complicated rules relating to the construction of houses found in the texts.[62] Of the many rules at least two provide for the sacrifice of a black cow or white goat.[63]

An interesting rite repeatedly mentioned in the texts of the later Vedic period is one relating to the reception of guests and is called *arghya*, or more popularly, *madhuparka*. The killing of the kine to honour guests seems to have been prevalent from earlier times. The *Ṛgveda* (X.68.3) mentions the word *atithinīr*, which has been interpreted as 'cows fit for guests',[64] and refers to at least one Vedic hero, Atithigva, meaning literally 'slaying cows for guests'.[65] The cow was also killed on festive occasions like marriage. A Ṛgvedic passage, for instance, refers to the slaughter of a cow on the occasion of marriage[66] and, later, in the *Aitareya Brāhmaṇa*, we are told, that 'if the ruler of men comes as a guest or any one else deserving of honour comes, people kill a bull or a cow'.[67] The word *madhuparka*, however, is first referred to by the *Jaiminīya Upaniṣad-Brāhmaṇa*[68] and discussed at length in several Gṛhyasūtras.[69] It was performed in honour of special guests such as the teacher, the priest, a *snātaka*, father-in-law, paternal and maternal uncles, a friend and a king. Their reception not only included the offering of a mixture of curds and honey (whence the term *madhuparka* was derived) but, more importantly, of a cow that was either immolated[70] or let loose according to their wishes, though in no case was the rite performed without beef or some other meat.[71] Several Gṛhyasūtras describe *madhuparka* independently[72] as well as part of the marriage ceremonies in which cow was slain more than once in honour of guests.[73] Pāṇini, therefore, uses the term *goghna* for a guest.[74]

The Gṛhyasūtras also attest to the use of the hide of the bull or the cow in domestic rituals[75] like the *sīmantonnayana* (the parting of the hair of the woman upwards) ceremony performed in the fourth month of pregnancy[76] and the *upanayana*[77] (investiture ceremony preceding the beginning of one's studenthood). Cattle, in fact, seem to have been killed even on what would appear to many of us to be flimsy grounds. Thus if one were eager to have a learned son with a long life, he could find a solution in the Upaniṣadic precept which permitted such a person to eat a stew of veal or beef (or other flesh) with rice and ghee,[78] though six months after the birth the child could be fed on the flesh of birds (e.g. *Bhāradvājī*, *tittira*, *kṛkasā*, etc.) and fish.[79]

Cattle slaughter was also intimately connected with the cult of the dead, which occupies considerable space in the Vedic and post-Vedic texts. One[80] of the several Ṛgvedic passages[81] relating to cremation, for example, refers to the use of the skin and the thick fat of the cow to cover the dead body, and the *Atharvaveda* in one place seems to speak of a bull being burnt along with the dead to ride with in the next world.[82] The Gṛhyasūtras, elaborately describing the funerary procedure, provide ample evidence of cattle killing at the time of cremation and of the practice of distributing different limbs of the animal on those of the corpse.[83] Cremation was followed by several rites in honour of the ancestors, variously mentioned as *pitṛyajña*, *mahāpitṛyajña* and *aṣṭakā* in the Vedic passages and as some other types of *śraddha* in the post-Vedic texts (especially the Gṛhyasūtras).[84] The detailed rules pertaining to the different types of *śraddha* need not detain us here; for the relevant point is that the Manes had to be well fed and this was possible only if beef was offered to them. Therefore, apart from other animals, cows and/or bulls were slain in *śrāddhas*.[85] Of the latter the *ābhyudayika* (also called *nandīmukha*) was performed to please the ancestors as a preliminary to festive occasions like the birth of a son and the marriage of the son or daughter. In another type of *śrāddha* called the *aṣṭakā* or the *ekāṣṭakā,* of which the Gṛhyasūtras[86] speak at length, the killing of the cow is explicitly mentioned. The performer of the *aṣṭakā* rite, we are told, prepared the cow for immolation and offered its cooked omentum to the Manes,[87] though the degree of satisfaction they derived from the *śraddha* seems to have varied according to the animal offered. For, we are told, the flesh of the cow gratified the *pitṛs* (dead ancestors) for a year (*saṃvatsaraṃ gavyena prītiḥ*), that of the buffalo, wild animals like hares and domesticated animals like goats for more than a year and the Manes remained satisfied for an endless period of time if the flesh of rhinoceros, *śatabali* (a kind of fish) and *vārddhrīṇasa* were offered to them.[88] However, not everything depended on their choice and preference for beef was generally unquestioned. After all the *śrāddha,* apart from being a ritual to please the ancestors, was also a feast for the community members, especially the brāhmaṇas, whose preference for beef is clearly indicated in the texts, and it was only in the absence of meat that vegetables could be offered to the *pitṛs.*[89]

There were also occasions, other than the *śrāddha,* when cattle were slaughtered for the community. The *gavāmayana,* a sessional sacrifice performed by the brāhmaṇas, was, for example, marked by animal slaughter. It culminated in an extravagant and frolicsome festival, *mahāvrata,* in which three barren cows were offered to Mitrāvaruṇa and other deities,[90] though going by the textual descriptions of this bacchanalian festival it seems likely that many more cattle were slaughtered. Similarly the *gṛhamedha,* which has much in common with earlier and later rituals and has been discussed in several Śrautasūtras,[91] was some kind of a lavish communal feast in which an unspecified number of cows were slain (*gā abhignate*), not in the strict ritual mode but in the crude and profane manner.[92] Evidently then, judging by the copious textual references, there is little doubt that the early Aryans in the northwestern part of the Indian subcontinent and their successors in the middle Gangetic valley slaughtered animals and cattle including the cow whose flesh they ate with relish.[93] Although flesh eating was forbidden for a Vedic teacher during the months between *upākarma* and *utsarjana*,[94] according to a Dharma-sūtra text the flesh of cows and bulls was pure and may be eaten.[95] Not surprisingly, beef was the favourite food of the much-respected sage of Mithilā, Yājñavalkya, who made the obdurate statement that he would continue to eat the flesh of cows and oxen so long as it was tender (*aṃsala*). This may, however, also imply that already in his time an opinion against beef eating was gaining ground.[96]

Several authorities attest that it was lawful to eat the meat of cattle. According to one law book, bull flesh was fit for offerings,[97] and according to another 'animals slain for the fulfilment of the sacred law' were to be eaten by priests and other brāhmaṇas,[98] though it is stated in one place that the killing of a milch-cow and a full grown ox, without reason, required the performance of a penance.[99] It has been therefore argued that only sacrificed or consecrated beef or animal flesh was eaten.[100] But this seems doubtful. The term *śasana* occurring in the *Ṛgveda* means 'slaughter' or 'killing'[101] and has also been interpreted to mean a slaughter house,[102] which may imply the consumption of a variety of unconsecrated meats including that of the milch cattle. This is probable because, in addition to birds, fish and other aquatic animals, the Vedic texts as well as the Dharmasūtras provide an impressive list of animals/beasts whose flesh could be eaten, and this includes the *khaḍga* (rhinoceros), wild boar *sūkara* (hog), *varāha* (boar/bull),[103] and *śarabha* (elephant?)[104] without reference to consecration.[105] An examination of the inventory of edible animals mentioned in the Vedic Saṃhitās and subsequent texts makes it improbable that eating of flesh of all kinds was always linked with rituals,[106] though the *Chāndogya Upaniṣad* seems to restrict injury to living beings to sacrificial occasions.[107]

The Myth of the Holy Cow

Whether or not the Vedic Aryans ate consecrated or sacrificed beef or other animal flesh, the heart of the matter is that the milch cattle including the cow was not sacred during the Vedic and post-Vedic centuries. The term *aghnya/aghnyā* (lit. not to be slain) has been used at four places in the *Ṛgveda* and the *Atharvaveda* 'as a masculine noun equivalent to bull or ox and 42 times with a feminine ending to mean a cow'.[108] Attention has also been drawn to the use of words for cow as epithet or in simile and metaphor with reference to entities of highest religious significance,[109] though these occurrences do not indicate their primary sense with reference to the actual animal. Neither of the two types of evidence adduced in favour of the sacredness of the Vedic cow, therefore, points to the basically unslayable character of cows. On the contrary the references seem to emphasize their economic value.[110] When slaughtered they provided food to the people and their priests and the *Śatapatha Brāhmaṇa* states unambiguously that 'meat is the best kind of food'.[111] When milked, cows gave additional nourishment not only through milk but also a variety of milk products, which formed part of the diet as well as of the Vedic sacrificial oblation (*havis*). Oxen were used as draught animals; they pulled the plough and are also referred to as pulling Sūryā's[112] bridal car. Cattle hide was used in a variety of ways. The bowstring (*jyā*) was made of a thong of cowhide—a practice that may have continued in later times.[113] The different parts of the chariot were tied together with leather straps, also needed for binding the arrow to the shaft. The goad for driving the animals was made of cow hide or tail. Leather thongs were used not only for making snares but also for a musical instrument called *godhā*.[114] The utility and importance of cattle therefore inspired warriors to fight wars (*gaviṣṭi*) for them and it is likely that part of the cattlestock of the vanquished tribes was killed in the course of raids. While all this goes against the popular notion of the inviolability of the cow through the Vedic period and proves that it was certainly killed for sacrifice (*yajña*) and food as well as for other requirements, the extent to which the economic value of the cow contributed to its supposed sacredness is difficult to ascertain.[115]

It is, however, pertinent to point out that cow being a symbol of riches, the Vedas liken it with Aditi (mother of gods, but lit. 'boundless heaven'), the earth (*pṛthivī*), the cosmic waters whose release by Indra after the slaying of Vṛtra established the cosmic law (*ṛta*), maternity and,—most important—to poetry/speech (*vāc*)[116] which was the monopoly of brāhmaṇas. Of all the animals, the cow is used most frequently in similes and metaphors[117] and these came to be taken as literal in the course of time. Poetic imagery ran away from the poets and this may have provided a basis for the supposed sanctity of the cow in subsequent times.[118] But the cow was neither sacred nor unslayable in the Vedic period, notwithstanding some Atharvavedic passages, which have been interpreted as 'a strong voice of protest against the slaughter of the cow'.[119] What seems likely is that the cow belonging to a brāhmaṇa came to acquire a certain degree of inviolability. It is known that the cow was an ideally preferred form of *dakṣiṇā*[120] (sacrificial fee) given to the brāhmaṇa priest. There are many references to the Vedic brāhmaṇa's interest in his *dakṣiṇā* (the good milch cow),[121] and to 'the dire consequences that will befall one who withholds it or injures or misappropriates it and the corresponding benefit accruing to him who bestows it'.[122] In one place in the *Atharvaveda* we come across a warning: 'O king (*nṛpati*), the gods did not give that [cow] to you to eat; O warrior (*rājanya*), do not desire to eat the brāhmaṇa's cow, [she is] not to be eaten (*anādyam*).'[123] In another part of the same text it is said that Vaitahavyas who ate the brāhmaṇa's cow perished.[124] It appears, therefore, that the cow could be inviolate only if owned by a brāhmaṇa or given to him as *dakṣiṇā,* though the twinning cow (*yaminī*), considered inauspicious in the *Atharvaveda* and given to a brāhmaṇa, was killed and offered in sacrifice.[125] The special importance attached to the brāhmaṇa's cow, however, cannot be stretched to argue that the Vedic cow was inherently sacred.

The practice of killing cattle including the cow is amply attested by archaeological material dispersed widely over time and space. We have it on the authority of H.D. Sankalia, that throughout the pleistocene period ranging from about a hundred thousand years to ten thousand years 'bones of the cow/ox have been discovered more frequently and at a large number of places in the river and other deposits than of any other animal'.[126] Found in association with stone tools, these bones indicate that the primitive man hunted them for food. Excavations clearly prove that the authors of the Harappan civilization ate cattle flesh, of which the relevant archaeological evidence is spread over a vast area covering Sind, Punjab, Uttar Pradesh, Rajasthan, Kutch, Saurashtra and coastal Gujarat. Outside the Harappan cultural zone there is ample faunal evidence indicative of the Chalcolithic diet, marked by the practice of eating beef.[127]

Archaeological evidence also testifies to the continuity of this practice through the first millennium BC. Excavations of Painted Grey Ware sites, whose cultural assemblage mostly belongs to the later Vedic phase when the Aryan settlements became stable in the Indo-

Gangetic divide, are very clear on the point. At Hastinapur (Meerut), for example, the bones of buffalo, sheep, goat, pig, elephant, and, most important, cattle of the smaller, humpless, short-horned variety of today, have been found. A substantial number of them range in date from the eleventh to about the third century BC. Many cattle bone fragments are either charred or bear definite cut marks, which suggests that these animals were cooked and eaten.[128] At Allahpur (Meerut), where a later Vedic settlement was excavated, charred bones along with horns were found.[129] Similar evidence is much more impressive from Atranjikhera (Etah district) where the total number of identified bone fragments goes to 927. Of these more than 64 per cent account for the cow, often with cut marks, and predate the fifth century BC. Beef, thus, appears to have been a favoured item of food, though mutton, venison, pork, fish, river turtles and fowl and the flesh of wild animals like *barasingha, nilgai* and leopard were also consumed.[130] In Haryana, at Bhagwanpura (Kurukshetra district) a large number of charred bones of cattle have been found.[131] In Punjab, the later phase of the Painted Gray Ware settlement at Ropar (600-200 BC) has yielded bones of domesticated cattle, buffalo, sheep, goat, pig, horse, dog, fowl, tortoise and chital with cut marks and signs of charring.[132] Interestingly, evidence of this type also comes from the second phase of habitation (*c.* 400-200 BC) at Mathura, whose association with the cattle protector Kṛṣṇa is well known.[133] In fact, of all the osteological remains, cattle bones are the most common at the PGW sites excavated so far and this leads us to the unmistakable conclusion that cattle domestication was linked with dietary as well as non-dietary uses. Consumption of beef is, thus, attested at a number of later Vedic and post-Vedic sites scattered over large parts of northern India, especially western UP, Haryana, Punjab and Rajasthan. But instead of making a count of animal bones with cut marks or signs of charring, suffice it to say here that the Vedic references to cattle flesh as an important dietary item tie up very well with archaeological evidence.

Towards Non-violence

The killing of cattle and eating of meat were fairly common among the Vedic Indians. But the Vedic texts were not always unanimous in recommending the killing of animals for sacrifice and other purposes. Already in the *Ṛgveda* indications of an effort to find substitutes for ritual killing of cattle are available. It is stated, for example, that 'a devout offering of praise or of a fuel stick or of cooked food was as good as a more solemn sacrifice'[134] and that 'oblations of food to the accompaniment of heart-felt hymns become like bulls, oxen and cows in sacrifice'.[135] This growing tendency towards ritual substitution seems to have gained ground from the later Vedic period onwards, and should be seen against the background of the gradual weakening of the Ṛgvedic pastoralism, which gave way to settled agriculture.[136] Important technological developments leading to the clearance of forest and consequent dispersal of agriculture and the emergence of stable agrarian settlements created a new social and economic milieu in which cattle, otherwise useful for dairy products, now became valuable for various agricultural operations.[137] Several later Vedic and post-Vedic texts began to recommend the offering of animal effigies (*piṣṭapaśu*) in lieu of livestock, and according to some of them the offering of rice and barley was equal to an animal sacrifice.[138] Attention has also been drawn to the fact that, in the *varuṇapraghāsa*[139] ritual of the *cāturmāsyas*, the ram and the ewe made of barley were offered and some texts describe them as *anṛtapaśu* (untrue animals).[140] The idea of ritual substitution, though often overemphasized,[141] may have been strenghthened by the view expressed in some Brāhmaṇa texts that the animal would eat its eater in the other world;[142] for the *Kauṣitaki Brāhmaṇa* 'threatens man being eaten in the next world by animals which he devoured in this'.[143] Ideas such as these were rooted in the theory of *karma* and transmigration often referred to in the Brāhmaṇas and Upaniṣads, according to which the acts committed in this life determined the man's place in the next. The Upaniṣadic texts went so far as to question the efficacy of animal sacrifice and gave primacy to asceticism as a means of achieving self-realization,[144] read new meanings in the sacrifice,[145] and propounded the notion of *ahiṃsā*,[146] though some of them continued to betray approval of the sacrificial cult.[147] However, despite the divergent perceptions of ritual butchery noticeable in the Vedic and post-Vedic texts, the general Upaniṣadic idea of ritual killing of animals as futile gained in strength and may have culminated in the doctrine of *ahiṃsā,* which is the defining trait of Buddhism and Jainism. These two religions, as is well known, forcefully challenged the Vedic sacrificial slaughter of animals and provided the ideological background to the emergence of stable agrarian settlement, state society and other related developments,[148] though, as will be shown in the sequel, the undermining of the world of Brāhmaṇic sacrifice did not lead to the disappearance of beef or any other meat from the Indian diet.

NOTES

1. It is neither necessary nor possible to mention the vast literature dealing with the Aryan problem. But the following recent works may be consulted with profit: I.M. Diakonov, 'On the Original Home of the speakers of Indo-European', *Journal of Indo-European*

Studies, XIII (1985), pp. 92-174; Colin Renfrew, *Archaeology and Language: The Puzzle of Indo-European Origins*, Penguin, Harmondsworth, 1989; J.P. Mallory, *In Search of the Indo-European Language, Archaeology and Myth*, Thames & Hudson, London, 1991; A.H. Dani and V.M. Mason, eds., *History of Civilizations of Central Asia*, I, UNESCO Publishing, Paris, 1992; Romila Thapar, 'The Theory of Aryan Race and Politics', *Transactions of the International Conference of Eastern Studies*, XL (1995), pp. 41-66; George Erdosy, ed., *The Indo-Aryans of Ancient South Asia*, Munshiram Manoharlal, Delhi, 1997; Thomas R. Trautmann, *Aryans and the British India*, Vistar Publications, Delhi, 1997; R.S. Sharma, *Looking for the Aryans*, Orient Longman, Chennai, 1994; idem, *Advent of the Aryans in India*, Manohar, Delhi, 1999; Rajesh Kochhar, *The Vedic People: Their History and Geography*, Orient Longman, Delhi, 1999.

2. Bruce Lincoln, *Priests, Warriors and Cattle*, University of California Press, Berkeley and Los Angeles, 1982, pp. 65-6.
3. Mallory, op. cit., pp. 228-9. Several archaeological cultures 'discovered in the former Soviet Central Asia are broadly similar to the Vedic and Avestan cultures . . . in respect of animal sacrifice, funeral rites, settlement patterns and economic activities', R.S. Sharma, *Looking for the Aryans*, 1995, p. 64.
4. R.S. Sharma, *Material Culture and Social Formations in Ancient India*, Macmillan, Delhi, 1983, p. 24.
5. Doris Srinivasan, *Concept of Cow in the Ṛgveda*, Motilal Banarsidass, Delhi, 1979, p. 1.
6. *ṚV*, II.41.7; VI.45.21; VII.27.5, 77.5, 94.9; IX.41.4, 61.3, etc.
7. *ṚV*, III.47.4; V.63.5; VI.31.3, 47.20, 59.7; VIII.24.2; IX.76.2, etc.
8. *ṚV*, VIII.53.8; IX.97.15.
9. *ṚV*, VII.23.3; VIII.17.15; *AV*, V.20.11.
10. *ṚV*, VI.50.11; VII.35.14; X.53.5.
11. R.S. Sharma, *Looking for the Aryans*, p. 42. According to Fritz Staal (*Agni: The Vedic Ritual of the Fire Altar*, I, Asian Humanities Press, Berkeley, 1983, p. 49), 'the animal that is sacrificed, called *paśu*, is generally a goat'. This may have been only partially true because in some later Vedic texts the goat is specified as the sacrificial victim (e.g., *BhāradvājaSS*, VII.9.7; *HiraṇyakeśiSS*, 4.4; *KātyāyanaSS*, VI.3.18).
12. *The Zend Avesta*, SBE XXIII, pt. 2, pp. 62-3, 79; ibid., SBE IV, pp. 232-3.

13. Indra, to whom the largest number of hymns are dedicated in the *Ṛgveda*, figures only twice in the *Avesta*, as a demon and not as a god, though his Vedic epithet *vṛtrahan* (slayer of Vṛtra), applied to him seventy times in the *Ṛgveda*, occurs in the latter as *verethraghna*. Agni is the Avestan Atar and Soma is Haoma of the *Avesta*. Several scholars have discussed the similarity of the names of the Avestan Iranian gods and the Vedic ones. See, for example, A.A. Macdonell, *Vedic Mythology*, Strassburg, 1897, Indian rpt., Indological Book House, Varanasi, 1963; A.B. Keith, *The Religion and Philosophy of the Veda and Upanishads*, Harvard Oriental Series 31, Cambridge, Massachusetts, 1925, Indian rpt., Motilal Banarssidass, 1970; Louis Renou, *Vedic India*, Indian rpt., Indological Book House, Varanasi, 1971.
14. *ukṣaṇo hi me pañcadaśa sākam picanti viṃsatim//*, *ṚV*, X.86.14ab.
15. *pacanti te vṛṣabhaṃ atsi //* *ṚV*, X.28.3c.
16. *amā te tumraṃ vṛṣabhaṃ pacāni*, *ṚV*, X.27.2c.
17. *pacac chataṃ mahiṣān indra tubhyam*, *ṚV*, VI.17.11b.
18. *sakhā sākhye apacat tūyam agnir asya kratvā mahiṣā triśatāni*, *ṚV*, V.29.7ab.
19. *yadi pravṛddha satpate sahasram mahiṣān aghaḥ*, *ṚV*, VIII.12.8ab.
20. A.B. Keith, op. cit., p. 154.
21. Macdonell, op. cit., pp. 88-100; Keith, op. cit., pp. 154-62. In the epics and Purāṇas, however, Agni is 'an unscrupulous seducer of women' as well as an 'ascetic heat' (fire of *tapas*): See W.D. O'Flaherty, *Asceticism and Eroticism in the Mythology of Śiva*, Oxford University Press, London, 1973, p. 91; Fritz Staal, op. cit., pp. 75-6.
22. *ukṣānnāya vaśānnāya somapṛṣṭhāya vedhase/stomairvidhemagnaye*, *ṚV*, VIII.43.11 cited in P.V. Kane, *History of Dharmaśāstra*, II, pt. 2, Bhandarkar Oriental Research Institute, Poona, 1974, p. 772, fn. 1847.
23. Harry Falk, 'Zur Tierzucht im alten Indien', *Indo-Iranian Journal*, 24 (1982), p. 176.
24. Doris Srinivasan (op. cit., pp. 58-60) thinks that only the barren cow (*vaśā*) was sacrificed—a view held by many scholars. But Stephanie W. Jamison has contested this view and agrees with H. Falk, who has shown that the *vaśā* is a cow (or other female domestic animal) that has been bred but has not calved, *The Ravenous Hyenas and the Wounded Sun*, Cornell University Press, Ithaca and London, 1991, pp. 258-9.
25. *yasminnaśvāsa ṛṣabhāsa ukṣṇo vaśāmeṣā avasṛṣṭāsa āhutāḥ*, *ṚV*,

X.91.14ab. Also see Rajnikant Shastri, *Hindu Jati Ka Utthan aur Patan*, Kitab Mahal, Allahabad, 1988, pp. 101-2.

26. *ajo bhāgas tapasā taṃ tapasva taṃ te socis tapatu taṃ te arciḥ*, *ṚV*, X.16.4ab; *agner varma pari gobhir vyavasya saṃ prorṇusva pīvasā medasā ca*, *ṚV*, X.16.7ab. Also see Keith, op. cit., p. 419.
27. For divergent views on the birth and attributes of Soma see Macdonell, op. cit., pp. 102-14. The botanical identity of the soma plant has remained a matter of inconclusive, though lively, debate. Scholars have sought to suggest its identification with different intoxicating or hallucinogenic plants. Recent archaeological discoveries, however, indicate the possibility that soma may be identical with ephedra twigs which appear in the vessels found in the premises of the temple of Togolok-21 in Margiana (south-eastern Turkmenia). See R.S. Sharma, *Looking for the Aryans*, p. 51; Harry Falk, 'Soma I and II', *BSOAS*, 52 (1989), pp. 77-90; Asko Parpola, 'The Problem of the Aryans and the Soma: Textual-linguistic and Archaeological Evidence', and Harri Nyberg, 'The Problem of the Aryans and the Soma: The Botanical Evidence', in G. Erdosy, ed., *The Indo-Aryans of Ancient South Asia*.
28. Louis Renou, op. cit., p. 104.
29. A.B. Keith, op. cit., p. 327.
30. Ibid., p. 87. Teetotalism was unknown to the Vedic gods and Indra, pot bellied from excessive drinking, is said to have drunk three lakes of soma before slaying the dragon Vṛtra. Macdonell (*The Vedic Mythology*, p. 56) cites substantial evidence to prove his excessive weakness for soma juice.
31. G.U. Thite, *Sacrifice in the Brāhmaṇa Texts*, University of Poona, Poona, 1975, Chap. VI. Thite suggests that the Brāhmaṇas elevated some of the popular (non-Aryan?) fertility rites to a higher status and incorporated them into the Vedic sacrificial system.
32. R.S. Sharma, *Material Culture*, p. 119. Also see A.B. Keith, op. cit., pp. 324-6.
33. L. Renou, op. cit., p. 102. J.C. Heesterman translates a *Kāṭhaka Saṃhitā* passage (8.7: 90.10) relating to the *agnyādheya* ritual as follows: 'they kill a cow, they play dice for [shares in] her, they serve up to those seated in the assembly hall'. See his *The Broken World of Sacrifice*, University of Chicago Press, Chicago, 1993, pp. 194, 283, n. 32.
34. Kane, op. cit., II, pt. 2, p. 990.

35. In *ṚV*, I.162, 163, the details of the horse sacrifice are available for the first time.
36. Renou, op. cit., p. 109.
37. *TS*, V.6.11-20. *tasmādaṣṭādaśino rohito dhūmrarohita ityādibhiranuvākairuktāḥ pratyanuvākamṣṭādaśasaṅkhyā militvā 'gotyadhikaśatasaṅkhyakāḥ paśava ālabdhanyāḥ*, Sāyaṇa's commentary on *TB*, III.9.1.1 cited in R.L. Mitra, *Indo-Aryans: Contributions to the Elucidation of Ancient and Mediaeval History*, 2 vols., rpt., Indological Book House, Varanasi, 1969, p. 362. Cf. *TS*, III.8-9 and various passages in *ŚB*, XIII, *TS*, V, and *TB*, III.
38. R.L. Mitra (*Indo-Aryans*, p. 361) has pointed out that *gosava* formed an integral part of the *rājasūya* and *vājapeya*. *Gosava* was a kind of cow sacrifice which, according to the *Mahābhārata* (3.30.17), should not be performed in the Kali age. See V.S. Apte, *The Practical Sanskrit-English Dictionary*, Kyoto, 1998, s.v. *gosava*. According to *TB*, II.7.6, one who desires *svarājya* should perform this sacrifice. The *ĀpDS* states that for a year after performing *gosava* the sacrificer should be *paśuvrata* (act like cattle), i.e. he should drink water like them and cut grass (with his teeth) and even have sexual relations with his mother: *teneṣṭvā saṃvatsaraṃ paśuvrato bhavati/upāvahāyodakaṃ pivettṛṇāni cācchindyāt/upa mataramiyādupa svasāramupa sagotrāṃ*, XXII.12.12-20; 13.1-3, cited in Kane, op. cit., II, pt. 2, p. 1213, n. 2644. Also see Thite, op. cit., pp. 97-100.
39. Thite, op. cit., p. 77.
40. L. Renou, op. cit., 105; Kane, op. cit., II, pt. 2, p. 1158. Kane also draws attention to a passage (*Kāt*, X.9. 14-15) which says that instead of the cow a bull or only *payasyā* may be offered to Mitra and Varuṇa, Kane, op. cit., II, pt. 2, pp. 1200-1.
41. R.L. Mitra, op. cit., p. 363. He also cites a passage from the *Tāṇḍya Brāhmaṇa* of the *Sāma Veda* which recommends cattle of different colours for each successive year (loc. cit.). P.V. Kane discusses in detail the *darśapūrṇamāsa* (op. cit., II, pt. 2, Chap. XXIX) on the basis of the Brāhmaṇas and the Sūtra texts without referring to the killing of cattle. Musashi Tachikawa has also discussed the structure of this ritual on the basis of its reenactment in Pune in 1979, without reference to any animal sacrifice. ('*Homa* in the Vedic Ritual: The Structure of the *Darśapūrṇamāsa*', in Yasuhiko Nagano and Yasuke Ikari, eds., *From Vedic Altar to Village Shrine*, National Museum of Ethnology, Osaka, 1993, pp. 239-67.)

42. *ŚB*, I.1.1. 9-10, cited in Thite, op. cit., p. 193.
43. Monier-Williams, *Sanskrit-English Dictionary*, s.v. *paśu*. Cf. Macdonell and Keith, *Vedic Index*, I, pp. 580-2. Hindi translation by Ramkumar Rai, Chowkhamba Vidyabhavan, Varanasi, 1962. The Sanskrit *paśu* = Avestan *pasu* means domestic animals, livestock and sacrificial animals but also frequently indicates simply cattle as the domestic animal and the sacrificial animal par excellence, Bruce Lincoln, *Priests, Warriors and Cattle*, p. 65 and fn. 98. Mayrhofer, *A Concise Etymological Dictionary*, II, pp. 239-40, s.v. *paśuḥ*.
44. A.B. Keith, op. cit., p. 323; J.C. Heesterman, *The Ancient Indian Royal Consecration*, Mouton, The Hague, 1957, p. 28. For a detailed discussion of *cāturmāsya* see P.V. Kane, op. cit., II, pt. 2, Chap. XXXI. Although Shingo Einoo has discussed the *cāturmāsya* only in relation to vegetal offerings (*Die Cāturmāsya oder die altindischen Tertialopfer dargestellt nach den Vorschriften der Brāhmaṇas und der Śrautasūtras*, Monumenta Serindica no. 18, Tokyo, 1988), G.U. Thite has asserted that some *cāturmāsyas* could also be performed in the soma-sacrifice category (op. cit., p. 73) which may imply the killing of animals as in the case of most of the soma sacrifices. This is supported by the fact that some post-Vedic Sūtra texts prescribe *paśukacāturmāsya* characterized by animal sacrifice, *Śrautakośa*, vol. I, Eng. Section, pt. 2, Vaidik Samsodhaka Mandala, Poona, 1962, pp. 894-8.
45. The *sautrāmaṇi*, the rite dedicated to Sutraman (Indra), was performed after the *rājasūya* and the *agnicayana* sacrifices. But it was also performed independently for the benefit of a person indisposed by excess imbibing of soma. In this rite the bull was the sacrificial victim, Kane, op. cit., II, pt. 2, p. 1224; for details see ibid., Chap. XXXV; Thite, op. cit., pp. 83-9. Also see 'animal' in the index to M.B. Kolhatkar, *Surā: The Liquor and the Vedic Sacrifice*, D.K. Printworld, Delhi, 1999.
46. Keith, op. cit. p. 324; Kane, op. cit., II, pt. 2, Chap. XXXII, discusses the details of the sacrifice on the basis of *SB*, *TS*, and several Sūtra texts belonging to the post-Vedic period. According to several scholars a goat (*chāga*) was the victim in this sacrifice but the use of the word *paśu*, which is the generic term for domesticated animals, would imply that the killing of the kine may have been quite common. The animal slaughter was accompanied by the recitation of specific hymns called the

Āprī hymns, Kane, op. cit., II, pt. 2, p. 1118; *Indo Iranian Journal*, 28 (1986), pp. 95-115, 169-89.

47. *gamālabhate yajño vai gauḥ . . . atho annaṃ vai gauḥ*. *TB*, III.9.8. Indirect evidence of cow killing is also provided by *TS*, II.1.1.4-5; V.5.1.3.
48. K.T. Achaya, *A Historical Dictionary of Indian Food*, Oxford University Press, Delhi, 1999, p. 145.
49. Asko Parpola, agreeing with Ronnow ('Zur Erklärung des Pravargya, des Agnicayana der Sautrāmaṇi', *Le Monde Oriental*, 23, 1929, pp. 145-9) interprets the term to mean 'the sacrificed human victim' who occupied an important place in the 'pre-Vedic, asuric religion'. For identity of the *kiṃpuruṣa* see Parpola's discussion in Frits Staal, ed., *Agni*, II, Berkeley, 1983, pp. 61ff.
50. For different meanings of the word see V.S. Apte, *The Practical Sanskrit-English Dictionary*, s.v. *śarabha*.
51. *ta eta utkrāntamedhā amedhya paśavastasmādeṣāṃ nāśnīyat*, *AitB*, VI.8. cited in Kane, op. cit., II, pt. 2, p. 773. For references to sacrificial victims including the cattle/cow also see *TS*, II.1.1. 4-5; V.5.1.1.3; *ŚB*, I.2.3.6; VI.2.1. 15-18; VI.2.2.15. The *Vādhūla-sūtra*, apart from mentioning the five sacrificial victims including the cow, also uses the term *gomedha*, W. Caland, 'Eine vierte Mitteilung über das Vādhūlasūtra', *Acta Orientalia*, 6 (1928), pp. 116-17. Shingo Einoo informs me that this is the only mention of the term in the Vedic literature. According to a recent view there is a hierarchical gradation in the list of five sacrificial victims (Brian K. Smith and Wendy Doniger, 'Sacrifice and Substitution: Ritual Mystification and Mythical Demystification', *Numen*, XXXVI (1989), p. 199.
52. According to one view, the Vedas refer to more than 250 animals and of these about 50 were deemed fit for sacrifice and, by inference, for eating. K.T. Achaya, *A Historical Dictionary of Indian Food*, p. 145.
53. The entrails of a dog were cooked in a situation of extreme destitution (*avartyā śūna āntrāṇi pece*, *ṚV*, IV.18.13a). In the post-Vedic period the notion of impurity of the flesh of several other animals figures in the Sūtra literature, Om Prakash, *Food and Drinks in Ancient India*, Munshiram Manoharlal, Delhi, 1961, pp. 39-40.
54. *TS*, VI.3.10.2-6. For a detailed description also see Naoshiro Tsuji (alias Fukushima), *On the Relation of Brāhmaṇas and*

Śrautasūtras, The Tôyô Bunko Ronsô, Series A, vol. XXXII, English Summary, The Tôyô Bunko, Tokyo, 1952, pp. 87-100.

55. For a discussion of the crucial *TB* passage see R.L. Mitra, op. cit., pp. 373-4.
56. *GB* (*Purvabhāga*), I.3.18. Charles Malamoud, *Cooking the World: Ritual and Thought in Ancient India*, Oxford University Press, Delhi, 1996, pp. 169-80.
57. For sacrificial animals thought of as food see *ŚB*, *paśavo hy annaṃ*, III.2.1.12; *annaṃ vai paśavaḥ*, V.2.1.16; *annaṃ paśavaḥ*, VII.5.2.42; VIII.3.1.13, VIII.3.3.2-4, VIII.5.2.1, VIII.6.2.1, 13; *paśubhir evainam annena prīṇāti*, IX.2.3.40. Also *atho annaṃ vai gauḥ*, *TB*, III.9.8.3.
58. *paramam annādyaṃ yan māṃsam*, *SB*, XI.7.1.3.9.
59. Brian K. Smith, 'Eaters, Food, and Social Hierarchy in Ancient India', *Journal of the Academy of Religion*, LVIII, no. 2 (1990), p. 181. Also see idem, *Reflections on Resemblance, Ritual, and Religion*, Oxford University Press, New York, 1989.
60. L. Renou, op. cit., p. 114 and R.L. Mitra (op. cit., pp. 363ff.) have interpreted *śūlagava* as a sacrifice of 'spitted ox' or roast beef. The word *śūla* is found in the *Ṛgveda* only once, but occurs more often in the later Brāhmaṇas and the Gṛhyasūtras (V.M. Apte, *Social and Religious Life in the Gṛhyasūtras*, The Popular Book Depot, Bombay, 1939, pp. 109-12). According to Baudhāyana if a person cannot secure an ox he may sacrifice a goat or a ram or a dish of cooked rice (*atha yadi gāṃ na labhate meṣamajaṃ vālabhate/ īśānāya sthālīpākaṃ vā śrapayati tasmādetatsarvaṃ karoti yadbhavā kāryam*, II.7. cited in Kane, op. cit., II, pt. 2, p. 832, fn. 1966). Kane, on the basis of the commentary of Devapāla on the *KāṭhGS* (52.1) has pointed out that in this sacrifice only a goat is offered and the bull is let off. But Devapāla belongs to the eleventh century (*Das Kāṭhaka-Gṛhya-Sūtra*, ed. Caren Dreyer, Stuttgart, 1986, p. xxx) and his interpretation reflects a later view and not the one prevalent in Vedic and post-Vedic times. For a discussion of the *śūlagava* (also called *Īśānabali*) see Kane, op. cit., II, pt. 2, pp. 831-2; J. Gonda, *Vedic Ritual: The Non-Solemn Rites*, E.J. Brill, Leiden, 1980, pp. 435-7.
61. A.B. Keith, op. cit., p. 364.
62. For textual references to *Vāstu-pratiṣṭhā* (construction and occupation of a new house) see Kane, op. cit., II, pt. 2, p. 833; J. Gonda, *Vedic Ritual*, pp. 154-7, 405-6.

63. V.M. Apte (*Social and Religious Life in the Gṛhyasūtras*, p. 144) points out that of the various Gṛhyasūtra texts only those of Gobhila and Khādira prescribe an animal sacrifice for *Vāstospati* on the completion of house construction. There are several other minor rites, which may have involved animal sacrifice. See A.B. Keith, op. cit., pp. 363ff.; Kane, op. cit., II, pt. 2, Chap. XXIV.
64. Herman W. Tull, 'The Killing That is not Killing: Men, Cattle and the Origins of Non-violence (*Ahiṃsā*) in the Vedic Sacrifice', *Indo-Iranian Journal*, 39 (1996), p. 229. The meaning given by Tull is his own interpretation. Karl Friedrich Geldner interprets the word as 'cows which bring guests' in his translation of *ṚV*, X.68.3 (Geldner, *Der Rig-Veda*, Harvard Oriental Series, vol. 35, 1951, p. 244) and so does Herman Oldenberg (*Ṛgveda: Textkritische und exegetische Noten*, Weidmannsche Buchhandlung, Berlin, 1912, p. 272). Also see Paul Thieme, *Der Fremdling im Ṛgveda*, Deutsche Morgenländische Gesellshaft, Leipzig, 1938, Kraus Reprint Ltd., Nendeln, Liechtenstein, 1966, p. 86; Jacob Wackernagel, *Altindische Grammatik*, vol. II, pt. 2, Vandenhoeck and Ruprecht, Gottingen, 1954, p. 330; Louis Renou, *Études Védiques et Pāṇinéennes*, Éditions E. De Boccard, Paris, 1966, p. 73. That the word is usually understood as '(a cow) which brings guests' is clear: Manfred Mayrhofer, *Etymologisches Wörterbuch des Altindoarischen*, vol. I, Heidelberg, 1986, p. 57, s.v. *atithi*.
65. Macdonell and Keith, op. cit., II, p. 145. Also see Kane, op. cit., II, pt. 2, pp. 749-56. The epithet Atithigva is also often used for the Ṛgvedic chief Divodāsa and has been interpreted by Bloomfield as 'he who (always) has a cow for a guest', *JAOS*, 16 (1894), p. cxxiv.
66. *aghāsu hanyate gāvo, ṚV*, X.85.13c.
67. *tad yathaivādo manuṣyarāja āgate'nyasmin vārhati ukṣāṇaṃ vā vehataṃ vā kṣadante, AitB*, III. 4, cited in Kane, op. cit., II, pt. 1, p. 542, n. 1254. Also see *ŚB*, III.4.1.2 according to which an ox or a goat was cooked for a guest, a king or a brāhmaṇa.
68. *taṃ hovāca kiṃ vidvān no dālbhyānāmantrya madhuparkaṃ pibasīti, Jaiminīya Upaniṣad-Brāhmaṇa*, I.59.3.
69. Kane, op. cit., II, pt. 1, Chap. X.; Ram Gopal, *India of Vedic Kalpasūtras*, National Publishing House, Delhi, 1959, pp. 456-8; R.L. Mitra, op. cit., pp. 379-83; A.B. Keith, op. cit., p. 363; Apte, op. cit., p. 230.
70. That the cow was offered to the guest of honour is mentioned in most of the Gṛhyasūtra texts but, according to the *ĀśGS*

(I. 24.30-1), the animal was slain only after he ordered its immolation with the words 'Om kuru' (accomplish, Om). Shingo Einoo has compiled a useful table showing the procedures of *madhuparka* and indicating the specific Sūtra passages which refer to the killing of cows in honour of guests: Einoo, 'The Formation of the Pūjā Ceremony', in Hanns-Peter Schmidt and Albrecht Wezler, eds., *Veda-Vyākaraṇa-Vyākhyāna: Festschrift Paul Thieme zum 90*, Verlag für Orientalitische Fachpublikationen, Reinbek, 1996, pp. 83-4.

71. *nāmāṃso madhuparko bhavati bhavati, ĀśGS*, I.24.33; *nāmāṃso madhuparkaḥ syāditi ha vijñāyate, KāṭhGS*, 24, 20; *nāmāṃsorghaḥ syāt, ŚāṅkhGS*, II.15.2; *na tvevāmāṃso' rghaḥ syād, PārGS*, I.3.29.
72. *ĀśGS*, I.24.1-33; *PārGS*, I.3.1-31; *KhādiraGS*, IV.4.5-23; *GobhGS*, IV.10.26; *HirGS*, I.4.12-13; *ĀpGS*, V.13.1-20. Cf. *ĀpDS* (V.IV.8.), which expressly provides for the offering of cow's flesh as a great delicacy to distinguished brāhmaṇa and kṣatriya guests (*athāpi brāhmaṇāya vā rājanyāya vābhyāgatāya mahokṣāṇaṃ vā mahājaṃ vā paced evamasmā ātithyaṃ kurvanti* cited in S.C. Banerji, *Dharma-Sūtras: A Study in Their Origin and Development*, Punthi Pustak, Calcutta, 1962, p. 157, fn. 39). Also see Kane, op. cit., II, pt. 2, p. 542; A.B. Keith, op. cit., p. 374.
73. There is textual evidence to indicate that the *madhuparka* ritual was conducted more than once in the course of marriage ceremonies. Āpastamba, for example, lays down that a cow should be killed for the bridegroom and another for those revered by him and Śāṅkhyāyana speaks of two *madhuparka* cows in marriage. *Vivāhe gauḥ/gṛheṣu gauḥ/tayā varamatithivadarhyet/yo 'syāpacitastamitarayā, ĀpGS*, I.3.5-8; *Vivāhe gāmarhayitvā gṛheṣu gāṃ te mādhuparkikyau, ŚāṅkhGS*, I.12.10. Cf. Kane, op. cit., II, pt. 1, p. 532.
74. *Aṣṭādhyāyī*, 3.4.73. See V.S. Agrawala, *India as Known to Pāṇini*, Prithvi Prakashan, Varanasi, 2nd edn., 1963, p. 100.
75. *tāṃ dṛḍhapuruṣa unmathya prāgvodagvā'nugupta āgāra ānaḍuhe rohite carmaṇyupaveśayati . . . PārGS*, I.8.10. The Vedic texts and the post-Vedic Sūtra literature provide numerous references to the ritual use of the hide of a cow or a bull. Interestingly the soma plant was pressed on the cow's or bull's hide to extract its juice.
76. *ĀśGS*, I.14.3.
77. The Gṛhyasūtras prescribe the use of upper garments of skins of different animals, depending on the caste of the student. If

one could not secure a skin suited to one's varṇa, he could wear an upper garment of cow-hide, because the cow is the chief among animals (*eiṇeyamajinamuttarīyaṃ brāhmaṇasya/rouravaṃ rājanyasya/ājaṃ gavyaṃ vā vaiśyasya/sarveṣāṃ vā gavyamasati pradhānatvāt, PārGS*, II.5.17-20. Also see Kane, op. cit., II, pt. 1, p. 278.

78. a*tha ya icchet putro me paṇḍito vigītaḥ, samitiṃ-gamaḥ, śuśrūṣitāṃ vācaṃ bhāṣitā jāyeta, sarvān vedān anubruvīta, sarvam āyur iyād iti, māṃsodanaṃ pācayitvā sarpiṣmantaṃ aśnīyātām; īsvarau janayita vai, aukṣṇena vārṣabheṇa vā, Br. UP.*; VI.4.18: *The Principal Upaniṣads* (with introduction, text and translation), ed. S. Radhakrishnan, Centenary edn., 4th impression, Oxford University Press, Delhi, 1991, p. 326.
79. Ram Gopal, op. cit., p. 278.
80. *ṚV*, X.16.7ab.
81. *ṚV*, X.14-18.
82. *AV*, XII.2, 48 cited in Keith and Macdonell, *Vedic Index*, I (Hindi translation by Ram Kumar Rai, Varanasi, 1962), p. 11. p. 9, s.v. *agni-dagdha*.
83. *KauśS*, 81, 20-9; *ĀśGS*, IV.3.19-21; *KauśGS*, V.2.13; V.3. 1-5, etc., cited in Ram Gopal, op. cit., pp. 360-1. For a detailed discussion of textual evidence from the *Śatapatha Brāhmaṇa* and other later Vedic texts as well as from the Gṛhyasūtras see Kane, op. cit., IV, pp. 189-266. The animal killed at the time of cremation was called *anustaraṇī*, which, according to Kane (ibid., p. 206, n. 486), means either a cow or a female-goat. But on the basis of Sāyaṇācārya's commentary and Tārānātha's *Vācaspatyam*, V.S. Apte interprets it as a cow sacrificed at the funeral ceremony (*The Practical Sanskrit-English Dictionary*, s.v. *anustaraṇam)*. A suggestion has also been made that the *anustaraṇī* cow is 'normally one that has not calved', W. Norman Brown, 'The Sanctity of the Cow in Hinduism', *Madras University Journal*, XXVIII, no. 2, 1957, p. 33, n. 17.
84. The word *śrāddha* is not found in the Vedic texts and, according to Kane, op. cit., IV, p. 350, first occurs in the *Kaṭhopaniṣad* (1.3.17). But it comes to occupy a very important place in the Dharmaśāstra literature and more than fifteen specialized treatises devoted to the procedures of *śrāddha* were produced in medieval times.
85. According to *ĀpDS*, II.7.16.25: 'the Manes derive very great pleasure from the flesh of the cow' S.C. Banerji, *Dharma-Sūtras:*

A Study in Their Origin and Development, p. 157. But the text also shows a preference for buffalo's flesh (II.7.16.27). According to the *PārGS*, on the eleventh day after death, the relatives of the dead should feed an odd number of brāhmaṇas a meal with meat; a cow could also be immolated in honour of the dead: *ekādaśyāmayugmān brāhmaṇān bhojayitvā māṃsavat/ pretāyoddiśya gāmapyeke ghnananti//* III.10.48-9. For a discussion of the different types of *śrāddha* see Kane, op. cit., IV, Chap. IX; Ram Gopal, op. cit., pp. 369-78.

86. *HirGS*, II.15.1; *BaudhGS*, II.11.51; *VaikhGS*, IV.3.
87. *ĀpGS*, VIII. 22.3-4.
88. *ĀpDS*, II.7.16.25—II.7.17.3, cited in Kane, op. cit., IV, p. 422. For different interpretations of *vārddhrīṇasa* see ibid., p. 422, fn. 951. Cf. *Yāj.* I. 258-72.
89. *ĀpDS*, II.8.19.18-9, cited by Om Prakash, op. cit., p. 39.
90. P.V. Kane, op. cit., II, pt. 2, p. 1245. The *mahāvrata* seems to have been some kind of a folk ritual marked by many bizarre practices. For a discussion of the *gavāmayana* and *mahāvrata* see ibid., pp. 1239-46; A.B. Keith, op. cit., pp. 351-2; Louis Renou, op. cit., p. 107; Jogiraj Basu, *India of the Age of the Brāhmaṇas*, Sanskrit Pustak Bhandar, Calcutta, 1969, pp. 162-5; Ram Gopal, op. cit., pp. 169- 71; G.U. Thite, op. cit., pp. 100-2.
91. For references to the *gṛhamedha* and its discussion see J.C. Heesterman, *The Broken World of Sacrifice: An Essay in Ancient Indian Ritual*, The University of Chicago Press, Chicago, 1993, pp. 190-3, 200-2.
92. Heesterman argues that in the case of *gṛhamedha*, the word used for cow slaughter is derived from the root *han* (to kill) which is different from the ritualistic killing indicated in the Vedic sacrifices by the term *ālambhana* (*The Borken World of Sacrifice*, pp. 189-201).
93. Apart from the bovine meat, the flesh of different animals formed part of diet as gleaned from the Vedic and post-Vedic texts. See Kane, op. cit., II, pt. 2, Chap. XXII.
94. Kane, op. cit., II, pt. 2, p. 777. The terms *upākarma* and *utsarjana* refer to the beginning and cessation of the Vedic studies. For details see ibid., Chap. XXIII.
95. *ĀpDS*, I.5.17.30-1. For a similar injunction see *VasiṣṭhaDS*, XIV.45.
96. *tasmāddhenvanaḍuhornāśnīyāt/ tadu hovāca yājñavalkyaḥ/ aśnāmyevāhaṃ māṃsalam cedbhavatiti/ ŚB*, III.1.2.21 quoted in R.S.

Sharma, *Material Culture,* p. 132, n. 19. The exact meaning of the word *aṃsala* is controversial. It has generally been translated as 'tender' but, according to M. Witzel, it might as well mean 'fatty' (Witzel, 'On the Sacredness of the Cow in India' (unpublished manuscript) abbreviated version published as *Ushi.wo meguru Indojin no kagae* (in Japanese), The Association of Humanities and Sciences, Kobe Gakuin University, 1991, no. 1, pp. 9-20.

97. *ĀpDS,* I.5.17.31.
98. *GautDS,* XVII. 37.
99. *ĀpDS,* I.9.26.1. Cf. According to *BaudhDS,* XVII.37-8 animals slain for the fulfilment of the sacred law and those killed by beasts could be eaten.
100. For a brief discussion of different views see Hanns-Peter Schmidt, 'Ahiṃsā and Rebirth', in Michael Witzel, ed., *Inside The Texts, Beyond The Texts: New Approaches To The Study of The Vedas,* Harvard Oriental Series, Opera Minora, vol. 2, Cambridge, 1997, pp. 209-10. Cf. J.C. Heesterman, 'Vrātya and Sacrifice', *Indo-Iranian Journal,* VI (1962), pp. 1-37.
101. Monier-Williams, *Sanskrit- English Dictionary,* s.v. *śasana.*
102. Om Prakash, op. cit., p. 16, fn.1.
103. Apte, *The Practical Sanskrit-English Dictionary,* s.v. *varāha.*
104. Ibid., s.v. *śarabha.*
105. Kane, op. cit., II, pt. 2, pp. 781-2; S.C. Banerjee, *The Dharmasūtras,* pp. 150-4. For a fuller list of animals, birds, fish and other aquatic animals mentioned in the Dharmasūtras see ibid., pp. 212-28.
106. Hanns-Peter Schmidt draws attention to Kauṭilya's *Arthaśāstra* (2.26), which mentions the slaughterhouse and to the first rock edict of Aśoka approving the killing of two peacocks and an antelope in the royal kitchen. He points out that neither of these refers to the consecration of meat. Yet, in his opinion, it is improbable to 'deduce a general toleration of random slaughter from the lack of reference to the consecration of the victim in certain Indian sources', Hanns-Peter Schmidt, 'Ahimsā and Rebirth', in Michael Witzel, op. cit., p. 210.
107. *Ch.Up.* 8.15 cited in Hanns-Peter Schmidt, 'The Origin of Ahiṃsā', in *Mélanges d'Indianisme a la memoire de Louis Renou,* Èditions E. Bocccard, Paris, 1968, p. 631.
108. W. Norman Brown, 'The Sanctity of the Cow in Hinduism',

Madras University Journal, XXVIII, no. 2 (1957), 33. Kane (op. cit., II, pt. 2, pp. 772-3) also cites Vedic passages mentioning the word *aghnyā*. I. Proudfoot rightly observes: '. . . *aghnyā* has nothing more to tell us about the sanctity of the cow than we would learn from a general study of the position of the cow in Vedic literature' (*Ahiṃsā and a Mahābhārata Story*, Australian National University, Canberra, 1987, p. 14).

109. A.A. Macdonell (*Vedic Mythology*, pp. 150-1) makes the valid point that the cow entered the conceptions of Vedic mythology—a view repeated by him and Keith in the *Vedic Index*, II, p. 146. But on Macdonell's own admission, this was owing to the great utility of the cow. For a convincing refutation of the above view see Norman Brown, op. cit.
110. See Doris Srinivasan, op. cit., Chap. II.
111. *ŚB*, XI.7.1.3, cited in Kane, op. cit., II, pt. 2, p. 773.
112. Sūryā has been interpreted as the wife and daughter of Sūrya: V.S. Apte, *The Practical Sanskrit-English Dictionary*, s.v. *sūrya*.
113. S.D. Singh, *Ancient Indian Warfare with special reference to the Vedic Period*, E.J. Brill, Leiden, 1965, p. 93, n. 2, p. 93.
114. Doris Srinivasan, op. cit., p. 14.
115. M. Witzel asserts: 'Cows are not sacred at all. This is a Christian term that has no bearing on ancient or modern India. Cows do not intercede as for example Catholic saints do, with god or the gods, to arrange eternal bliss for men in heaven', ('On the Sacredness of the Cow in India', op. cit.).
116. Witzel (ibid.) points out that poetry and speech are identified with the cow in the Vedas as well as in Zoroastrian poetry. Cf. Hanns-Peter Schmidt, *The Cow in the Pasture*, Leiden, 1976 cited by Witzel.
117. For Ṛgvedic references see Doris Srinivasan, op. cit., pp. 37ff. Also see Norman Brown, op. cit., pp. 40-1. The Vedic synonym dictionary, the *Nighaṇṭu*, lists 21 names of the cow (Witzel, 'On the Sacredness of the Cow . . .').
118. Norman Brown, op. cit., p. 42. Cf. W. Crooke ('The Veneration of the Cow in India', *Folklore*, XXIII (1912), pp. 280-1) errs in thinking that the cow had already acquired 'a considerable degree of sanctity' among the Indo-Aryans.
119. Ram Gopal treats *AV*, XII.4.38, 53 and XII.5.36-7 as a protest against the killing of the cow (op. cit., p. 472).

In our view these passages indicate that the Vedic texts did contain ideas that did not favour ritual killing of cattle and may be taken to suggest that the Vedic tradition was not a monolith.

120. *Dakṣiṇā* imparts power or strength to the receiver (*dakṣakaraṇī hi dakṣiṇā/ dakṣaśca balaṃ, Śabarabhāṣya* on *Mimāṃsāsūtra*, 10.3.45, cited in Apte, *The Practical Sanskrit-English Dictionary*, s.v. *dakṣiṇā*). It is used in the sense of a good milch cow or 'the richly milking one' in the Vedic texts because it gave wealth and hence strength to the priest. See Thite, op. cit., pp. 151-61; I. Proudfoot, op. cit., p. 3 and on p. 185, n. 22.
121. M. Bloomfield, *Religion of the Veda*, New York, 1908, pp. 69ff.
122. Norman Brown, op. cit., p. 43 draws attention to several passages in the *Ṛgveda* and *Atharvaveda* to prove this point. Also see Herman W. Tull, 'The Killing That Is Not Killing: Men, Cattle and the Origins of Non-Violence in the Vedic Sacrifice', *Indo-Iranian Journal*, 39 (1996), 236-7.
123. *AV*, 5.18.1.
124. *AV*, 5.18.10.
125. N.J. Shende, *The Religion and Philosophy of the Atharvaveda*, rpt. of 1952 edn., Bhandarkar Oriental Research Institute, Poona, 1985, p. 124.
126. H.D. Sankalia, '(The Cow) In History', *Seminar*, no. 93 (May 1967), 13.
127. Idem, *Prehistory and Protohistory of India and Pakistan*, 2nd edn., Deccan College, Poona, 1974, pp. 461, 484.
128. B.B. Lal, 'Excavations at Hastinapur and Other Explorations in the Upper Ganga and Satlej Basins', *Ancient India*, nos. 10-11 (1954-5); B. Nath, 'Animal Remains from Hastinapur', *Ancient India*, nos. 10-11 (1954-5), 107-20; B.P. Sahu, *From Hunters to Breeders*, Anamika Prakashan, Delhi, 1988, pp. 233-5.
129. Vibha Tripathi, *Painted Grey Ware: An Iron Age Culture of Northern India*, Concept Publishing Company, Delhi, 1976, p. 24.
130. R.C. Gaur, *Excavations at Atranjikhera*, Motilal Banarsidass, Delhi, 1983, pp. 461-71.
131. According to J.P. Joshi the assemblage at Bhagwanpura 'consists of a large number of charred bones, particularly belonging to that of cattle' ('A Note on the Excavation at Bhagwanpura', *Purātattva*, no. 8, 1975-6, p. 180). He maintains this position in his final report on the site (*Excavation at Bhagwanpura* 1975-6, Archaeological Survey of India, Delhi, 1993, p. 29), though his technical assistant asserts

'Surprisingly there is not a single piece of bone having a cut or butchering mark' (ibid., p. 143).

132. B. Nath, 'Animal Remains from Rupar and Bara sites . . .', *Indian Museum Bulletin*, III, nos. 1-2, pp. 69-116; B.P. Sahu, op. cit., pp. 235-6.

133. A.K. Sharma, 'Faunal Remains from Mathura', in J.P. Joshi et al., eds., *Facets of Indian Civilization: Recent Perspectives: Essays in Honour of Prof. B.B. Lal*, Aryan Books International, Delhi, 1997, III, 824.

134. *ṚV*, VIII.19.5; VIII. 24.20 cited in Kane, op. cit., II, pt. 2, p. 775.

135. *ā te agna ṛcā havirhṛdā taṣṭaṃ bharāmasi/te te bhavantūkṣaṇa ṛṣabhāso vaśā uta*, *ṚV*, VI.16.47, cited in Kane, op. cit., II, pt. 2, p. 775, f. 1854.

136. The linkage of technological developments (e.g., the knowledge of iron technology) and the dispersal of agriculture was indicated by D.D. Kosambi (*Introduction to the Study of Indian History*, Popular Prakashan, Bombay, 1956) but has been convincingly established by R.S. Sharma (*Material Culture*). For a summary of the relevant evidence see D.N. Jha, *Ancient India in Historical Outline*, Manohar, Delhi, 1998, Chaps. 3 and 4. Brian K. Smith and Wendy Doniger have discussed the practice of substitutions within a sacrificial ritual ('Sacrifice and Substitution: Ritual Mystification and Mythical Demystification', op. cit., pp. 189-223).

137. R.S. Sharma, *Material Culture*, Chap. V.

138. *AitB*, II.8-9; *ŚB*, I.2.3.6-9; *MS*, III.10.2 cited by Hanns-Peter Schmidt, 'Ahiṃsā and Rebirth', op. cit., p. 211. On the basis of his analysis of the Vādhūla text J.C. Heesterman speaks of a link between the growth of agriculture and the vegetal sacrifice, *The Inner Conflict of Tradition*, Oxford University Press, Delhi, 1985, p. 62. But this seems somewhat farfetched and does not go well with those passages of the *Vādhūlaśrautasūtra* (1.1.1.1, 1.1.1.3) which clearly indicate the possibility of sacrifice of animals including the cow, M. Sparreboom and J.C. Heesterman, *The Ritual of Setting up the Sacrificial Fires According to the Vādhūla School, Vādhūlaśrautasūtra*, Verlag Der Österreichischen Akademie der Wissenschaften, Wien, 1989.

139. For a detailed discussion of the *Varuṇapraghāsa* see Kane, op. cit., II, pt. 2, pp. 1095-100.

140. Hanns-Peter Schmidt, 'The Origin of Ahiṃsā', in *Mélanges d'Indianisme a la memoire de Louis Renou*, pp. 629-30; idem, 'Ahiṃsā and Rebirth', op. cit., pp. 211ff.; cf. Brian K. Smith and Wendy Doniger, 'Sacrifice and Substitution: Ritual Mystification and Mythical Demystification', op. cit., 189-224.
141. An examination of detailed sacrificial procedures does not seem to suggest a frequent use of surrogates in animal sacrifices. See *Śrautakośa* (English Section), Vaidik Samsodhana Mandala, Poona, 1962, vol. I, pt. 1, pp. 26-30; ibid., vol. I, pt. 2, pp. 770-893.
142. *KB*, 11.3; *ŚB*, 12.9.1.1. The clearest exposition of the idea of the sacrificer being eaten by the sacrificial victim is found in the Bhṛgu legend mentioned in *ŚB*, 11.6.1 and *JB*, 1.42-4. Bhṛgu considered himself superior in knowledge to his father Varuṇa who, wanting to teach his son a lesson, sent him to the yonder world. There Bhṛgu was appalled to see a man cutting another into pieces, a man eating another who was crying aloud, and a man eating someone who was silent. His curiosity was ultimately satisfied by his father who told him that the first man was a tree and was doing to the woodcutter what he had done to it in this world, the second man was an animal that was slaughtered and eaten earlier and the third man was a plant that had been eaten and was now eating the eater. For further references and discussion see Hanns-Peter Schmidt, 'The Origin of Ahiṃsā', op. cit., pp. 644-5; idem, 'Ahiṃsā and Rebirth', op. cit., pp. 214-15.
143. A.B. Keith, op. cit., p. 410.
144. That the Upaniṣadic position on sacrifice was different from that of the Vedic texts is clear from many passages (e.g., *Br.Up.*, 1.4.10; 3.9.6; 3.9.21; *Ch.Up.*, 1.10-12; 4.1-3) to which attention has been drawn by several scholars like Deussen (*The Philosophy of the Upaniṣads*, London, 1906), and A.B. Keith (op. cit.). More recently this point has been touched upon, albeit briefly, by Romila Thapar, 'Ideology and the Upanisads', in D.N. Jha, *Society and Ideology in India: Essays in Honour of Professor R.S. Sharma*, Munshiram Manoharlal, Delhi, 1996, pp. 11-27.
145. For example, A.B. Keith (op. cit., p. 585) points out that 'the allegory of life as a Soma sacrifice postulates that the fee shall be asceticism, liberality, right dealing, non-injury to life, and truthfulness. . . .'

146. The word *ahiṃsā/ahimsāyai* finds mention in several later Vedic and post-Vedic texts like the *Atharvaveda, Taittirīya Saṃhitā, Maitrāyaṇī Saṃhitā, Kāṭhaka Saṃhitā, Kapiṣṭhala Kaṭha Saṃhitā, Aitareya Brāhmaṇa, Taittirīya Āraṇyaka* and *Śatapatha Brāhmaṇa* (for reference to specific passages see Vishva Bandhu, *A Vedic Word-Concordance,* Vishveshvaranand Vedic Research Institute, Hoshiarpur, I, pt. 1 (1976) and II, pt. 1 (1973), s.v. *ahiṃsā.* There is however a wide divergence of scholarly opinion on the origin of the idea of non-violence (*ahiṃsā*). According to Hanns-Peter Schmidt ('The Origin of Ahiṃsā', op. cit., p. 653) the word *ahiṃsā* first occurs in the sense of a new doctrine in the teachings of Ghora Āṅgīrasa found in *Ch.Up.*, III.17.4. According to Ludwig Alsdorf (*Beiträge zur Geschichte von Vegetarismus und Rinderverehrung in Indien,* Akademie der Wissenschaften and der Literatur, Wiesbaden, 1962) the doctrine of *ahiṃsā* originated in the Indus Valley civilization, though J.C. Heesterman views his exercise as amounting to pushing 'the problem out of sight, into the limbo of an as yet undeciphered past'. Like Schmidt, Heesterman locates the origin of the doctrine within the Vedic-Brāhmaṇical tradition ('Non-Violence and Sacrifice', *Indologica Taurinensia,* XII (1984), p. 120). Independently of these scholars Witzel has asserted that the origin of *ahimsā* lies in the horror of killing and in this sense non-violence 'is a selfish action, not altruism and love for all beings . . . a prudent action taken in one's own interest . . . not necessarily a Jaina, Buddhist, or an "aboriginal" development at all, but one which has its roots in much earlier Brāhmaṇical thought' (Witzel, 'On the Sacredness of the Cow in India', op. cit.). There is, however, a strong opinion in favour of the *śramana* traditions as being the source of *ahiṃsā* doctrine. See William Norman Brown, *Man in the Universe,* University of California Press, Berkeley, 1966, p. 56; Louis Dumont, *Homo Hierachicus,* Oxford University Press, Delhi, 1988, p. 150; Brian Smith, 'Eaters, Food, and Social Hierarchy in Ancient India', *Journal of the American Academy of Religion,* LVIII, 2(1990), p. 198.

147. In the first passage of the *Kaṭhopaniṣad* (I.1.1) Vājaśrava is said to have performed the Viśvajit sacrifice for worldly gain, and his son, Naciketā, though hurt by its formalism and hypocrisy, did not hesitate to burn at Yamas' behest, the three fires that came to be known after him (I.1.13,17). Similarly

the *Śvetāśvatara Upaniṣad* (II.6) extols the fire offering: ***agnir yatrābhimathyate vāyur yatrādhirudhyate/somo yatrātiricyate tatra saṃjāyate manaḥ***: Where the fire is kindled, where the wind is directed, where the soma flows over, there the mind is born. See S. Radhakrishnan, *The Principal Upaniṣads*, p. 720. Again, the *Maitrāyaṇīya Upaniṣad* speaks of the importance of sacrifice (I.1) and of the knowledge of the Vedas (VII.8-10).

148. R.S. Sharma, *Material Culture*, Chaps. V-VII.

2

The Rejection of Animal Sacrifice: An Assertion of the Sacredness of the Cow?

Buddhism Negates Vedic Sacrifice

Early Buddhism, despite its antagonism to animal immolation, has a somewhat negative attitude to animals. According to the Buddhist canonical texts animals are inferior to human beings. Lacking the faculty of insight (*prajñā*), they cannot understand the Buddhist doctrine and therefore cannot attain liberation (*nirvāna*). Like man, they are subject to suffering, and their existence is extremely unhappy. Morally they are inferior and wicked on account of promiscuity and incest.[1] Despite such a negative evaluation of animals and their existence, the Buddhists preached the idea of non-injury to them as to all living beings. In this, they were guided, at the theoretical level, by such ethical principles as those of right speech and right action.[2] The application of the principle of right speech is seen in the case of the ox Nandivisāla who protested against the abusive language used by his brāhmaṇa master.[3] The tenet of right action in the context of animal–human relationships meant 'abstinence from conscious destruction of any sentient being from human to smallest animalcule'[4]—an idea emphasized in the canonical as well as the post-canonical Buddhist texts.[5] The precept regarding non-killing of animals determined the Buddhist attitude to animal sacrifice, which the Buddha rejected unequivocally. The *Aṅguttara Nikāya* relates the story of a wealthy brāhmaṇa, Uggatasarīra, who made preparations for a sacrifice in which numerous animals were to be killed. He released them, however, on the advice of the Buddha.[6] At another place in the same text we come across two brāhmaṇas, Ujjaya and Udāyī, asking the Buddha whether he thought well of sacrifice. The Buddha told each of them that he did not commend sacrifices that involved butchery.[7] The *Saṃyutta Nikāya* tells us that at the time of his visit to Śrāvastī, Prasenajit, the king of Kosala, started a great sacrifice of 500 oxen, 500 male calves, 500 female calves and 500 sheep, but abandoned it on the advice of the Buddha.[8] The *Sutta Nipāta* records the story that several old and decrepit but rich brāhmaṇas once visited the Buddha at Jetavana to ask him whether their practices were in conformity with those of earlier times. The Buddha however answered in the negative and taught them that cattle should not be killed for sacrifice;[9] for, like our parents and other kin, cattle are our great friends and give us food, strength, beauty, and happiness. Thereupon the brāhmaṇas are stated to have given up the killing of cows.[10]

Despite Ahiṃsā Meat Remains a Favourite Food

Despite the Buddha's opposition to the killing of animals for sacrifice or food, the early Pāli texts provide numerous references to cow slaughter. In the *Majjhima Nikāya,* for example, similes speaking of skilled cow-butchers (*dakkho goghātako*) or their apprentices (*goghātakantevāsī*) are repeatedly used.[11] The *Vinaya Piṭaka* compares the place where Soṇa Koḷivisa Thera walked in excitement after ordination with bleeding feet as 'a slaughter-house for oxen'.[12] The *Sutta Nipāta* states that death took its toll of living beings like cows meant for slaughter;[13] it speaks of the king Ikṣvāku who killed hundreds and thousands of cows in a sacrifice performed on the advice of brāhmaṇas.[14] The evidence drawn from the Buddhist texts thus unambiguously shows that eating animal flesh including beef was prevalent during the age of the Buddha and ties up with injunctions found in the Dharmasūtras and Gṛhyasūtras most of which belong to the post-Vedic/pre-Mauryan period and have been referred to earlier.

Although the Buddha himself was unambiguously against animal sacrifice, the killing of animals for rituals as well as for food was very common in his times. It was so prominent an aspect of contemporary life that, contrary to popular perception, even the Buddha and his followers do not seem to have abstained from meat. There are at least two passages in the early Buddhist texts that support the view that he ate pork. According to the story of the last meal recorded in the *Mahāparinibbāna Sutta,* at Pāvā he stayed in a mango grove of the smith Cunda who, according to the wishes of his honoured guest, offered him excellent food, hard and soft, and a large amount of *sūkaramaddava,*[15] or tender boar. The interpretation of this term as pork has been questioned,[16] but apart from this reference there is other clear evidence of the Buddha partaking of pork. In the *Aṅguttara Nikāya* we are told that

Ugga Seṭṭhi of Vaiśālī offered to the Buddha, a meal of rice cakes and pork (*sūkara māṃsa*) cooked with a good jujube sauce. Ugga himself considered this meal good, but realized it was unsuitable for the Tathāgata, who, however, accepted it out of pity.[17] There is indeed nothing to show that the Buddha and the early Buddhists abhorred meat. On the contrary, the Buddha is reported to have told the physician Jīvaka that he forbade the eating of meat only when there was evidence of one's eyes or ears as grounds for suspicion that the animal was slain for one's express use[18] and that no meat should be consumed without enquiry as to its provenance (*na ca bhikkhave appativkkhatvā masaṃ paribhuñjitabbaṃ*)[19]—unseen, unheard and unsuspected meat became 'the three pure kinds of flesh' in Buddhist tradition! Interestingly, he also permitted monks to eat the flesh of bear, fish, alligator, swine and ass during illness.[20] The absence of beef in this list does not mean that the cow was not slain for food or sacrifice in the age of the Buddha; for the Vaiśāliyan general Sīha is said to have killed an ox for him.[21] In a Jātaka story also the Bodhisat himself is said to have eaten beef (*gomāṃsam*).[22] One scholar has even pointed out that 'people once found a Buddhist friar killing . . . a calf and several times they complained that "followers of the Buddha" hurt and killed living things'.[23]

Early Buddhist texts refer to the various types of animal food like beef, venison and the flesh of sheep, goats, pigeons, poultry and so on[24] and Buddhist birth stories provide substantial basis for the view that flesh eating was widespread. In one Jātaka story, for example, the Bodhisat as Sakka, is said to have permitted the eating of flesh (*maṃsodanaṃ sappīpāñca bhuñja*);[25] in another he himself is depicted eating the meat of monkey and using its skin as a robe.[26] The flesh of deer was admitted to be the natural food of warriors and in one Jātaka story a king is said to have hunted deer and wild boar (*migasūkarādayo vadhitvā*) and eaten broiled venison (*aṅgārapakkaṃ migamaṃsam*),[27] though in another a king is persuaded to stop killing deer and all other animals.[28] A forest ascetic ate flesh without qualms,[29] thieves made use of meat, fish and liquor (*macchamaṃsasurādīni*) to cheat women of their ornaments,[30] and a demon fed a beautiful lady of Benares rice, fish and flesh to woo her.[31] Meat was generally eaten as a delicacy,[32] and the lizard was considered good,[33] though even the crow's flesh was not spared.[34] Pork seems to have been a favourite; roast pig was therefore offered to guests at weddings.[35] The slaughter of animals can be inferred also from several Jātaka references to large bags,[36] chariot harnesses[37] and the wandering ascetic's clothing (*cammasāṭako paribbājako*) of leather,[38] a meat shop in Mithilā,[39] and slaughter houses and fishermen at other places.[40] Nevertheless, the *Vinaya Piṭaka* tells us that the Buddha, on hearing that monks had eaten the flesh of elephants, horses, dogs, snakes, and tigers in times of famine and distress, declared these animals inedible. So too a ban on human flesh was imposed after a lay devotee Suppiyā offered the flesh of her thigh to a sick monk who ate it, perhaps unknowingly.[41] The golden peacock, believed to be a source of eternal youth and immortality, also seems to have been a forbidden food in the Jātakas,[42] though it was permitted by the Brāhmaṇical texts.[43]

Despite these exceptions, there is little doubt that the early Buddhists ate meat as a matter of course and 'to take a vow not to eat meat was unusual'[44] even if a fondness for it sometimes may have earned a monk the derogatory epithet of 'false ascetic' (*dussīlatapaso*).[45] The monastic order was practical enough to realize that it was living in a flesh eating non-Buddhist society and that it was not easy to break away completely from contemporary dietary norms and practices. The pragmatism of early Buddhism is best reflected in Kassapa Buddha's statement that 'defilement comes not from eating meat but from sin'[46] and encapsulated in the doctrine of the Middle Path preached by Gautama Buddha, who refused to make vegetarianism compulsory for monks,[47] even if he attached importance to animal husbandry and cattle herding (*gorakkhā*) as one of the noble professions for the laity.[48]

The Buddhist conservationist attitude is seen in the edicts of the Buddhist emperor Aśoka, who repeatedly appealed to his subjects to treat animals with kindness and care, and claimed to have made arrangements for their medical treatment.[49] In one of his edicts Aśoka prohibited animal sacrifice and festive gatherings,[50] in another exempted certain species of animals from slaughter, though the list is somewhat puzzling. The relevant decree reads:

> When I had been consecrated for twenty-six years I forbade the killing of the following species of animals, namely: parrots, *maināas*, red-headed ducks (?), *cakravāka*-geese, swans, *nandīmukhas* (birds encountered in rice fields?), pigeons, bats, ants, tortoises, boneless fish, *vedaveyakas*, *pupuṭas* of the Ganges (fish?), skate, porcupines, squirrels, deer, lizards, domesticated animals, rhinoceros, white pigeons, domestic pigeons, and all quadrupeds which are of no utility and are not eaten. She-goats, ewes, and sows which are with young or are giving suck are not to be killed, neither are their young up to the age of six months.[51]

Of the exempt animals some are difficult to identify, others like parrots, *maināas*, bats, ants, squirrels are not in the category of edible species. The prohibition of the killing of birds and fish, she-goats, sheep, and swine (pig) is indicative of the fact that their flesh was generally eaten; so was the case with the flesh of the bull (*saṇḍaka*) and other cattle—and Aśoka's silence about the cow certainly indicates that it had not achieved the sanctity that it came to acquire in later times. The imperial order, no doubt, bears testimony to Aśoka's compassion for animals, and has been stretched a little too far to indicate the establishment of animal homes by Aśoka.[52] But he did not and perhaps could not ban meat *per se*.

Interestingly, in one of his edicts Aśoka informed his subjects that two peacocks and a deer continued to form part of the royal cuisine every day, though he had the noble intention of stopping even their killing in the future.[53] One cannot therefore make too much of his proclamation. At best it was an example worth emulating, and it will be puerile to think that the emperor succeeded in banning a practice which was common, as can be inferred from Kauṭilya's *Arthaśāstra,* whose kernel belongs to the Mauryan period and which essentially is a Brāhmaṇical text. Kauṭilya advises the king to 'to make provision for pasture grounds on uncultivable tracts',[54] and devotes a section each to the superintendent of the slaughterhouse (*sūnādhyakṣa*)[55] and the superintendent of cows (*go'adhyakṣa*).[56] He lays down punishment for any person who entraps, kills, or molests deer, bison, birds and fish under state protection (*abhayavanavāsīnām*)[57] but does not take into account animals outside state custody. On the other hand he mentions a vendor of cooked meat and enjoins butchers to sell only the fresh and boneless meat of beasts (*mṛgapaśu*).[58] He states that domestic animals like cows, buffaloes, goats, sheep, asses and camels are to be maintained by herdsmen presumably under the supervision of the superintendent of cows who was required to classify the different types of animals. In this context he speaks of a category of cattle that are fit only for the supply of flesh (*sūnāmahiṣāḥ*).[59] The cow seems to have been important mainly for hide and dairy products, for we are told that cowherds were required to pay a certain quantity of clarified butter per year together with the branded hides of cows that died during the year.[60] Kauṭilya does not permit the killing of the calf, bull or milch cow. However, this seems to have been a minor offence for which he prescribes a nominal fine of 50 *paṇas*[61] and recommends the use of cow bones and dung, along with the hog's fat, as manure.[62] In fact there is nothing in his treatise to show that the cow was sacred and inviolate and that its flesh could not form part of human diet. On the contrary, he permits the cowherd to sell its flesh or dried flesh after its natural death.[63] Thus the continuity of the practice of eating the flesh of animals (including milch cattle) during the Mauryan period is borne out both by the *Arthaśāstra* of the brāhmaṇa Kauṭilya and the Buddhist texts.

There is no doubt that the early Buddhists and the Buddha himself did eat meat including beef, though, according to the post-Mauryan text *Milindapañho,* he did not die because of the pork meal which was 'in good condition, light, pleasant, full of flavour, and good for digestion' but on account of 'the extreme weakness of his body'.[64] When, however, their religion split into Hīnayāna and Mahāyāna the propriety of eating flesh became a subject of major debate among Buddhists. From the point of view of the Mahāyānists the eating of pork by the Buddha and the consumption of any meat by the monks involved a moral question and in the new set of monastic rules that they framed, meat was forbidden altogether.[65] The earliest indication of this prohibition is seen in the Mahāyānist remodelling of the *Mahāparinibbāna Sutta*; in its Sanskrit version the Buddha is stated to have said: 'I order the various disciples from today that they cannot any more partake of meat'.[66] This prohibition is equally categorical in the Mahāyāna version of the *Brahmajāla Sūtra* and the *Laṅkāvatāra Sūtra.* The latter, a Mahāyāna text datable to the third or fourth century,[67] devotes an entire chapter (*Māṃsabhaksaṇa*) to flesh eating, advances arguments against it, and describes the Buddha as telling the Bodhisattva Mahāmati to refrain from eating meat,[68] though, interestingly, he permitted his followers to eat eggs.[69]

Although the Mahāyānist vegetarian explanation of the Pāli canon seems to represent a distinct strand in Buddhist thought, it does not have any unity. This is clear from the fact that more or less at the time when Buddhaghoṣa interpreted the Buddha's last meal as consisting of pork, Fa-hsien[70] (fifth century), the Chinese Buddhist traveller to India, provided a Chinese version of the remodelled *Mahāparinibbāna Sutta* in which he ruled out the consumption of meat by the Enlightened One. He reported that the killing of animals was unknown throughout Madhyadeśa, though he admitted that meat was sold only by the cāṇḍālas outside the city.[71] Even if Fa-hsien's statement is ignored, the non-vegetarianism of Buddhists is borne out by other evidence. The Chinese text, *Fan-wang Ching*, which east Asian Buddhists consider the foundation of their monastic rules, regarded flesh eating not a major sin but merely one of the forty-eight 'light defilements'[72] like losing one's temper. Hsüan Tsang, the Buddhist traveller who came to India in the early seventh century, tells us that the flesh of oxen, asses, elephants, horses, pigs, dogs, foxes, wolves, lions, monkeys and apea was forbidden and those who ate such food became pariahs,[73] though, on his own admission, there were Mahāyānists who allowed the meat of geese, deer and calves.[74] He adds that his patron king Harṣavardhana 'forbade the slaughter of any living thing or flesh as food throughout the Five Indies on pain of death without pardon'[75] but the Hīnayāna Buddhists of A-k'ini (Turfan in Central Asia?) ate meat.[76]

The testimony of Hsüan Tsang is, however, weakened by Indian evidence. While he may have noticed a sentiment against animal food in some sections of society, it is unlikely that Harṣavardhana, despite his Buddhist predilection, issued any decree banning animal killing. For according to Bāṇabhaṭṭa, the biographer of Harṣa, his army procession included 'bearers of . . . goats attached to thongs of pig-skin, a tangle of hanging sparrows and fore-quarters of venison, a collection of young rabbits. . . .'[77] Thus, although one comes across divergent and often contradictory views on the question of meat eating, there is reason to believe that Buddhists continued to eat flesh meat in later times when the original 'three kinds' of pure flesh' was increased to nine.[78]

The tendency among Buddhists to be non-vegetarian invited the wrath of Jainas. According to the Jaina scholar Devasena (tenth century),[79] the Buddhists regarded as pure whatever fell into their begging bowls, ate flesh and drank wine.[80] Somadeva (tenth century), who mentions them first among the communities who advocate the eating of flesh food, says that a wise man cannot respect them because they are addicted to flesh and wine.[81] Hemacandra (twelfth century) is no less harsh in his denunciation of Buddhists whom he considers no better than gluttons who could not practice austerities as, he tells us, they ate day and night, and made no distinction between lawful and unlawful food.[82] Although much of the Jaina tirade against Buddhists was rooted in sectarian rivalry, it is likely that compared to their adversaries, the Buddhists were more pragmatic and conformed to local conditions. When, for example, the Mahāyāna Tāntric Buddhism reached Tibet through Padmasambhava and subsequently Atīśa Dīpaṅkara, it accommodated the indigenous religious beliefs and practices[83] as well as the local food habits. Not surprisingly, the people of Tibet, overwhelmingly Buddhist, eat cows, sheep, pigs and chickens, and yak;[84] nearer home, in Lahul, where Buddhism has been a dominant religion, the cow was eaten, albeit secretly, not long ago.[85] In pre-Han China (before 200 BC) the commoners ate vegetables and the ruling class enjoyed beef, mutton, pork and fish, but such social barriers in dietary culture may have become weak with Buddhism's great thrust into Chinese thought and life.

Although Buddhism in Japan, where it came from China and Korea, played a role in legitimizing the ideology that made outcasts of those associated with slaughtering, butchering and tanning, it may not have aimed at prohibiting animal food (deer, rabbit, or pork) but may have encouraged the inclusion of fish (especially raw fish) as an important item of the Japanese cuisine from the eighth century onwards. In Myanmar, where Theravāda Buddhism continues to remain the dominant religion, goats, pigs and poultry are raised for food, and beef eating is not uncommon,[86] though devout Buddhists may refrain from killing even mosquitoes. Similarly in Sri Lanka, another Theravāda country, various kinds of meat such as peacock-flesh (*mayūramaṃsa*), venison and pork (*miga-sūkara-maddava*), hare (*sasa-maṃsa*) and chicken (*kukkuṭa-maṃsa*) were 'favourite and delicious dishes'.[87] Beef also seems to have been eaten, though apparently the killing of cows was an offence punishable with a fine. According to a late Buddhist text, the *Vibhaṅgaṭṭhakathā*, king Bhātiya (AD 38-66) degraded some people who ate beef (*gomāṃsa*) to the position of scavengers for their failure to pay the fine for killing the cow, though it does not figure as a sacred animal in the text.[88] In Sri Lanka beef occupies a low position in the hierarchy of meat types but this has been attributed to the 'entrepreneurial antagonisms' between the Muslims who control the meat business and the aggressive Buddhist mercantile and professional class belonging to the caste of fishermen.[89] Notwithstanding their religious objections to killing animals and raising livestock for slaughter, Sri Lankan Buddhists continue to eat meat, including beef and fish.[90]

All this implies that while theoretical debates on meat eating and diversity in dietary practices persisted among the Buddhists, the flesh of various animals including milch cattle continued to please their palate. There is, therefore, not much basis for the view that meat eating was and is a taboo among Buddhists. Nor is there any evidence to show that the cow was inherently sacred and inviolable in Buddhist thought and tradition—which explains the inconspicuous involvement of Buddhists with establishing cattle homes in India.[91] As is well known, throughout its history the religion of the Buddha emphasized the precept of the Middle Path, which meant moderation: neither license nor exaggerated self-mortification. This was intended to keep life practicable for the monk as well as for the laity.

The Jaina Philosophical Basis of Ahiṃsā

Jainism, like Buddhism, rejected the Vedic sacrifice and placed emphasis on the creed of non-violence (*ahiṃsā*). It shared the attitude of Buddhism to animals because, in its view also, they were not capable of achieving liberation.[92] But Jainism emphasized the plurality of life forms and, going much beyond the concerns of human beings, it encouraged respect for both plant and animal life. It lacked the inherent flexibility of Buddhism and, at least in theory, remained uncompromising on the basic precepts that should govern life. The Jaina ascetic life is based on five 'great vows' (*mahāvratas*) to which initiates were required to commit themselves. The first of them, the vow to harm no living beings, was the most important for the initiate as well as the laity. The Jaina canonical rules relating to food are detailed. They not only prohibit meat, but everything that may contain the germs of life. Therefore monks were not allowed even juices, honey, ghee, curds or molasses.[93] The prohibition of killing was carried to its extreme and the *ahiṃsā* doctrine was practised much more rigorously in Jainism than in Buddhism.[94]

Be that as it may, the Jaina canonical works provide evidence for the eating of meat. The *Acārāṅgasūtra*[95] enjoins that if a monk inadvertently accepted as alms meat or fish containing many bones, he should not refuse it—though the same text indicates that Jaina ascetics did not accept any food involving *himsā*.[96] There is a similar reference in the *Daśavaikālikasūtra* that has been interpreted as evidence of meat and fish being eaten by Jaina monks in early times.[97] References to seasoned meat and various other kinds of meat are found in early Jaina texts like the *Vipākasūtra*[98] (II.14; III.22) and *Sūtrakṛtāṅgasūtra* (II.6, 9). According to A.L. Basham's interpretation of a passage of the *Bhagvatīsūtra*, Mahāvīra, recuperating from his duel of yogic power with his rival Makkali Gosāla (who shared his *ahiṃsā* doctrine with him) asked his disciple to prevent a laywoman from cooking two pigeons for him and asked her to cook instead the meat of a cockerel (*kukkuḍamaṃsa*) that had just been killed by a cat,[99] though this interpretation is unacceptable to many. Although the words *poggala*, *maṃsa* and *maccha* occurring in the above texts have been given a laboured vegetarian gloss by modern scholarship,[100] commentators like Haribhadrasūri (eighth century) and Śilaṅka (ninth century) have understood them in their primary sense.[101] As late as the eleventh century Abhayadeva interpreted these words literally, though he also read vegetarian meanings in them,[102] much as the later Buddhists glossed over the embarrassing pork meal of the Buddha. But the possibility of Jaina ascetics eating meat in later times cannot be ruled out. The *Bṛhat Kalpa Bhāṣya* of Saṅghadāsagaṇi (sixth century) informs us that in the Sindhu region, where the people were predominantly non-vegetarians, monks were asked to adjust their life to local conditions,[103] and one is tempted to imagine that they ate flesh oftener than the precept of abstaining from animal food would indicate. The text further tells us that in a settlement of robbers or in a deserted village where only meat was available, a monk was allowed to eat flesh as an exception to the general rule.[104] This accords well with the monastic rules laid down in the *Nisītha Cūrṇi*, a commentary on the *Nisītha Sūtram* by Jinadāsa (seventh century), according to which, in adverse circumstances, monks could eat meat, wine and honey, all of which were otherwise taboo.[105] This injunction is similar to the one found in the *Ācārāṅgaṭīkā*,[106] a commentary on the *Ācārāṅgaśutta*, which hints that flesh could be eaten in a situation of extreme distress. The *Niśītha Cūrṇi* advises monks that eating meat is better than accepting food specially prepared for them (*ahākammiya*) or eating at night (*addhāṇakappa*) in those regions where people are not familiar with the Jaina ascetic dietary practices. It also indicates that the Jaina precept could not stand in the way if one were suffering from fistula, for which meat was an effective cure.[107] Similarly, according to the interpretation of the *Daśavaikālika* by the Śvetāmbara Jaina logician-commentator Haribhadrasūri (AD 725-825), 'the monks . . . in the days of the Sūtras did not have any objection to eat flesh and fish which were given to them by the householders'.[108] Therefore it seems reasonable to hold that the Jainas, especially in the early phase of their history, were not strict vegetarians.[109]

There is, however, overwhelming evidence to prove that animal food remained a strong taboo among Jainas and their texts abound in stories in support of this. Sometimes the mere killing of animals could be a good enough reason to convert to Jainism as was the case with Ariṣṭanemi, who, according to the *Uttarādhyayanasūtra*, a Jaina canonical text, renounced the world on hearing the cries of animals being slaughtered at his wedding.[110] Some instances of aversion to meat are also known from later commentaries. The *Āvaśyakacūrṇi* of Jinadāsagaṇi Mahattara (seventh century) records the story of Jinadatta who defied medical advice to eat meat,[111] anticipating, as it were, the views of Ugrāditya (eighth–ninth century), the author of the Jaina medical treatise *Kalyāṇakāraka*, on the uselessness of a meat diet.[112] Amitagati (eleventh century) asserted that it was better to take poison than to eat meat.[113] The *Vyavahārabhāṣya* of Malayagiri (twelfth century?) also reports that some 500 monks starved themselves to death and exposed their bodies to jackals and vultures, when they could not get food in a famine.[114] All this shows that the Jainas viewed animal food with odium, though there is also much to suggest that this was not always the case.

Several Jaina works testify to the eating of meat outside the monastic circle. An early canonical text, *Uvāsagadasāo,* recounts the story of a rich merchant's wife Revatī, who known for her fondness for meat, asked her family retainers to kill each day two young bulls in her ancestral herd and bring them to her, so that she could enjoy their meat along with juice, liquor and spirits of various kinds.[115] A passage in the *Niśītha Sūtram* tells us that meat was a prominent item in the diet of the *mlecchas* and that cattle, goats, sheep and deer were killed for food.[116] The *Niśītha Cūrṇi,* a commentary on this text, tells us that hunters were paid for the flesh brought by them and makes specific mention of the meat of buffaloes, goats, dogs and cows.[117] The *Vasudevahiṇḍī* of Saṅghadāsagaṇi (late sixth century), the first Jaina version of the *Mahābhārata,* refers to the flesh of dogs, asses and crows as inedible; it records the story of king Sumitra, a champion of non-violence, who ate meat, though reluctantly, and incurred great sin.[118] In a story narrated in the *Ācārāṅgacūrṇi* of Jinadāsagaṇi (seventh century), when an ox died the master of the house, a *sucivādi* (?), instead of giving it to the cāṇḍālas, ordered his servants to take its hide, give the flesh to beggars, and make bow strings of the veins.[119] Udyotanasūri (eighth century) mentions a king who agreed with the Jaina ascetic practice of avoiding beef but not curds,[120] and refers to animal sacrifice and animal flesh as food.[121] At one place he says that when born as a rabbit, deer or buffalo one's flesh was liable to be torn to pieces and eaten.[122] Haribhadra (eighth century) speaks of the slaughter of fifteen buffaloes and of cooking them for brāhmaṇas;[123] elsewhere he tells us about a cook who killed a pig when a cat snatched away the meat prepared for the Manes.[124] He refers to special preparations like fried fish and roasted mutton and gives the impression that rulers ate fish and the flesh of buffalo and sheep, though he also draws attention to the evil consequences of that by narrating the story of a king who acquired bad *karma* even by eating the meat of an artificial cock.[125] Somadeva (tenth century), who was unsparing in his denunciation of Brāhmaṇical religion and ritual killing of animals, tells us in his *Yaśastilaka* about the Jaina king Yaśodhara, who argued with his mother against the efficacy of Vedic sacrifice, but ultimately agreed to kill a cock at the altar of Caṇḍikā and eat its flesh.[126] However, he makes a case against beef eating. He asserts that the gem supposed to be on the head of a snake counteracts poison, but snake-poison itself causes death; that the milk of a cow can be taken but not its flesh, just as the leaves of a poisonous plant may be taken for the cure of disease, while its roots may cause death.[127] Here he seems to anticipate and refute the idea found in a later Jaina play, *Moharājaparājaya*, in which a character argues that just as one drinks cow's milk one may eat cow meat without incurring any sin.[128] The *Prabandhacintāmaṇi* of Merutuṅgasūri (fourteenth century) refers to the use of animal food among brāhmaṇas and kṣatriyas[129] and to a physician who advised king Vikramāditya to eat the flesh of the crow (*kākamāṃsaṃ*), presumably as a cure for a disease.[130] Paṇḍita Dhanapāla, who figures prominently in one of his stories, even questions the sacredness of the cow.[131] The *Sūryaprajñapti*, a late Jaina work on astronomy, recommends different types of food (like the frog and clawed and aquatic animals) for various *nakṣatras*,[132] presumably for the common people. It also informs us that not only tribal people like the Pulindas and untouchables like cāṇḍālas, but brāhmaṇas too were allowed to eat impure flesh like that of the dog. Such evidence of flesh eating as has been cited above, even if occasionally contradictory, may become voluminous if one rummages through the vast amount of Jaina literature. Statements disapproving the practice of eating meat would not occur so frequently in the texts were it not for people who ate flesh regularly. But this cannot be construed to mean that the Jaina clergy and laity in later times were allowed to eat meat, bovine or otherwise.

The Jaina textual testimony is overwhelmingly against eating animal food of all types, which, as we shall show, the early medieval law books had in many cases declared inedible for the upper castes. The influence of Jaina dietary culture is best seen in western India where several kings adopted it. Hemacandra (twelfth century), the encyclopaedic Śvetāmbara Jaina scholar, advised his patron kings, Siddharāja and Kumārapāla, to give up wine and meat, and even inspired the latter to assiduously promote the doctrine of *ahiṃsā* throughout his kingdom.[133] Under his influence Kumārapāla is said to have prohibited animal slaughter and built Tribhuvanavihāra and thirty-two other temples 'for expiation of the sin of flesh eating to which he was addicted before his conversion to Jainism',[134] though the effectiveness of such a ban, if at all imposed, remains doubtful.[135] Later Jaina accounts claim that Harivijayasūri played a similar role in the court of Akbar who ordered the freeing of caged birds and banned animal slaughter on the Śvetāmbara festival of *Paryuṣaṇ*.[136] Jahangir, despite his inconsistent attitude towards Jainism, appointed a Śvetāmbara monk to teach his son, and issued, in 1616, an edict granting freedom of worship to the Jainas.[137] We are also told that Jahangir and Aurangzeb passed laws favourable for the protection of cows,[138] though this could not have resulted from any veneration of the animal.

This survey of limited evidence indicates that both Buddhism and Jainism found animal food unacceptable in normal circumstances. Both made major departures from Vedic beliefs and practices, but, curiously, neither held the cow as sacred.[139] The former, emphasizing the Middle Path, was comparatively flexible in its food regulations. It travelled to many Asian countries and therefore had to come to terms with diverse geographical, ecological and cultural milieus. The resultant glaring gaps between orthodoxy and practice in various strands of Buddhist thought are therefore easy to understand. As opposed to Buddhism, Jainism remained confined to the country of its origin throughout and hence the need for tuning itself up to diverse food cultures was not acutely felt. Its adherents, compared with Buddhists, have been much more rigid in their rejection of animal food and consider it a mark of their community identity.[140] Both religions permitted deviations from the prescribed dietary norms in exceptional circumstances. But there is no doubt that, in varying degrees, they strengthened the idea of non-violence (*ahiṃsā*), which appears in its rudimentary form in the Vedic and Upaniṣadic texts.[141]

NOTES

1. Lambert Schmithausen, *Buddhism and Nature,* Lecture delivered on the Occasion of the EXPO 1990, The International Institute for Buddhist Studies, Tokyo, 1991, pp. 14-15; idem, 'The Early Buddhist Tradition and Ecological Ethics', *Journal of Buddhist Ethics,* 4 (1997), http://jbe.ba.psu.edu/4/4cont.html.
2. James P. McDermott, 'Animals and Humans in Early Buddhism', *Indo-Iranian Journal,* 32 (1989), pp. 269ff.
3. *Vinayapīṭaka,* IV.5. Cf. *Jātaka,* I, 191 cited in McDermott, op. cit., p. 271; also Nandavisāla Jātaka (J. 28).
4. James P. McDermott, op. cit., p. 271.
5. James P. McDermott (op. cit., p. 272) cites a late sūtra

attributed to Gautama Prajñāruci (fourth-fifth century AD), available only in Chinese and Tibetan translations, to show that those who killed animals in diverse circumstances went to appropriate hells. Also see Daigan and Alicia Matsunaga, *The Buddhist Concept of Hell*, Philosophical Library, New York, 1972.

6. G.P. Malalasekera, *Dictionary of Pāli Proper Names*, s.v. Uggatasarīra.
7. Ibid., I, pp. 343, 376.
8. *pañca ca vasabhasatāni pañca ca vacchatarasatāni pañca ca vacchatarisatāni pañca ca ajasatāni pañca ca urabbhasatāni thūṇūpanitāni honti yaññatthāya, Saṃyutta Nikāya*, 3.9.23 (vol. I, p. 74).
9. *Sutta Nipāta*, Brāhmaṇadhammika Sutta, 12, p. 58.
10. *yathā mātā pitā bhātā aññe vāpi ca ñātakā gāvo no paramā mittā yāsu jāyanti osadhā, annadā baladā cetā vaṇṇadā sukhadā tathā, etamatthavasaṇ ñatvā nāssu gāvo haniṃsu te.* Ibid., 13-14, p. 58-60.
11. *dakkho goghātako vā goghātakantevāsī vā gāviṃ vadhitvā catumahāpathe bilaso vibhajitvā nisinno assa, Majjhima Nikāya*, 19.1.4. (vol. III, p. 153).
12. *Vinaya Piṭaka* (*Mahāvagga*), V.1.13 (SBE XVII, pt. 2, p. 6).
13. *govajjho viya niyyati, Sutta Nipāta*, Salla Suttam 7, p. 128.
14. *tato ca rājā saññatto brāhmaṇehi rathesabho, nekasatasahassiyo gāvo yaññe aghātayi, Sutta Nipata*, Brahmanadhammika-Suttam 25, p. 60.
15. *Dīgha Nikāya*, 3.19.62 (vol. II, pp. 98-9).
16. Whether or not the Buddha died of a meal of pork has been a theological problem among Buddhists and has led to much logic chopping even among serious scholars. T.W. Rhys Davids, who first translated the word as 'boar-tender', was not quite sure of the exact sense it conveyed (*The Questions of King Milinda*, SBE XXXV, pt. 1, p. 244, fn. 1). In his *Sumaṅgalavilāsinī* (Pali Text Society, London, 1971, vol. II, p. 568) Buddhaghoṣa (fifth century AD) interpreted the word *sūkaramaddava* as 'meat available (in the market) of an excellent (first-rate) pig, neither too young nor too old' but, in addition to his own explanation, he also referred to two views, held by others (Walpola Rahula in *JAOS*, 102.4 (1982), p. 602). Similarly, the *Paramatthajotikā* (Colombo, 1920), which is a commentary on the canonical Pāli text *Udāna*, explained the term on the basis of the *Mahāṭṭhakathā* as 'soft and fatty pork . . . available in the market' and mentioned

three other meanings ascribed to the term by some people (Walpola Rahula, op. cit., pp. 602-3). Both exegetical works thus support the interpretation of the *sūkaramaddava* as pork and if credence is given to them, the Buddha died because of eating pork. According to one view, however, the idea (Arthur Waley, 'Did Buddha die of Eating pork?: with a note on Buddha's image', *Mélanges Chinois et bouddhiques*, vol. 1931-2, Juillet [1932], p. 347), is 'wholly absent from the Chinese canon'. Several vegetarian explanations of the term *sūkaramaddava* are available in later Buddhist texts as well as in modern writings. A recent effort to equate *sūkaramaddava* with the Vedic *pūtika* and Santal *putka*, a kind of mushroom, does not carry conviction (R. Gordon Wasson, 'The Last Meal of the Buddha with Memorandum by Walpola Rahula of the Early Sources for the Meaning of *Sūkaramaddava*', *JAOS*, 102.4 (1982), pp. 591-603). But it must be conceded that whatever confusion centres round the actual meaning of the term stems from the fact that it does not occur anywhere else in the Buddhist Canon and Brāhmaṇical literature and is a hapax legomenon. For a discussion of whether or not the Buddha died of eating pork see Arthur Waley, op. cit., pp. 343-54.

17. Malalasekera, *Dictionary of Pāli Proper Names*, s.v. Ugga; *Aṅguttara Nikāya*, Manāpadāyīsuttam, 5.5.4 (vol. II, p. 314). The crucial *sutta*, where the story is related does not occur in the Chinese canon. Waley, op. cit., p. 347.
18. In the Jīvaka Sutta, the Buddha says: 'I allow the use of fish and meat blameless in three ways, unseen (*adiṭṭham*), unheard (*asutaṃ*) and unsuspected (*aparisaṅkitaṃ*).' *Majjhima Nikāya*, 5.1.2 (vol. II, p. 39). Cf. V.A. Gunasekara, 'Buddhism and Vegetarianism, The Rationale for the Buddha's Views on the Consumption of Meat', *Buddhasasana Home Page* (Eng. Section), *http://www.uq.net.au/slsoc/budsoc.html*.
19. V.A. Gunasekara, op. cit.
20. *Vinaya Piṭaka, Mahāvagga*, VI.2.1-2. (SBE XVII). The monks were also allowed the use of urine as medicine, *Vinaya Piṭaka*, I.30.4; VI.14.6.
21. Malalasekera, *Dictionary of Pāli Proper Names*, s.v. Sīha. Cf. *Aṅgutta Nikāya* (Sīhasenāpatisuttam), V.4.4 (vol. II, pp. 304-6); *J.144*.
22. Gahapati Jātaka (*J.* 199). Cf. Nanguttha Jātaka (*J.* 144).

23. E. Wahburn Hopkins, 'The Buddhist Rule Against Eating Meat', *JAOS*, XXVII (1907), pp. 457-8.
24. For references see Om Prakash, *Food and Drinks in Ancient India*, Munshiram Manoharlal, Delhi, 1961, p. 64.
25. Kumbha Jātaka (*J.* 512).
26. Mahābodhi Jātaka (*J.* 528).
27. Bhallāṭīya Jātaka (*J.* 504).
28. Nigrodhamṛga Jātaka (*J.* 12).
29. Bhikkhāparampara Jātaka (*J.* 496).
30. Sulasā Jātaka (*J.* 419).
31. Samugga Jātaka (*J.* 436).
32. Cakkavāka Jātaka (*J.* 434). Cf. Kāka Jātaka (*J.* 140).
33. Pakkagodha Jātaka (*J.* 333).
34. Punnanadi Jātaka (*J.* 214).
35. Munika Jātaka (*J.* 30); Saluka Jātaka (*J.* 286).
36. Brahācchatta Jātaka (*J.* 336).
37. Kukkura Jātaka (*J.* 22)
38. Cammasāṭaka Jātaka (*J.* 324).
39. Kumbhakāra Jātaka (*J.* 408).
40. Om Prakash, op. cit., p. 63, nn. 10, 11.
41. *Vinaya Piṭaka*, VI.4.1 (Hindi tr. Rahula Sankrityayana, Mahabodhi Sabha, Benaras, 1935), pp. 231-3.
42. Mora Jātaka (*J.* 159); Mahāmora Jātaka (*J.* 491).
43. For a list of birds whose flesh was forbidden or permissible item of food see S.C. Banerji, *Dharmasutras: A Study in their Origin and Development*, Punṭhi Pustak, Calcutta, 1962, pp. 153-4.
44. The *Pātimokkha* prohibits meat and fish on the ground that they are delicacies and the monks were not expected to indulge in them. The rules for novices contain no injunction against meat. But the Jātaka attitude is best seen in a verse attributed to the Bodhisat in the Telovāda Jātaka (*J.* 246), which is as follows: *bhuñjmāno pi sappañño na pāpena upalippati* (According to the context, if one has divine wisdom, eats fish or meat, even when he knows it is prepared for him, he does no wrong: E.W. Hopkins, op. cit., pp. 457, 462).
45. Godhā Jātaka (*J.* 138); Godhā Jātaka (*J.* 325).
46. In the *Āmagandha Sutta* a brāhmaṇa confronted the Buddha with his arguments against eating fish and flesh. But in his reply he uttered a number of verses listing acts of moral defilement and at the end of each verse uttered the refrain: 'this is the stench

giving defilement, not the consumption of meat' (*easāmagandho na hi maṃsabhojanaṃ*) *Sutta Nipāta*, p. 48.

47. The story goes that Devadatta, who was keen to bring a schism in the Buddhist Order, asked him to impose on all monks the five rules including the ban on fish and meat. The Buddha, however, refused to oblige. This may be an indication of an early, though temporary, division in the Sangha. Malalasekera, *Dictionary of Pāli Proper Names*, s.v. Devadatta; Richard Gombrich, *Theravāda Buddhism: A Social History from Ancient Benares to Modern Colombo*, Routledge & Kegan Paul, London-New York, 1988, p. 94.
48. For a discussion of *gorakkhā* (cattle herding) see James P. McDermott, op. cit., pp. 276-7. In a story recorded in the *Dīgha Nikāya*, a king is advised to grant seed and fodder to those in his country who take up agriculture and cattle breeding, A.K. Warder, *Indian Buddhism*, Motilal Banarsidass, Delhi, 1970, p. 172.
49. II Rock Edict, lines 5-6, D.C. Sircar, *Select Inscriptions Bearing on Indian History and Civilization*, I, 2nd edn., University of Calcutta, Calcutta, 1965, p. 17; VII Pillar Edict, line 13, D.C. Sircar, op. cit., p. 63.
50. Rock Edict I, lines 3-4, Sircar, op. cit., p. 15.
51. Pillar Edict 5, Sircar, op. cit., pp. 59-60.
52. Deryck O. Lodrick, *Sacred Cows and Sacred Places: Origins and Survivals of Animal Homes in India*, University of California Press, Berkeley, 1981, pp. 57-8.
53. Rock Edict I, lines 11-12, Sircar, op. cit., p. 16.
54. *AŚ*, II.2.1.
55. *AŚ*, II.26.
56. *AŚ*, II.29.
57. *AŚ*, II.26.1.
58. *AŚ*, II.26.7.
59. *AŚ*, II.29.5 (*Kauṭilya's Arthaśāstra*, tr. R. Shamasastry, 7th edn., Mysore, 1961, p. 143). The word occurring in R.P. Kangle's edition is *sūnāmahisāḥ* (*AŚ*. II.29.8) which has been translated as slaughter of buffaloes.
60. *AŚ*, II.29.5.
61. *AŚ*, II.26.11. Also see Aparna Chattopadhyay, 'A Note on Beef-Eating in Mauryan Times', *Indo-Asian Culture*, XVII, no. 2 (1968), pp. 49-51.
62. *AŚ*, II.24.24.

63. *AŚ*, II.29.26.
64. *Mililidapañho*, IV.3.22. Also see *The Questions of King Milinda*, SBE XXXV, pt. 1, p. 244, fn. 1.
65. Arthur Waley, op. cit., p. 347.
66. V.A. Gunasekara, op. cit.
67. For a brief discussion of the date of the *Laṅkāvatāra Sūtra* see Maurice Winternitz, *A History of Indian Literature*, II, 2nd edn., rpt., Munshiram Manoharlal, Delhi, 1977, p. 337.
68. V.A. Gunasekara, op. cit.
69. P.C. Divanji, '*Laṅkāvatārasūtra* on Non-Vegetarian Diets', *Annals of the Bhandarkar Oriental Research Institute*, 18 (1940), p. 317.
70. Arthur Waley, op. cit., pp. 347-8.
71. James Legge, *Fahien's Record of the Buddhistic Kingdoms*, Oxford, 1886, p. 43.
72. The *Fan-wang Ching* is supposed to be an extract from a long Sanskrit work but it may have been translated into Tibetan from Chinese some time after AD 507. See Arthur Waley, op. cit., p. 349 and n. 5.
73. Thomas Watters, *On Yuan Chwang's Travels in India*, London, 1904-5, 2nd Indian edn., Munshiram Manoharlal, Delhi, 1973, Chap. V, p. 178.
74. Thomas Watters, op. cit., Chap. III, p. 57.
75. Samuel Beal, *Si-Yu Ki: Buddhist Records of the Western World*, London, 1884, Indian rpt., Motilal Banarsidass, Delhi, 1981, Book V, p. 214.
76. Thomas Watters, op. cit., Chap. III, pp. 53-60. Also see Devahuti, *Harsha: A Political Study*, 2nd edn., Oxford University Press, Delhi, 1983, p. 6.
77. *Harṣacarita* (with the commentary of Śaṅkara), ed. K.P. Parab, 5th edn., Nirnaya Sagar Press, Bombay, 1925, text p. 211; tr. E.B. Cowell and F.W. Thomas, London, 1929, p. 208.
78. Thomas Watters, op. cit., p. 55, fn. 3.
79. J.K. Nariman (*Literary History of Sanskrit Buddhism*, 2nd edn., rpt., Pilgrims Book Pvt. Ltd., Delhi, 1972, p. 289) draws attention to Devasena's *Darśanasāra* which contains 'a virulent attack on the Buddhists charging them . . . with the consumption of animal food. . . .' Cf. Jagdish Chandra Jain, *Prākrit Sāhitya Kā Itihās*, Chowkhamba Vidya Bhavan, Varanasi, 1961, p. 319.
80. K.K. Handiqui, *Yaśastilaka and Indian Culture*, Jaina Saṃskriti Saṃrakshaka Maṇḍala, Sholapur, 1949, p. 373.
81. Ibid., pp. 371-2.

82. Ibid., p. 373.
83. An idea of how Buddhism adapted itself to conditions prevailing in Tibet is provided by Eva K. Dargyay, 'Buddhism in Adaptation: Ancestor Gods and Their Tantric Counterparts in the Religious Life of Zanskar', *History of Religion*, 28, no. 2 (1988), pp. 123-34.
84. L.A. Waddell, *The Buddhism of Tibet or Lamaism*, 2nd edn., Cambridge, 1939, pp. 216, 219, 225. Writing in 1924 Charles Bell reported as follows: 'Dalai Lamas do not drink wine or spirits, but they may and do eat meat, a necessary article of diet in Tibet, where the climate is cold and fruit and vegetables are scarce, often indeed unobtainable. As, however, the taking of life, even for food, is to Buddhists a sin, a religious ceremony is performed on behalf of the animals so killed and this is held to insure their rebirth in a higher state of existence. Thus the loss of their lives means a gain to them', Charles Bell, *Tibet Past and Present*, Oxford University Press, Oxford, 1924, rpt., Delhi, 1990, p. 50.
85. A.F.P. Harcourt, *The Himalyan Districts of Kooloo, Lahoul and Spiti* (Selections from the Records of the Government of the Punjab, New Series no. X), Vivek Publishing Company, Kamla Nagar, Delhi, rpt., Delhi, 1982, p. 65.
86. E. Washburn Hopkins (op. cit., p. 455) refers to H. Fielding Hall's *People at School* (1906) to imply that it was customary among the Burmese Buddhists to eat meat and that, in doing so, they were inspired by the British beef eaters. Incidentally Burma became a part of the British empire in 1886.
87. *Rasavāhinī*, ed. Saranatissa Thera, Colombo, 1920, II, pp. 10, 91, 128, 181 cited in Walpola Rahula, *History of Buddhism in Ceylon*, M.D. Gunasena, 2nd edn., Colombo, 1966, p. 247.
88. *Vibhaṅgaṭṭhakathā* (Simon Hewavitarne Bequest Series, Colombo), p. 310 cited in Walpola Rahula, *History of Buddhism in Ceylon*, p. 231.
89. H.L. Seneviratne, 'Food Essence and the Essence of Experience', in R.S. Khare, ed., *The Eternal Food: Gastronomic Ideas and Experiences of Hindus and Buddhists*, State University of New York Press, Albany, 1992, p. 195.
90. N.D. Wijesekera, *The people of Ceylon*, 2nd edn., M.D. Gunasena, Colombo, 1965, pp. 114, 141 cited in Frederick J. Simoons, *Eat Not This Flesh*, 2nd edn., University of Wisconsin Press, Madison, 1994, p. 370, n. 62.

91. Deryck O. Lodrick, op. cit., pp. 146-7.
92. Paul Dundas, *The Jains*, Routledge, London and New York, 1992, p. 90.
93. *Acārāṅgasūtra*, II.1.8. Cf. II.1.1.1-6. Also see S.B. Deo, *History of Jaina Monachism*, Deccan College Research Institute, Poona, 1956, p. 172.
94. The idea of *ahiṃsā* was carried to such lengths in Jainism that fasting became and remains central to its practice. For this reason the question whether or not the Tirthaṅkar should eat, has been a point of serious debate. See Paul Dundas, 'Food and Freedom: The Jaina Sectarian Debate on the Nature of the Kevalin', *Religion*, XV (1985), pp. 161-98.
95. *bahu-y-aṭṭhiyaṃ vā maṃsaṃ macchaṃ vā bahu-kaṇṭagaṃ* (II.1.10.5) cited in Ludwig Alsdorf, *Beiträge zur Geschichte von Vegetarianismus und Rinderverehrung in Indien*, Akademic der Wissenschaften and der Literatur, Wiesbaden, 1962, p. 8, fn. 3. Also see S.B. Deo, op. cit., p. 172.
96. *sebhikkhū ca sejaṃ maṃsaṃ va bhajijjamāṇaṃ pehāe tillapūyaṃ va āe sāe uvakkhaḍijjamāṇaṃ pehāe no khaddhaṃ uva saṅkavittu o bhā siñjā nannatha gilāṇa ṇisāe*, *Acārāṅgasūtra*, II.1.3. *sāsiāo avidala kaḍāo atiriccha cchiṇāo avvācchināo taruniyaṃ vā chivāḍiṃ aṇabhivakata mabhābhijjataṃ pehāe aphasuyaṃ aṇe saṇijjanti*, ibid., I.525 cited in Om Prakash, op. cit., p. 67, fn. 2.
97. S.B. Deo, op. cit., pp. 172-3.
98. *Vipākasūtra*, II.14; III.22. Among the variety of meat preparations occurring in this text mention may be made of *saṅkhaṇḍiya, vaṭṭakhaṇḍiya, dīhakhaṇḍiya, rahassakhaṇḍiya, himapakka, jammapakka, vegapakka, māruyapakka, kāla, heraṅga, mahiṭṭha*, *Vipākasūtra*, III, p. 46. See Om Prakash, op. cit., p. 66, fn. 4; Jagdish Chandra Jain, *Jaina Āgama Sāhitya men Bhāratīya Samāja*, Chowkhamba Vidya Bhavan, Varanasi, 1965, p. 200.
99. A.L. Basham, *History and Doctrines of the Ājīvikas*, Luzac and Company, London, 1951, p. 67. The Jaina idea of *ahiṃsā* was shared in great measure by the Ājīvikas, though, according to the *Bhagavatīsūtra*, they ate animal food and a passage of the *Vāyu Purāṇa* indicates that they used wine and meat in their religious ceremonies (A.L. Basham, *History and Doctrines of the Ājīvikas*, p. 122).
100. H.R. Kapadia, 'Prohibition of Flesh Eating in Jainism', *Review of Philosophy and Religion*, IV (1933), pp. 232-9; idem, *A History*

of the Canonical Literature of the Jainas, Author, Surat, 1941, p. 123.

101. Ludwig Alsdorf, op. cit., pp. 8-11.
102. Ludwig Alsdorf, op. cit., p. 12. Also see Jagdish Chandra Jain, *Prākrit Sāhitya Kā Itihās*, Chowkhamba Vidya Bhavan, Varanasi, 1961, p. 73, fn. 1.
103. S.B. Deo, op. cit., p. 417. A passage of the *Bṛhat Kalpa Bhaṣya Vṛtti* has been cited to show that meat eating was common also in Konkan (Jagdish Chandra Jain, *Prakrit Narrative Literature: Origin and Growth*, Munshiram Manoharlal, Delhi, 1981, pp. 167-8).
104. Ibid., p. 417.
105. *madhu-majja-maṃsā avavāte daṭṭthavva, Niśītha Cūrṇi*, II, p. 394 cited in Madhu Sen, *A Cultural Study of the Niśītha Cūrṇi*, Sohanlal Jaindharma Pracharka Samiti (Amritsar), available at P.V. Research Institute, Varanasi, 1975, p. 139, n. 4. For further references see ibid., pp. 139-40.
106. *Ācārāṅgaṭīkā*, II.i.4.247, cf. 9.274 cited in Om Prakash, op. cit., p. 67, n. 5.
107. *poggalaṃ maṃsaṃ, taṃ gaheūṇa bhagandale pavesijjati, te kimiyā tattha lagganti, Niśītha Cūrṇi*, I, p. 100 cited in Madhu Sen, op. cit., p. 140, n. 3. Cf. Dalsukh Malavaniya, *Niśītha: Ek Adhyayana*, Sanmati Jñāna Pīth, Agra, n.d., pp. 62-5. Malavaniya has also drawn attention to instances of Jaina monks indulging in violence and killing not only animals (e.g. lions) but also human beings for the defence of their faith and monastic order (ibid., pp. 59-61).
108. This has been cited by H.R. Kapadia, ('Prohibition of Flesh Eating in Jainism', op. cit., p. 235), if only to contest the assertion. Others who sharply disagree with the view that the early Jainas ate meat are: Pandit Hiralal Jain Dugar, *Shramaṇa Bhagavān Mahāvīra tathā Māṃsāhāra Parihāra*, Shri Atmānand Jain Mahāsabhā (Panjab), Shri Jainendra Press, Delhi, 1964; *Prāchīn Bhārat men Gomāṃsa—Ek Samīkshā*, Gita Press, Gorakhpur (It is interesting that the name of the author is not mentioned!). These works are examples of faith overcoming reason.
109. Paul Dundas, *The Jains*, p. 153.
110. Jagdish Chandra Jain, *Jaina Āgama Sāhitya men Bhāratīya Samāja*, p. 201.

111. *Āvaśyakacūrṇi*, II, p. 202 cited in S.B. Deo, op. cit., p. 418; *Sūtrakṛtāṅgasūtra*, II.6.37.42 cited in Om Prakash, op. cit., p. 67, fn. 4.
112. Jyoti Prasad Jain, *The Jaina Sources of the History of Ancient India*, Munshiram Manoharlal, Delhi, 1964, pp. 204-6.
113. *Subhāṣitasandoha*, 21.16 cited in Om Prakash, op. cit., p. 215.
114. *Vyavahārabhāṣya*, 10, 557-60 cited in S.B. Deo, op. cit., p. 418, fn. 205.
115. *Uvāsagadasāo*, VIII.242-4, tr. A.F. Rudolf Hoernle, Asiatic Society, Calcutta, 1989, p. 157. Also see J.C. Jain, *Jaina Agāma Sāhitya men Bhāratīya Samāja*, pp. 201-2.
116. D.C. Jain, *Economic Life in Ancient India As Depicted in Jain Canonical Literature*, Research Institute of Prakrit, Jainology and Ahiṃsā, Vaishali, 1980, p. 28.
117. Madhu Sen, op. cit., pp. 137-8.
118. The text narrates the story of Sumitra in the sixteenth section which contains a discussion on the propriety or otherwise of eating meat, under the heading *maṃsabhakkhaṇavisayaṃ vāyatthalaṃ*. See *The Vasudevahiṇḍī* of Saṅghadāsagaṇi, ed. with introduction and Hindi tr., Dr. Shreeranjan Sūrideva, Pandit Rampratap Shastri Charitable Trust, Beawar, Rajasthan, 1989, pp. 810-13.
119. *Ācārāṅgacūrṇi* cited in J.C. Jain, *Prākrit Sāhitya Kā Itihās*, p. 235.
120. *go-māse paḍiseho eso vajjei maṅgalaṃ dahiyaṃ/khamaṇaya-sīlaṃ rakkhasu majjha vihāreṇa viṇṇa kajjaṃ/ Kuvalayamālā* 206.13 cited in Prem Suman Jain, *Kuvalayamālā Kahā Kā Sāṃskritik Adhyayana*, Institute of Prakriti, Jainology and Ahiṃsā, Vaishali, 1975, p. 383, fn. 2.
121. Prem Suman Jain, op. cit., pp. 356-7, 388.
122. *Kuvalayamālā*, Part I, ed. A.N. Upadhye, Bombay, 1959, p. 40. Cited in Shanta Rani Sharma, *Society and Culture in Rajasthan c AD 700-900*, Pragati Publications, Delhi, 1996, p. 169.
123. *vāvāiyā pannarasa mahisayā/ baṃbhaṇajaṇabhoyaṇatthaṃ*, *Samarāiccakahā*, ed. H. Jacobi, vol. I (text and introduction), Calcutta, 1926, p. 260 cited in Shanta Rani Sharma, op. cit., p. 169.
124. *paccchannameva vāvāiūṇa visasio kolo, Samarāiccakahā*, p. 475 cited in Shanta Rani Sharma, op. cit., p. 169.
125. Shanta Rani Sharma, op. cit., pp. 169-70.
126. K.K. Handiqui, op. cit., p. 325.

127. *Yaśastilaka*, VII.24 cited in K.K. Handiqui, op. cit., p. 376.
128. K.K. Handiqui, op. cit., p. 376.
129. Kumud Bala Shrivastava (*Prabandhacintāmaṇi kā Sāṃskritik Adhyayana*, Ph.D. thesis, Benaras Hindu University, 1985) cites several instances of flesh eating but her work does not inspire much confidence.
130. *Prabandhacintāmaṇi*, ed. Muni Jinavijaya, Singhi Jain Series, I, Santiniketan, 1933, text p. 9.
131. 'For what good quality, O King, is the cow worshipped? If the cow is to be worshipped because it is able to give milk, why not the female buffalo? There is not seen in the cow even the slightest superiority to the other.'
Prabandhacintāmaṇi, English tr. C.H. Tawney, rpt., Indian Book Gallery, Delhi, 1982, p. 58. Muni Jinavijaya refers to the original Sanskrit passage (*Prabandhacintāmaṇi*, p. 40, line 10) but does not reproduce it in the text edited by him.
132. Jagdish Chandra Jain, *Prākrit Sāhitya Kā Itihās*, p. 115; idem, *Jaina Āgama Sāhitya men Bhāratīya Samāja*, p. 201.
133. Jainism exercised great influence on kings like Māṇḍalika, Siddharāja and Kumārapāla whose names the Jaina community loves to recall with respect even today. The depiction of Kumārapāla's enthusiasm for Jainism has sometimes assumed hyperbolic proportions. For he is said to have imposed a heavy fine on a merchant who killed a louse. See Paul Dundas, *The Jains*, pp. 115-16; Lodrick, op. cit., p. 63. H.R. Kapadia, 'Prohibition of Flesh Eating in Jainism', op. cit., pp. 234-5.
134. *Moharājaparājaya*, IV, p. 93 cited in Om Prakash, op. cit., p. 216.
135. King Kumārapāla is said to have imposed the death penalty on an unfortunate merchant who was found in possession of meat near a sanctuary in the capital city of Anhilwāḍapāṭan (*Prabhāvakacarita*, 22.823-30, cited by William Norman Brown, op. cit., p. 38). A.L. Basham has drawn attention to the story of Kumārapāla as well as to the one relating to a Coḷa king who ordered the execution of his own son for the accidental killing of a calf but rightly takes these as indications of current opinion, *The Wonder That Was India*, 27th impression, Rupa and Co., Delhi, 1996, p. 120.
136. Paul Dundas, *The Jains*, p. 126.
137. Ibid., p. 126. Also see Deryck O. Lodrick, op. cit., pp. 64-5.

138. Sundara Ram, *Cow Protection in India*, The South Indian Humanitarian League, Madras, 1927, p. 123.
139. P.S. Jaini asserts that the Jainas were 'distinguished from the Brāhmaṇical tradition by their rejection of the sacredness of food, of sacrificial meat, but also of ghee and, by extension, rejection of the cow as a sacred animal', *Collected Papers on Jaina Studies*, Motilal Banarsidass, Delhi, 2000, p. 283.
140. Some Jainas claim their descent from Rajputs. For example the Khaṇḍelvāls are believed to have descended from a Cauhāna Rajput king of Khaṇḍela just as the Śrīmāls and the Oswāls claim descent from the kṣatriyas of Śrīmāl and Osiya respectively. This means that before entering the Jaina fold they were accustomed to Rajput ways of life, which included meat eating. According to Lawrence A. Babb, this is a case of the convergence of two different identities, Rajput and Jaina (*Ascetics and Kings in a Jain Ritual Culture*, Motilal Banarsidass, Delhi, 1998, Chap. 4). But it is worth investigating whether such merging of community identities invariably results in a total change in diet.
141. Hanns-Peter Schmidt, however, argues that the *ahiṃsā* doctrine had originally nothing to do with vegetarianism. This, according to him, is obvious from 'the strict animism of the Jaina doctrine according to which the whole world is animated'. He also agrees with Ludwig Alsdorf that the Jaina *ahiṃsā* is based on 'a magico-ritualistic dread of destroying life in any form' (op. cit., p. 15) and that 'the "non-violence" movement is part of the all-Indian religious development and cannot be credited to the reform-religions of the Buddha and the Jina' (op. cit., p. 49): Hanns-Peter Schmidt, 'The Origin of Ahiṃsā', in *Mélanges d'Indianisme a la memoire de Louis Renou*, Paris, 1968, pp. 625-6.

3

The Later Dharmaśāstric Tradition and Beyond

Despite the role of Upaniṣadic thought, Buddhism, and Jainism in the development of the *ahiṃsā* doctrine, the ritual and random killing of animals for sacrifice and food continued to enjoy Brāhmaṇical and Dharmaśāstric approval. Kauṭilya's general dictum[1] of non-injury (*ahiṃsā*) being the duty of all classes and Aśoka's pious wishes to disallow animal flesh in the royal kitchen did not stand in the way of cow slaughter. The Mauryan evidence, as we have seen, is explicit about the killing of animals including cattle. In post-Mauryan times several lawgivers indicate the continuity of the earlier practice, even though, far from being univocal, they are full of internal contradictions.

Vedic Killing is Not Killing

The law book of Manu (200 BC-AD 200), the most representative of the legal texts having much to say on lawful and forbidden food, contains several passages on meat, which have much in common with earlier and later Brāhmaṇical juridical works. Like the earlier law books, it mentions those animals whose flesh may be eaten: the porcupine, hedgehog, iguana, rhinoceros, tortoise and the hare; all those domestic animals with teeth in one jaw only, the only exception being the camel,[2] and, significantly, not the cow. Among the aquatic animals specific types of fish (e.g. *pāṭhīna* and *rohita* offered to the gods and ancestors, and *rājīva, siṃhatuṇḍa* and *saśalka* on all occasions) are classed with the comestibles.[3] Eating meat on sacrificial occasions, Manu tells us, is a divine rule (*daivo vidhiḥ smṛtaḥ*), but doing so on other occasions is demonic (*rākṣaso vidhirucyate*).[4] Accordingly, one does not do any wrong by eating meat while honouring the gods, the Manes and guests (*madhuparke ca yajñe ca pitṛdaivatakarmaṇi*), irrespective of the way in which the meat was procured.[5] Yet, eating flesh on other occasions or even in times of distress (*āpadyapi*) is forbidden.[6] Manu asserts that animals were created for the sake of sacrifice, that killing (*vadha*) on ritual occasions is non-killing (*avadha*),[7] and injury (*hiṃsā*) as enjoined by the Veda (*vedavihitahiṃsā*) is known to be non-injury (*ahiṃsā*).[8] He assures that plants, cattle, trees—and birds, which have met their death in sacrifice, attain higher levels of existence (*yajñārthaṃ nidhanaṃ prāptāḥ prāpnuvantyutsṛtīḥ punaḥ*).[9] This benefit is available not only to the victim but also to the sacrificer; for he tells us that 'a twice-born man who knows the true meaning of the *Veda* and injures animals for these purposes (hospitality, sacrifice to gods and ancestor spirits) makes himself and the animal go to the highest state of existence (in heaven)'.[10] If, however, he refuses to eat consecrated meat, he will be reborn as a beast for twenty-one existences.[11] In one context the lawgiver categorically states that a twice born person must not cause injury to any creature except on sacrificial occasions, not even in times of distress.[12] But elsewhere he asserts equally unambiguously that one may eat meat 'when it has been sprinkled with water . . . when brāhmaṇas desire, when one is engaged according to the law, *when one's life is in danger*'[13] (emphasis added). Regarding behaviour in times of distress, Manu recalls the legendary examples of the most virtuous brāhmaṇas of olden days who ate oxen and dogs to escape starvation.[14] Manu's latitudinarian attitude is clear from his recognition of the natural human tendency to eat meat, drink liquor and indulge in sexual intercourse, even if abstention brings great rewards.[15] He further breaks loose the constraints when he says,

> Prajāpati created this whole world to be the sustenance of the vital spirit; both the immovable and the movable (creation is) the food of the vital spirit. What is destitute of motion is the food of those endowed with locomotion; (animals) without fangs (are the food) of those with fangs, those without hands of those who possess hands, and the timid of the bold. The eater who daily even devours those destined to be his food, commits no sin; for the Creator himself created both the eaters and those who are to be eaten.[16]

This injunction removes all restrictions on meat eating and gives freedom to all who like it. Perhaps even the food of ascetics included meat,[17] though brāhmaṇas are advised to avoid village pigs and fowl.[18] Manu contradicts his own position on dietary rules by extolling the virtues of *ahiṃsā*,[19] which he declares, like Kauṭilya, to be the common duty of all classes.[20] While the inconsistent injunctions of Manu indicate that his law book has several chronological layers spread over several centuries, there is no doubt that he permitted meat at least on certain specified ritual occasions like the *madhuparka* and *śrāddha*, on which the killing of the cow was, according to his commentator Medhātithi, in keeping with Vedic and post-Vedic practice.[21]

Yājñvalkya (AD 100-300), like Manu, discusses the rules of lawful and forbidden food. Although his treatment of the subject is less detailed, he does not differ radically from Manu.[22] Like Manu, Yājñavalkya also mentions the specific animals (deer, sheep, goat, boar, rhinoceros, etc.) and birds (e.g. partridge) whose flesh satisfies the Manes.[23] According to him a student, teacher, king, close friend and son-in-law should be offered *arghya* every year and a priest should be offered *madhuparka* on all ritual occasions.[24] He further enjoins that a learned brāhmaṇa (*śrotriya*) should be welcomed with a big ox or goat, delicious food and sweet words.[25] This indicates his endorsement of the earlier practice of killing cattle to welcome honoured guests. Yājñavalkya, like Manu, permits eating of meat when life is in danger, or in sacrifice and funerary rites.[26] But unconsecrated meat (*vṛthāmāṃsam, anupākṛtamāṃsāni*), according to him is a taboo[27] and anyone killing animals solely for his own food and not in accordance with the Vedic practice is doomed to hell for as many days as the number of hair on the body of the victim.[28]

Bṛhaspati (AD 300-500) too recommends abstention from liquor (*madya*), flesh (*māṃsa*) and sexual intercourse only if they are not lawfully ordained.[29] The lawgivers generally accept those sacrifices that, according to them, had Vedic sanction. The sacrificial slaughter of animals and domesticated animals including the cow, as we have seen, was a Vedic practice and possibly common in Brāhmaṇical circles during the early Christian centuries and even well into the later half of the first millennium AD. It would, however, be unrealistic to assume that the dharmic precept of restricting animal slaughter to ritual occasions was always obeyed by brāhmaṇas for whom they were meant or by other sections of society.[30] It is not surprising, therefore, that Bṛhaspati, while discussing the importance of local customs, says that in Madhyadeśa artisans ate cows.[31] Beef and fish were usual items of dietary menu also in south India as is evident in the Sangam texts. One of them, in fact, refers to the brāhmaṇa priest Kapilar speaking with relish and without fear of social ostracism about consuming liquor and meat.[32]

The Purāṇas, whose compilation ranges in date from the early Christian centuries to about the eighteenth century, have much in common with the lawbooks mentioned above. They do not impose a ban on flesh food, and even the later ones among them, continue to refer to the use of meat in rituals.[33] According to the *Viṣṇu Purāṇa* the meat of the hare, goat, hog, antelope, deer, gayal and sheep at a *śrāddha* was meritorious.[34] The *Mārkaṇḍeya Purāṇa*, more or less in the vein of Dharmaśāstra texts, postulates that 'whoever eats meat commits no sin either when it has been consecrated or when it serves as a remedy'.[35] According to one authority, several Purāṇic texts bear testimony to feeding brāhmaṇas beef at a funeral ceremony.[36] They also refer to the performance of animal sacrifice in the festival of the goddess, known variously as Durgāpūjā, Navarātra, Navarātri, Daśara and Dasai. The *Devī*, *Garuḍa*, *Skanda* and *Bhaviṣya* Purāṇas clearly recommend the killing of buffaloes during the festival,[37] though a passage from the *Nāradīyamahāpurāṇa* prohibits the killing of cows in honour of guests or in sacrifice.[38] This was no more than a disapproval of a prevalent practice. In any case, the very fact that the Purāṇas prescribed butchery of buffaloes indicates that they did not show any special veneration for the bovids, notwithstanding their unprecedented glorification from the second half of the first millennium AD onwards[39] of the practice of making donations to the priestly class thus undermining the Vedic religion characterized by sacrifices and the large scale killing of animals.

Evidence from the Epics

The practice of eating flesh is amply attested by the *Mahābhārata* and the *Rāmāyaṇa*, finally redacted during the post-Maurya and Gupta times, to which chronological segment the early Smṛtis and Purāṇas also belong. The *Mahābhārata*, especially the *Vanaparvan*, gives the impression that kṣatriyas hunted wild life oftener for food than for sport,[40] and also provides evidence of the slaughter of domesticated animals for the kitchen. Yudhiṣṭhira, who deplores *hiṃsā*[41] is described as regularly hunting *ruru* deer and *kṛṣṇamṛga* to feed his brothers and Draupadī, as well as the brāhmaṇas living in the forest,[42] though in the story of Kalmāṣapāda in the *Ādiparvan*, meat was clearly a normal part of a brāhmaṇa's diet.[43] Draupadī is said to have offered Jayadratha and his companions a meal of fifty deer promising that Yudhiṣṭhira would provide them with black antelope, spotted antelope, venison, fawn, *śarabha*, rabbit, *ṛṣya*, *ruru*, *śambara*, gayal, many deer, boar, buffalo and every other kind of game.[44] The Pāṇḍava heroes are said to have killed deer with unpoisoned arrows and eaten venison after offering it to the brāhmaṇas.[45] According to the *Vanaparvan*, two thousand cows were slaughtered every day in the kitchen of the king Rantideva who achieved unrivalled fame by distributing beef with food grains to brāhmaṇas.[46] The river Carmavatī (modern Chambal) originated from the blood of the slaughtered cows,[47] though it is mentioned as Carmaṇanvatī even earlier by Pāṇini.[48] In the *Anuśāsanaparvan* Nārada declares that one should give meat, rice, ghee and milk to brāhmaṇas,[49] and Bhīṣma enumerates the foods to be offered to the Manes in the ascending order [50] of effectiveness as sesame, rice, barley, beans, water, roots and fruits, fish, mutton, rabbit, goat, boar, fowl, venison (*pārṣata, raurava*), gayal, buffalo, beef,[51] *pāyasa, vārddhrīṇasa,* rhinoceros (*khaḍga*), basil and red-skinned goat. On the other hand, in the same *parvan* of the *Mahābhārata,* Bhīṣma, before stating that meat may be eaten when the animal has been slaughtered as part of a Vedic sacrifice, waxes eloquent in his praise of *ahiṃsā.*[52] Although the exaltation of *ahiṃsā* strikes a discordant note in the general non-vegetarian food ambience of the Great Epic, eating of the animal food including beef and other bovine flesh was fairly common among brāhmaṇas and kṣatriyas in ancient India. The much trumpeted abstemiousness of the former could not have stood between them and the wide variety of flesh food offered at Yudhiṣṭhira's *aśvamedha* in which a large number of animals, including bulls (*ṛṣabha*), are said to have been killed,[53] even if, according to one view expressed in the *Mahābhārata,* meat was eaten only by the lowest sections of society.[54]

Like the *Mahābhārata,* the *Rāmāyaṇa* of Vālmīki contains numerous references to the practice of killing animals including cattle for sacrifice as well as for food. It tells us that Daśaratha, desirous of progeny, performed a sacrifice in which the sages brought forth numerous animals (e.g. horses, snakes and aquatic animals) permitted by the śāstras to be killed in rituals. It adds that three hundred animals along with the horse, which had roamed the earth, were tied to the sacrificial poles (*yūpas*),[55] obviously for ritual slaughter. While announcing the news of his exile to Kauśalyā, Rāma seems to be assuring her that he would live for fourteen years in the forest on honey, roots and fruit, abstaining from meat,[56] as indeed he initially does. This is why he refuses food offered by the Niṣāda chief Guha.[57] But the epic makes frequent references to Rāma and Lakṣamaṇa killing game for consumption as well as for sacrifice and the former's image of a habitual hunter is corroborated by numerous Rāmāyaṇa episodes.[58] Similarly Sītā's fascination for meat can be inferred from several passages of the text. While crossing the Gangā she promises to offer her rice cooked with meat and thousands of jars of liquor on her safe return with her husband.[59] While being ferried across the Yamunā, Sītā says that she will worship the river with a thousand cows and a hundred jars of wine when her husband accomplishes his vow.[60] Sītā's love of deer meat makes her husband chase and kill Mārīca disguised as the fabulous golden deer; and even while thinking of its evil consequences he does not hesitate to kill a *chital* and take its meat;[61] in the later part of the story Rāma also gives the pregnant Sītā different kinds of wine (*madhu* and *maireya*) when his servants serve them with meat and fruit.[62] Kabandha tells us that the hero of the *Rāmāyaṇa* can easily kill birds and fish on his way to Sugrīva,[63] though Hanumān, describing Rāma's behaviour during his separation from Sītā, informs her that Rāghava does not eat meat nor does he use honey or liquor.[64] Guha offers fish, meat and honey (*matsaymāṃsamadhūni*) to Bharata, and fresh and dried meat along with other things to his army.[65] Bharadvāja also extends generous hospitality to Bharata's troops, regaling them with meat and wine,[66] and 'welcomes Rama by slaughtering the "fatted calf"'.[67] The flesh of deer, buffalo, boar, peacock, jungle fowl and goat are the highlights of the convivial banquet of Rāvaṇa[68] and the colossal non-vegetarian meal of Kumbhakarṇa.[69] Vālin, struggling for life, accepts the slaughter of animals, though he is not unaware of the Dharmaśāstric maxim about the five types of five-nailed animals that may be eaten.[70] Vālmīki's text abounds in references to the eating of the flesh of animals declared edible by the Dharmaśāstras, though, of course, dog meat was abhorred.[71] Thus the

Rāmāyaṇa, despite its condemnation of meat eating,[72] upholds the non-vegetarian dietary tradition; and Sītā, as we have seen, even promises to offer a thousand heads of cattle to the river Yamunā. It will not be out of place to point out that Sītā's liking for meat figures even in the *Adhyātma Rāmāyaṇa,* which is ascribed to Rāmānanda (fourteenth century) and has strong Vaiṣṇava *bhakti* affiliations.[73]

Prophylaxis and Cure

The non-vegetarian culinary tradition is also reflected in the classical Indian texts on medicine. The treatises of Caraka (first-second century) and Suśruta (third-fourth century), available to us in their later redacted form, and of Vāgbhaṭa (seventh century) mention no less than three hundred animals[74] (not all of them kosher ones!) and bear ample testimony to the therapeutic use of meats. The *Caraka Saṃhitā* provides a list of at least twenty-eight animals whose flesh is recommended for the cure of various ailments[75] and the *Suśruta Saṃhitā* catalogues one hundred and sixty-eight meat types endowed with pharmaceutical properties,[76] though references to various meat diets in the *Aṣṭāṅga Hṛdayam* of Vāgbhaṭa may be comparatively less. The meat types mentioned in the classical Indian medical texts give an idea of their authors' familiarity with a wide range of ancient fauna. But, more importantly, they also include almost all those animals whose flesh was declared edible by the lawgivers: goats, *rohita* fish, tortoises, deer, parrots, quails, partridges, hares, peacock and alligators were considered good.

Although the list of animals and birds whose flesh is recommended by the classical Indian medical texts is fairly long,[77] these treatises extol the importance of *ahiṃsā,* which, according to Caraka, is 'the most perfect of all means of increasing the longevity of living beings. . . .' But the *ahiṃsā* doctrine does not seem to have been a major concern for him and subsequent Indian authorities on medicine. For, according to the requirements of the art of healing, Caraka, like Suśruta and other later experts, recommends a large variety of meats and meat soups to patients suffering from different diseases. No doubt, he traces the origin of diarrhoea to the eating of flesh of cows killed in a sacrifice performed by one of Manu's numerous sons, Pṛṣadhara, whose legends, centring on the murder of the cow, occur later in the Purāṇic texts[78] and even goes to the extent of asserting that the unhealthiest of the meats of the quadrupeds is the meat of the ox.[79] But elsewhere in his text Caraka unhesitatingly recommends a gruel prepared with beef gravy soured with pomegranates as a remedy for intermittent fevers.[80] He is unequivocal in describing the virtues of beef for disorders of wind, catarrh and irregular fever.[81] Similarly, Suśruta tells us that beef 'proves curative in dyspnoea, catarrh, cough, chronic fever and in cases of a morbid craving for food (*atyāgni*)' and, going a step further, describes it as 'holy' (*pavitra*)[82] and coveted. He speaks of pregnant women craving for ox meat—a craving that was predictive of the vigour and endurance of the child in the womb.[83] Several centuries later, Vāgbhaṭa (seventh century) speaks in a similar vein about the curative powers of beef.[84] Laudatory references to the properties of beef continue till late.[85] Halāyudha (tenth century) preserves the memory of Suśruta's therapeutic use of beef.[86]

None of the above-mentioned works on medicine, even by implication, suggest that the cow was inherently sacred or inviolable or that beef was taboo. One may, of course, argue that medical texts deal with emergency situations and hence, like the law books laying down norms for times of distress (*āpaddharma*), recommend various meat diets depending on their prophylactic and curative powers.[87] But this is far from convincing. The classical

Indian works on medicine give due place to vegetarian dietetics in their taxonomy of food. Vegetarianism, in fact, coexists with non-vegetarianism in them and the recommended diet depended both on the physician's preference and the patient's choice. Had animal food of any kind been taboo, it would not be talked of highly in the medical texts.

This is corroborated by astrological works. Varāhamihira (sixth century), for example, not only gives the impression that meat eating was common but also says that the flesh of elephants, buffaloes, sheep, boars, cows or bulls, hares, deer, lizards and fish could be eaten.[88] He also recommends to a monarch 'the ceremonial eating of the fish, the flesh of buffalo, bull, he-cat, goat, deer' and so on.[89] The extent to which his advice was followed in practice, however, remains a matter of speculation. For, several centuries later the Cālukya king Someśvara (twelfth century), whose *Mānasollāsa* deals mainly with various aspects of the life of royalty, recommends several animals (*sāraṅga, hariṇa, śaśa*) for food but indicates his preference for pork[90] and fish, and beef does not figure in his list of inedibles.[91] Be that as it may, there is substantial evidence against the inherent sanctity of the bovine including the cow.

Poets, Playwrights and Philosophers Support the Vedic Practice

That the prescriptive texts allow the killing of animals including cattle is beyond doubt. Secular literature bears testimony to the continuity of the practice of killing animals including cattle for food till very late. To begin with, mention may be made of Kālidāsa's *Meghadūta*, a lyrical poem of little more than a hundred graceful stanzas containing the message sent by the lovelorn Yakṣa to his wife pining across the northern mountains in Alakā through the clouds. In an obvious allusion to the *Mahābhārata* legend, Yakṣa asks the cloud-messenger to show respect to Rantideva who sacrificed numerous cows whose blood flew in the form of a river.[92] Bhavabhūti (AD 700), in *Mahāvīracarita*, while dealing with the early life of Rāma, describes a scene where Vasiṣṭha requests the angry Paraśurāma to accept king Janaka's hospitality, that included the killing of a heifer (*vatsatarī*).[93] In another play, the *Uttararāmacarita*, Vasiṣṭha himself is depicted as feasting on the 'poor tawny calf' in the hermitage of Vālmīki; for, one of the latter's disciples says that according to the holy law it is the duty of a householder to offer a heifer or a bull or a goat to a *śrotriya* guest (*samāṃso madhuparka ityamnāyaṃ bahumanyamānaḥ śrotriyāyābhyagatāya vatsatarīm mahokṣaṃ vā mahājaṃ vā nirvapanti gṛhamedhinaḥ*).[94] In the *Bālarāmāyaṇa* of Rājaśekhara (tenth century) Satānanda courteously receives Rāvaṇa and reiterates the old practice of killing an ox or goat for a *śrotriya*,[95] though at one place in the *Kāvyamimāṃsā*, the poet refers to pork eating as prevalent among uncultured people.[96] Śrīharṣa's *Naiṣadhacarita* (twelfth century), one of the longest *mahākāvyas* of the classical period, gives a graphic description of a marriage feast in which tasty curries of fish, and broths of venison and flesh of birds and goat[97] were served, and provides at least two interesting references to cow killing. The Canto XVII of this text records that Kali, having failed to attend the *svayaṃbara* of Damayantī and thus missing the chance of getting the charming lady's hand, becomes desperate, and, determined to wreak vengeance on Nala, goes to destroy his capital. But he finds that place a sanctuary of piety and a centre of Vedic religious practices. Once Kali rejoiced to see a cow meant for sacrifice and rushed forward, but the cow, devoted to the religious virtue inherent in the Soma sacrifice, repelled him.[98] At another place Kali is said to have run joyfully to a cow, which was being killed, but returned after realizing that it was for the guests.[99] All this may be at variance with the gastronomic preferences of king Someśvara who liked pork and fish, as well as with Jayānaka's contempt for the beef eater Muhammad Ghuri.[100] But the early medieval literature not only strongly supports the tradition of non-vegetarianism but also provides clear evidence of the continuity of the tradition of killing cattle on certain occasions. This is borne out by the commentaries on some of the passages cited above. Cāṇḍupaṇḍita, who commented on the *Naiṣadhīya* XVII.173 in the late thirteenth century, does not differ from the translation of the crucial passage as given above.[101] Narahari (fourteenth century) and Mallinātha (fourteenth-fifteenth century) also understand the passage to mean the killing of cow.[102] The latter has also understood the *Naiṣadhīya* verse XVII.197 as referring to the killing of a cow as part of the reception of guests.[103] While commenting on Kālidāsa's couplet he recalls the *Mahābhārata* legend of Rantideva who slaughtered a large number of cows every day, and their blood flew in the form a river called Carmaṇvatī.[104] As late as the early eighteenth century Ghanaśyāma interpreted the dialogue between Dāṇḍāyana and Saudhātaki in the *Uttararāmacarita* to mean that the killing of cow in honour of a guest was the ancient norm.[105]

It follows that whether or not cows were generally slain by members of the upper caste, the commentators on the crucial passages from the secular texts were familiar with the earlier practice of cow killing and preserved its memory until at least the eighteenth century and perhaps later without feelings of guilt. In other words, non-killing of cows and abstention from eating flesh could not have been a mark of community identity for brāhmaṇas or the Brāhmaṇical social order.

Non-vegetarianism received support from some early medieval philosophers and logicians. For, even while 'the Vedic sacrificial religion was fast becoming a relic of the past, the authority of the Veda was constantly reaffirmed by Mimāṃsakas, Smārtas, and Nyāya-Vaiśeṣikas alike'.[106] Kumārilabhaṭṭa[107] (AD 650-750) defends the Vedic ritual violence and the Vedānta philosopher Śaṅkara[108] (eighth century) rejects the opinion that animal sacrifice is sinful. Even the Vaiṣṇava philosopher Madhva[109] (twelfth century) does not consider Vedic animal sacrifice as blameworthy.

Although it is difficult to ascertain whether all this perpetrated the ritual killing of the kine, the Dharmaśāstra texts continue to uphold the tradition of flesh eating. As late as the seventeenth century Viśvanātha Nyāya-Pañcānana, a great logician who also wrote on the Smṛtis, vehemently advocates the eating of flesh by brāhmaṇas on occasions like sacrifices, *śrāddha* and *madhuparka* and when life is in danger; he also ridicules the south Indian brāhmaṇas, who deprecate meat, as followers of the Buddhist tenets.[110] Even though the schools of *Mimāṃsā* and *Nyāya* represent a distinct strand of thought in Indian tradition, their defence of Vedic animal sacrifice, which traditionally included cattle sacrifice, provided an ideological prop to non-vegetarian food habits unambiguously supported by the Smṛtis, and whose all pervasive influence on contemporary life remains unquestionable. It is therefore not surprising that the *Śaṅkhasmṛti*, a late smṛti, gives a list of edible birds, aquatic and other animals[111] and goes to the extent of describing animals like the rhinoceros and rabbit as very dear to Yama.[112]

NOTES

1. *AŚ*, I.3.13.
2. *Manu*, V.18.
3. *Manu*, V.16.

4. *Manu*, V.31.
5. *krītvā svayaṃ vāpyutpādya paropakṛtameva vā/ devānpitṛ'scāryitvā khādanmāṃsaṃ na duṣyati//Manu*, V.32. *madhuparke ca yajñe ca pitṛdaivatakarmaṇi/ atraiva paśavo hiṃsyā nānyatretyabravīnmanuḥ//Manu*, V.41.
6. *Manu*, V.43.
7. *yajñārthaṃ paśavaḥ sṛṣṭāḥ svayameva svayaṃbhuvā/ yajña'sya bhūtyai sarvasya tasmād yajñe vadho'vadhaḥ//Manu*, V.39.
8. *yā vedavihitā hiṃsā niyatāsminścarācare/ ahiṃsāmeva tāṃ vidyādveddādharmo hi nirbabhau//Manu*, V.44.
9. *Manu*, V.40.
10. *esvarthesu paśūnhiṃsanvedatattvārthaviddvijaḥ/ ātmānaṃ ca paśuṃ caiva gamayatyuttamāṃ gatiṃ, Manu*, V.42. Also see *Manu*, V.41. For the periods up to which the Manes remain satisfied with fish and the flesh of goats, gazelles, kids, spotted deer, black antelope, ruru deer, boar, buffalo, hare, tortoise, *vārddhrīṇasa*, rhinoceros and birds see *Manu*, III.268-72.
11. *Manu*, V.35.
12. *Manu*, V.43.
13. *prokṣitaṃ bhakṣayenmāṃsaṃ brāhmaṇānāṃ ca kāmyayā/ yathāvidhi niyukttastu prāṇānameva cātyaye//Manu*, V.27.
14. Francis Zimmermann, *The Jungle and the Aroma of Meats*, University of California Press, Berkeley, 1987, p. 189. *Manu* (X.105-9) tells us that the hungry Ajīgarta sought a remedy by slaying his son without incurring sin. Vāmadeva, tormented by hunger, desired to eat the flesh of a dog. Bharadvāja, starving with his son in a lonely forest, accepted many cows from a carpenter. And a famished Viśvāmitra ate part of a dog offered by a cāṇḍāla.
15. *na māṃsabhakṣaṇe doṣo na madye na ca maithune/ pravṛttireṣā bhūtānāṃ nivṛttistu mahāphalāḥ//Manu*, V.56.
16. *prāṇasyānnamidaṃ sarvaṃ prajāpatirakalpayat/ sthāvaraṃ jaṅgamaṃ caiva sarvaṃ prāṇasya bhojanam// carāṇāmannamacarā danṣṭrṇāmapyadanṣṭrṇaḥ/ ahastāśca sahastānāṃ śūrāṇāṃ caiva bhīravaḥ// nāttā duṣyatyadannādyānprāṇino'hanyahanyapi/ dhātraiva sṛṣṭā hyādyāśca prāṇino'ttāra eva ca//Manu*, V.28-30.
17. That the food of ascetics was not always vegetarian has been inferred by Hanns-Peter Schmidt ('The Origins of Ahiṃsā',

Mélanges d'Indianisme a la memoire de Louis Renou, Paris, 1968, p. 629) from the following verse: *phalamūlāśanair medhyair munyannānāṃ ca bhojanaiḥ/ na tat phalam avāpnoti yat māṃsaparivarjanāt//* 'By eating (only) kosher fruits and roots and by eating (only) the food of silent ascetics, one does not gain the same fruit as by complete avoidance of meat', *Manu,* V.54.

18. *Manu,* V.19.
19. Several works have appeared on the evolution of the *ahiṃsā* doctrine and only some of them are mentioned below: Ludwig Alsdorf, *Beiträge zur Geschichte von Vegetarismus und Rinderverehrung in Indien,* Akademic der Wissenschaften und der Literatur, Wiesbaden, 1962; Unto Tahtinen, *Ahiṃsā: Non-Violence in Indian Tradition,* Rider and Company, London, 1976; Hanns-Peter Schmidt, 'The Origins of Ahiṃsā', op. cit.; idem, 'Ahiṃsā and Rebirth', in Michael Witzel, ed., *Inside The Texts Beyond The Text: New Approaches To The Study of The Vedas,* Cambridge, 1997; J.C. Heesterman, 'Non-violence and Sacrifice', *Indologia Taurinensia,* 12(1984), pp. 119-27; I. Proudfoot, *Ahiṃsā and a Mahābhārata Story,* Australian National University, Canberra, 1987; Guiseppe Spera, *Notes on Ahiṃsā,* Torino, 1982.
20. *Manu,* X.63. Cf. *AŚ,* I.3.13.
21. *govyajamāṃsamaprokṣitaṃbhakṣayedityanenaitadanupākṛtānāmevāsadrūpama nūdyate* (Medhātithi on *Manu,* V.27 *Mānava-Dharma-Śāstra,* ed. V.N. Mandalik, Bombay, 1886, p. 604); *madhuparkovyākhyātaḥ tatra govadhovihitaḥ* Medhātithi on *Manu,* V.41, ibid., p. 613.
22. *bhakṣyāḥ pañcanakhāḥ sedhāgodhākacchapaśallakāḥ/*
    śaśaśca matsyeṣvapi hi siṃhatuṇḍakarohitāḥ//
    tathā pāṭhīnarājīvasaśalkāśca dvijātibhiḥ/
    ataḥ śṛṇudhvaṃ māṃsasya vidhiṃ bhakṣaṇavarjane// Yāj. I.177-8.
23. *Yāj.* I.258-61.
24. *pratisaṃvatsaraṃ tvarghyāḥ snātakācāryapārthivāḥ/ priyo vivāhyaśca tathā yajñaṃ pratyṛtvijaḥ punaḥ/ / Yāj.* I.110.
25. *mahokṣaṃ vā mahājaṃ vā śrotriyāyopakalpayet/satkriyā'nvāsanaṃ svādu bhojanaṃ sūnṛtaṃ vacaḥ/ / Yāj.* I.109.
26. *prāṇātyaye tathā śrāddhe prokṣite dvijakāmyayā/devānpitṛnsamabhyarcya khādanmāṃsaṃ na doṣabhāk/ / Yāj.* I.179.
27. Ibid., I.167, 171.
28. *Yāj.* I.180. Cf. *Manu,* V.51.
29. *madyaṃ māṃsaṃ maithunaṃ ca bhūtānāṃ lalanaṃ smṛtam/*
    tadeva vidhinā kurvan svargamāpnoti mānavaḥ// cited in *Kṛtyakal-*

pataru of Lakṣmīdhara, tṛtiyabhaga, ed. K.V. Ranagaswami Aiyangar, Baroda Oriental Institute, Baroda, 1950, p. 326.

30. Francis Zimmermann (op. cit., p. 180ff.) asserts that only consecrated meat was eaten and Hanns-Peter Schmidt seems to be in agreement with him ('Ahiṃsā and Rebirth', op. cit., p. 209). But the evidence from the Buddhist Jātakas, Kauṭilya's *Arthaśāstra,* and Aśokan inscriptions, etc., does not support this view.
31. *madhyadeśe karmakarāḥ śilpinaśca gavāṣinaḥ*/ 128b *Bṛhaspatismṛti,* Gaekwad Oriental Series, Baroda, 1941.
32. K.T. Achaya, *A Historical Dictionary of Indian Food,* Oxford University Press, Delhi, 1999, p. 146; K.K. Pillay, *A Social History of Tamils,* I, University of Madras, 1975, pp. 291-2.
33. *MatsyaP,* 93.20d, 268.23, 26cd-30; *ViṣṇudharmottaraP,* 2.104.106-7ab, 2.105.21-2, 3.318.3, 3.318.29cd-30ab; *KālikāP,* 35.21-2, 59.88b, 60.47ab, 60.51ab; *AgniP,* 93.23a, 93.27-8ab, 93.29cd; *BṛhaddharmaP,* 1.19.28; *DevīP,* 65.93; *SkandaP,* 3.2.17.7d-8a; *BhaviṣyaP,* 4.61.48ab, 4.62.3cd, 4.73.8cd-9, 4.87.13-16, 4.140.53ab, 4.144.18, 4.192,6cd-7ab. I owe these references to Professor Shingo Einoo.
34. K.T. Achaya, *A Historical Dictionary of Indian Food,* pp. 145-6.
35. *MārkaṇḍeyaP,* XXXII, 4 (tr. Pargiter, p. 181) cited in Francis Zimmermann, op. cit., p. 187.
36. J.C. Banerjea, 'Social Life in the Pouranic Age', *Hindustan Times,* vol. 38, no. 227, July 1918, p. 34 cited in Pradipto Roy, 'Social Background', *Seminar: no. 93: The Cow* (May 1967), p. 19, fn. 5.
37. For references see Shingo Einoo, 'The Autumn Goddess Festival described in the Purāṇas', in Masakazu Tanaka and Musashi Tachikawa, eds., *Living With Sakti: Gender, Sexuality and Religion in South Asia,* National Museum of Ethnology, Osaka, 1999, pp. 33-70.
38. P.V. Kane, *History of Dharmaśāstra,* III, Bhandar Oriental Research Institute, Poona, 1973, p. 928; R.L. Mitra, *Indo-Aryans,* I, Indological Book House, Varanasi, 1969, p. 385.
39. *dānaṃ ekaṃ kalau yuge, KūrmaP,* 1.28.17 cited by R.C. Hazra, *Studies in the Purāṇic Records on Hindu Rites and Customs,* 2nd edn., Motilal Banarsidass, Delhi, 1975, p. 249. Also see Vijay Nath, '*Mahādāna*: The Dynamics of Gift-economy and the Feudal Milieu', in D.N. Jha, ed., *The Feudal Order: State, Society and Ideology in Early Medieval India,* Manohar, Delhi, 2000, pp. 411-40. Despite their emphasis on giving gifts to brāhmaṇas,

the Purāṇas, especially those of Śākta affiliation, extol Vedic sacrifice (R.C. Hazra, op. cit., pp. 239-42).

40. John Brockington, *The Sanskrit Epics*, E.J. Brill, Leiden, 1998, pp. 191-2.
41. *Mbh*, 3.257.9 cited in ibid., p. 192.
42. Brockington, *The Sanskrit Epics*, p. 192.
43. *Mbh*, 1.166.20. See John Brockington, *The Sanskrit Epics*, p. 225.
44. *Mbh.* III.251.12-13.
45. *Mbh.* III.50.4.
46. *rāhyo mahān se pūrvaṃ rantidevasya vai dvija/*
ahanyahīnavadhyete dvai sahasregavāṃ tathā//
samāṃsaṃ dadatohyannaṃ rantidevasya nityaśaḥ/
*atulākīrtirabhavannṛsya dvijasattama//*III.208.8-9 cited in Rajnikant Shastri, *Hindu Jāti kā Utthāna aur Patan*, Allahabad, 1988, p. 91, fn.1. For further references see S. Sorensen, *An Index to the Names in the Mahābhārata*, Motilal Banarsidass, Delhi, 1963, pp. 593-4.
47. S. Sorensen, loc. cit.
48. *Aṣṭādhyāyī*, VIII.2.12 cited in V.S. Agrawala, op. cit., p. 47.
49. *Mbh*, XIII.63.6.
50. Ibid., XIII.88.2-10. Cf. *Manu*, 3.266-72.
51. *māsānaṣṭau pārṣatena rauraveṇa navaiva tu/*
gavyasya tu māṃsena tṛptiḥ syāddaśamāsikī//
māsānekadāśa prītiḥ pitṛṇāṃ mahiṣena tu/
gavyena datte śrāddhe tu saṃvatsaramihocyate// *Mbh*, XIII.88.7-8.
52. Ibid., XIII.115-17. There are several passages in the *Mahābhārata*, which glorify the *ahiṃsā* doctrine. The god Bṛhaspati extols it as the foremost among the six gates to heaven (13.114) and the dialogue between the brāhmaṇa ascetic Jājali and the merchant Tulādhāra proclaims it as the highest morality (12.253-7). See John Brockington, *The Sanskrit Epics*, pp. 225-6; I. Proudfoot, op. cit.; Christopher Key Chapple, '*Ahiṃsā* in the Mahābhārata: a story, a philosophical perspective, and an admonishment', *Journal of Vaiṣṇava Studies*, 4.3 (1996), pp. 109-25.
53. *taṃ taṃ devaṃ samuddiśya pakṣiṇaḥ paśvaśca/*
ṛṣabhāḥ śāstrapaṭhitāstathā jalacarāśca ye/
sarvāṅstānabhyayuñjaste tatrāgnicayakarmaṇi/ 14.34.88 cited in Om Prakash, op. cit., p. 107.
54. 1.79.12 cited in John Brockington, *The Sanskrit Epics*, p. 225.
55. *śāmitre tu hayastatra tathā jalacarāśca ye/*

ṛtvijbhiḥ sarvamevaitanniyuktaṃ śāstrastadā//
paśūnāṃ triśataṃ tatra yūpeṣu niyataṃ tadā/
aśvaratnottamaṃ tasya rājño daśarathasya ca//Bālakāṇḍa, XIV.29-30. See *The Vālmīki Rāmāyaṇa*, ed. T.R. Krishnacharya, 1st edn., Kumbakonam, 1905, rpt., Sri Satguru Publications, Delhi, 1982.

56. *Rāmāyaṇa*, 2.17.15 cited in Brockington, *The Righteous Rāma: The Evolution of an Epic*, Oxford University Press, Bombay, 1984, p. 82.
57. Ibid., 2.44.20 cited in ibid., p. 83.
58. Ibid., 2.49.14; 2.50.16, etc.
59. *surāghaṭa sahasreṇa māṃsa bhūtoudanena ca/*
*yakṣye tvāṃ prayatāṃ devi purīṃ punrupāgatā//*Ibid., 2.52.89 (Kumbakonam edn.).
60. *svasti devi tarāmi tvā pārayenme pativrataṃ/ yakṣye tvāṃ gosahasreṇa surāghaṭaśatena ca//*Rāmāyaṇa, Kumbakonam edn., 2.55.19cd-20ab.
61. *Rāmāyaṇa*, 3.42.21 cited in Brockington, *The Righteous Rāma*, p. 82.
62. Ibid., 7.41.13-14. Cf. Rajnikant Shastri, op. cit., pp. 84-5.
63. Ibid., 3.69.8-11 cited in Brockington, *The Righteous Rāma*, p. 82.
64. Brockington, *The Righteous Rāma*, p. 82.
65. Ibid., p. 82.
66. *Rāmāyaṇa*, 2.85.17.
67. R.L Mitra, *Indo-Aryans*, vol. I, p. 396.
68. *Rāmāyaṇa*, 5.9.11-14.
69. Ibid., 6.48.24-6.
70. Ibid., 4.17.33-5 cited in John Brockington, *The Righteous Rāma*, p. 82.
71. John Brockington, *The Righteous Rāma*, p. 83.
72. Ibid., p. 83; Brockington, *The Sanskrit Epics*, p. 416.
73. Rajnikant Shastri (*Hindū Jāti kā Utthāna aur Patan*, pp. 82-4) cites the original Sanskrit passages from the *Ayodhyākāṇḍa* and *Araṇyakāṇḍa*, which bear striking resemblance with Vālmīki's work. For English translation of the crucial passages see: *The Adhyātma Rāmāyaṇa*, Eng. tr. Lala Baij Nath, Panini Office, Allahabad, 1913, p. 44, verses, 21-2; p. 80, verses, 38-9.
74. Francis Zimmermann, op. cit., p. 97.
75. Brahmanand Tripathi, ed., *Caraka Saṃhitā*, Chowkhamba Surabharati Prakashan, Varanasi, 4th edn., 1996, p. 1376.
76. Francis Zimmermann, op. cit., p. 98, 103-11. Cf. P. Ray, H.N. Gupta and M. Roy, *Suśruta Saṃhitā* (Scientific Synopsis), Indian

National Science Academy, Delhi, 1980, Table I, pp. 110-19.

77. Om Prakash, op. cit., p. 141.
78. *Caraka, cikitsā,* XIX.4. Zimmermann, op. cit., p. 189.
79. *Caraka, sūtra,* XXV.39.
80. *gavyamāṃsarasaiḥ sāmlā viṣamajvaranāśinī, Caraka, sūtra,* II.31.
81. *gavyaṃ kevalavāteṣu pīnase viṣamajvare, Caraka, sūtra,* XXVII.79.
82. *śvāsa-kāsa-pratiśyāya-viṣamajvara-nāśanam/ śramātyāgni-hitaṃ gavyaṃ pavitraṃ anilāpaham. Suśruta, sūtra,* XLVI.89d, cited in Alsdorf, op. cit., p. 618, fn.1.
83. *godhā-māṃsāśane putraṃ suṣupsaṃ dhāraṇātmakam/gavaṃ māṃse tu balinaṃ sarva-kleśa-sahaṃ tathā. Suśruta, śarīra,* III.25, cited in Alsdorf, op. cit., p. 618, fn. 2. Also see Alsdorf, op. cit., pp. 617-19. Cf. Francis Zimmermann, op. cit., pp. 185-6.
84. *śuṣkakāsaścamātyāgniviṣamajvarapīnasān/kārśyaṃ kevalavātāñśca gomāṃsaṃ sanniyacchati. Aṣṭāṅga Hṛdayam, sūtra,* VI.65. K.R. Srikantha Murthy, ed. and tr., *Aṣṭāṅga Hṛdayam,* vol. I, Krishnadas Academy, Varanasi, 1996.
85. For a different view see Zimmermann, op. cit., pp. 186-7.
86. *'gokarṇamāṃsaṃ madhuraṃ snigdhaṃ mṛdu kaphāpahaṃ/vipāke madhuraṃ cāpi raktapittavinaśanam'—iti suśrute. Halāyudhakośaḥ* (*Abhidhānaratnamālā*), ed. Jaishankar Joshi, Uttar Pradesh Hindi Sansthan, Lucknow, 3rd edn., 1993, p. 281.
87. Cf. Francis Zimmerman, op. cit., pp. 187-94.
88. *Bṛhatsaṃhitā,* L. 34-5 cited in Ajaya Mitra Shastri, *India As Seen in the Bṛhatsaṃhitā,* Motilal Banarsidass, Delhi, 1969, p. 214.
89. Ajaya Mitra Shastri, op. cit., p. 214.
90. Despite some lawgivers' abhorrence for pig flesh, it has continued to be sacrificed and eaten in India here and there (Frederick J. Simoons, *Eat Not This Flesh,* pp. 51-6; K.T. Achaya, *A Historical Dictionary of Indian Food,* p. 187). James Tod, writing in the early nineteenth century, reports the hunting and eating of wild boar among various groups including the Rajputs (*Annals and Antiquities of Rajasthan,* I, 1st Indian rpt., Delhi, 1983, pp. 451-2). However, the anti-pig sentiment, traceable to pre-Islamic times in West Asia, has been very strong among Indian Muslims, though certain Islamic groups in Mauritania, Morocco, Algeria, Tunisia, Kurdistan and Indonesia permit pork. It is interesting that two Persian doctors, Avicenna and Haly Abbas, spoke favourably of pork as food (Frederick J. Simoons, *Eat Not This Flesh,* p. 35; also p. 341, n. 180-2). Also see Marvin Harris, *Cows, Pigs, Wars and Witches,* Random House, New York, 1974;

Paul Diener and Eugene E. Robkin, 'Ecology, Evolution, and the Search for Origins: The Question of Islamic Pig Prohibition', *Current Anthropology*, 19, no. 3 (1978), pp. 493-540.

91. Om Prakash, op. cit., pp. 210-14; Shivashekhar Mishra, *Mānasollāsa: Ek Sānskritic Adhyayana*, Chowkhamba Vidya Bhavan, Varanasi, 1966, pp. 295-6; K.T. Achaya, *Indian Food: A Historical Companion*, Oxford University Press, Delhi, 1998, p. 90.
92. *ārādhyainaṃ śaravaṇabhavaṃ devamullaṅghitādhvā/ siddhadvandairjalakaṇabhayādvīṇibhirmuktamārgaḥ/ vyālambethāḥ surabhitanayālambhajāṃ mānayiṣyansrotomūrtyā bhuvi pariṇatāṃ rantidevasya kīrtim// Meghadūta*, I.48. That the reference here is to Rantideva's large-scale cow slaughter is clear from the commentary of Mallinātha (fourteenth-fifteenth century). See Meghadūta, ed. and tr. with the Commentary of Mallinātha by M.R. Kale, Motilal Banarsidass, 8th edn., rpt., 1979, p. 83.
93. *sañjñapte vatsatarī sarpiṣyannaṃ ca pacyate/ śrotriya śrotriyagṛhānagto'si juṣasva naḥ//Mahāvīracarita*, III.2. ed. with Hindi tr. Ramprataр Tripathi Shastri, Lok Bharati Prakashan, Allahabad, 1973, p. 60.
94. *Uttararāmacarita*, ed. and tr. with notes and the commentary of Ghanaśyāma, P.V. Kane and C.N. Joshi, Motilal Banarsidass, Delhi, 1962, Act IV, p. 86. The above interpretation of the dialogue between Dāṇḍāyana and Saudhātaki, the two disciples of Vālmīki, is based not only on the literal translation provided by the editors but also on Ghanaśyāma's commentary which belongs to as late a period as the early eighteenth century.
95. *mahākṣo vā mahājo vā śrotriyāya viśasyate/ Bālarāmāyaṇa*, I.38a. (*Bālarāmayaṇa* of Rājaśekhara, ed. Ganagasagar Rai, Chowkhamba, Varanasi, 1984, p. 18).
96. Om Prakash, op. cit., p. 216.
97. *Naiṣadhamahākāvyam*, ed. Haragovind Shastri with the commentary of Mallinātha, Chowkhamba, Varanasi, 1981, XVI.76, 86, 94.
98. *hiṃsāgavīṃ makhe vīkṣya riraṃsurdhāvati sma saḥ/ sā tu saumyavṛṣāsaktāḥ kharaṃ dūraṃ nirāsa tam//Naiṣadhamahākāvyam* (Chowkhamba edn.) XXVII. 173. Mallinātha (fourteenth-fifteenth century) gives different readings of the text but his own interpretation is as follows: *himseti/ saḥ kaliḥ, makhe gomedhākhyayajñe, hiṃsāyā gauḥ tāṃ hiṃsāgavīṃ ālambhārthāṃ gāṃ ityarthaḥ* (ibid., p. 1127). Cāṇḍupaṇḍita (AD 1297): *sa hiṃsā eva*

gaustāṃ vīkṣya riraṃsuḥ san dhāvati sma . . . makhe yāge paśuhiṃsāmiti bhāvaḥ. Narahari (late fourteenth century) in his commentary called *Dīpikā* says: *makhe gomedhākhye yajñe hiṃsāgavīṃ hiṃsāsaṃbandhinīṃ gavīṃ vīkṣya riraṃsuḥ hṛṣṭacittaḥ sa niṣiddhagohiṃsā matpriyā iti dhāvati sma/ sā tu hanyamānā gauḥ punaḥ saumye somadevatākadravyasādhye vṛṣe dharma āsakttā saumyo ramaṇīyaḥ pāraloukiko dharmastatsādhikā vā kharaṃ pāparūpatvādduḥsahaṃ dūrādeva nirāsa/*See *Naiṣadhacarita* of Śrīharṣa, Eng. tr. K.K. Handiqui, Deccan College, Poona, 1965, p. 472, notes on verse 177 which is the same as the verse cited above.

99. *adhāvat kvāpi gāṃ vīkṣya hanyamānāmayaṃ mudā/ atithibhyastu tāṃ buddhvā mandaṃ mando nyavarttata//* *Naiṣadhamahākāvyam*, XVII.197 (Chowkhamba edn.).
100. *Pṛthvīrājavijaya* [summary in Chandra Prabha, *Historical Mahākāvyas in Sanskrit (Eleventh to Fifteenth Century AD)*, Delhi, 1976, Chap. 9] cited in B.D. Chattopadhyaya, *Representing the Other? Sanskrit Sources and the Muslims*, Manohar, Delhi, 1998, p. 43.
101. Supra.
102. Supra.
103. *gāṃ saurabheyīṃ, hanyamānāṃ ālabhyamānāṃ, vīkṣya dṛṣṭvā, mudā harṣeṇa adhāvat drutamāgachhat/ tu kintu, tāṃ gāṃ, atithibhyaḥ atithyarthaṃ hanyamānāṃ, buddhvā jñātvā, mandaṃ śanaiḥ śanaiḥ, nyavarttat vyaramat, sakhedaṃ pratyāgachhadityarthaḥ/ 'mahokṣaṃ vā mahājaṃ vā śrotriyayopakalpayet' iti vidhānāditi bhāvaḥ/ Naiṣadhamahākāvyam*, Chowkhamba edn., p. 1137.
104. For Mallinātha's interpretation of the crucial passage see *surabhitanayānāṃ gavāmālambhena sanjñapanena jāyata iti tathoktāṃ/bhuvi loke srotomūrtyāṃ pravāharūpeṇa pariṇatāṃ rūpaviśeṣamāpannāṃ rantidevasya daśapurapatermahārājasya kīrtim/carmaṇvatyākhyāṃ nadīmityarthaḥ/ mānayiṣyaṅ satkārasyan vyālambeyithāḥ/ālambyāvatarerityarthaḥ/purā kila rājño rantidevasya 'gavālambheṣvekatra saṃbhṛtādraktaniṣyandāccarmaraśeḥ kācinnadī sasyande/sā carmaṇvatītyākhyāyata iti/Meghadūta*, ed. and tr. with the commentary of Mallinātha, M.R. Kale, 8th edn. rpt., 1979, p. 83.
105. Ghanaśyāma, a minister of a Tanjore king Tukkoji from 1728 to 1738, was a man of great erudition and quotes not only from the Vedas and Smṛtis to support his interpretation but also refers to about sixty lexicographers and lexicons in his

commentary. His comment on the Dāṇḍayāna–Saudhātaki dialogue is unambiguous: *yadāgateṣu vasiṣṭhamiśreṣu evamadyaiva pratyāgatāya rājarṣaye bhagavatā vālmīkinā dadhimadhubhireva nirvartito madhuparkaḥ vatsatarī punarvisarjitā:* see *Uttararāmacarita* of Bhavabhūti, ed. with notes and tr. P.V. Kane and C.N. Joshi, Motilal Banarsidass, Delhi, 4th revd. edn., 1962, text p. 87.

106. K.K. Handiqui, *Yaśastilaka and Indian Culture*, p. 390.

107. Wilhelm Halbfass, *Tradition and Reflection: Explorations in Indian Thought*, Sri Satguru Publicatiohs, Delhi, 1992, Chap. 4.

108. Śaṅkara on *Brahmasūtra* 3.1.25 and 3.4.28: see Hanns-Peter Schmidt, 'Ahiṃsā and Rebirth', op. cit., p. 228.

109. Ibid., p. 228.

110. *Māṃsatattvaviveka,* Sarasvatibhavan Series, Benaras, 1927, pp. 28-9 cited by Kane, op. cit., III, p. 946 fn. 1835. Cf. *Bhāṣā-Paricched with Siddhānta-Muktāvalī* by Visvanātha Nyāya-Pañcānana, tr. Swami Madhvānanda with an Introduction by Satkari Mookerjee, Advaita Ashrama, Calcutta, 1977, pp. xxiv-xxv.

111. *Śaṅkha,* VII.27-8.

112. *kālaśākaṃ saśalkaṃ ca māṃsaṃ vārdhrarṇisasya ca/ khaḍgamāṃsaṃ tathānantaṃ yamaḥ provāca dharmavit//*ibid., IV.26.

4

The Cow in the Kali Age and Memories of Beef Consumption

While animal food continued to occupy a place of importance, even among the upper castes, it remains true that, around the middle of the first millennium AD, the Dharmaśāstras began to show their disapproval of the killing of the cow. This change in the Brāhmaṇical attitude towards cow slaughter may be viewed against the general background of a transformation of rural society in early medieval times which saw an unprecedented agrarian expansion and shrinkage of trade. Agriculture, earlier viewed as a distinctive occupation of the vaiśyas, no longer remained confined to them. It came to be sanctioned unreservedly for the poor as well as for the landholding priestly aristocracy.[1] The ranks of the latter swelled on account of the widespread practice of making land donations to the priestly class and this in turn resulted in a qualitative change in agrarian society in which agriculture and animal husbandry played a pivotal role.[2] All this together with the gradual replacement of Vedic sacrifice by Purāṇic religion, buttressed by a new mechanism of gift-making with emphasis on the donation of land and other agrarian resources like the cattle made it necessary for the law givers to forbid the killing of kine.[3]

The changes outlined above may have been both cause and effect of a social crisis, encapsulated in the broad concept of the *kaliyuga* as described first in the Great Epic and the early Purāṇas[4] and elaborated in the later Purāṇic texts. The *kaliyuga,* whose dark aspects find frequent mention in the Purāṇas, begins to figure in early medieval land charters, which often give credit to the donor-kings for restoring *dharma* and driving away the evil influences of Kali. Not surprisingly, the law books and legal digests seem to have begun to modify earlier social norms, including the dietary rules. Early medieval jurists speak of customs that have to be given up in the kali age (*kalivarjyas*) and these include the killing of cattle[5]—a practice that now was considered odious. This disapproval, repeatedly mentioned as a *kalivarjya* in religious texts, tended to give special status to the cow, and to exclude beef from at least the brāhmaṇa's menu. The *Vyāsasmṛti* thus categorically states that a cow killer is untouchable (*antyaja*) and even by talking to him one incurs sin;[6] it thus made beef eating one of the bases of untouchability from the early medieval period onwards.

Parāśara, whose lawbook is believed to be especially applicable to the *kaliyuga,* speaks in a similar vein.

According to him a brāhmaṇa who eats beef or the food offered by a cāṇḍāla (*gomāṃsam cāṇḍālānnamathāpi vā*) is required to perform the *kṛcchracāndrāyana* penance[7] and one who kills a cow and hides his offence goes to the worst hell.[8] Parāśara therefore lays specific penances for the offence.[9] The law book of Devala avers that if a brāhmaṇa is forced by the mlecchas, cāṇḍālas and the dasyus to kill a cow he is required to perform a penance.[10] The condemnation of cow killing is borne out by numerous passages in other early medieval law books[11] and finds an echo in contemporary narrative literature.[12] One law book describes a cow killer as a leper (*kuṣṭhī govadhakārī*)[13] and another treats beef (*gomāṃsa*) as 'the worst form of cursed or abominable food'.[14] However, according to some lawgivers, no sin seems to have been incurred if the cow dies by accident or in the course of an illness.[15] The Dharmaśāstras are generally silent about whether the carcass was to be eaten or not, but the *Śaṅkhasmṛti* prescribes a fifteen-day penance for one who eats a dead calf,[16] though, curiously, a Jana Sangha (now BJP) ideologue permits, without equivocation, the eating of 'the flesh of cows dying a natural death'.[17]

The Brāhmaṇical rejection of cattle slaughter perhaps encouraged the establishment of cow shelters alongside temples, as can be inferred from several epigraphic records. An inscription dated AD 883-4 records the gift of a *gosāsa* (*goṣṭha* = cowshed?) by a certain Chidāṇṇa.[18] Another order issued in the third year of the later Pallava king Peruñjinga refers to gifts of cows to a *gośālā* (*kulottuṅgan-tiru-gośālai*) established at the time and in the name of the Coḷa king Kulottuṅga III (AD 1179-1216).[19] A clear link between the cow shelter and the temple is borne out by an inscription dated AD 1374-5 which speaks of the construction of a *gośālā* in the premises of the Padmanābhasvāmin temple at Thiruvananthapuram.[20] While it may be worthwhile to examine the relationship between the Brāhmaṇical rejection of cow slaughter and the founding of cow homes,[21] beef eating may not have been a taboo among the followers of Tāntric religion, whose texts call for a separate study.[22]

Memories of Cattle Killing

There is a clear lack of consistency on vegetarianism in the commentarial literature and digests of the eighth to the nineteenth centuries.[23] They provide substantial evidence to prove that animal food was not only permitted but also quite often preferred. Even though they generally disapprove of the killing of cows in the kali age, they retain a memory of the ancient practice and sometimes even sanction it. Medhātithi, commenting on Manu III.119, quotes a passage from the *Aitareya Brāhmaṇa* (III.4.) according to which a bull or ox was killed in honour of a ruler of men or any person who deserved to be honoured.[24] In his detailed gloss on Manu (V.26, 27), he states that meat can be eaten in specific circumstances and goes to the extent of permitting beef (*govyajamāṃsaṃ*) on ritual occasions.[25] Similarly Viśvarūpa's exegesis (ninth century) of Yājñavalkya's passage on *madhuparka* (receiving guests) more or less supports the killing of the bull in honour of the guest.[26] Vijñāneśvara (AD 1100) interprets the word *upakalpayet* used by Yājñavalkya as 'one should offer' a bull by saying to the guest, 'for you [it is] presented by us for your satisfaction', not as a gift, nor for killing either (. . . *na tu dānāya vyāpādanāya* vā,), viz., 'all this is your honour's' (*sarvaṃ etad bhavadīyam*), since for 'every learned brāhmaṇa a bull is impossible (*prati śrotriyaṃ ukṣāsambhavāt* . . .)'.[27] The motivation behind such an interpretation seems to have been the expense, not veneration of cattle. Yet, elsewhere Vijñāneśvara attaches great importance to the popular disapproval of the offering of a big bull or goat to the venerable priest or slaying a cow for Mitra and Varuṇa.[28] In the twelfth century Haradatta on Gautama (XVII.30) quotes the *Aitareya Brāhmaṇa* passage, cited earlier by Medhātithi, to explain a statement of Gautama. Lakṣmīdhara in his *Kṛtyakalpataru* (twelfth century) explains the crucial passage of Yājñavalkya as well as a statement of Vasiṣṭha that in ancient times it was the duty of the householder to kill the cow for a learned brāhmaṇa, but not so in the *kaliyuga*.[29] Lakṣmīdhara quotes in support of his contention a passage from the *Brahmapurāṇa* prohibiting cow slaughter by the twice-born on the occasion of marriage in the kali age.[30] Unlike several medieval lawgivers, Lakṣmīdhara endorses the old rule of flesh eating in *śrāddha*, and cites the dictum of Vasiṣṭha condemning an ascetic who declines to eat the meat served on this occasion.[31] He goes to the extent of stating, '. . . substances like the flesh of cows and buffaloes which are recommended for special advantage (*phalaviśeṣārthaṃ*) can be used (in *śrāddha*) only by those who desire those special results. . . . The meat of buffaloes and the like, which are neither recommended nor rejected, may still be used in the absence of articles that are prescribed for use.'[32] Several centuries later we find Mitra Miśra (AD 1610-40) quite unequivocal on the point. He takes the word *upakalpayet* used by Yājñavalkya in the context of receiving guests to mean '*should cook*' (*pacet*) as a meal, and quotes a *śruti* passage in support.[33]

As opposed to all this, Alberuni (AD 1017-30) mentions the cow along with animals and birds (horses, mules, asses, camels, elephants, domestic fowl, crows, parrots and nightingales) as inedible for the brāhmaṇas, who, however, were allowed to eat the meat of other animals like sheep, goats, gazelles, hares, rhinoceros, buffaloes, fish, and such birds as are 'not loathsome to man nor noxious'.[34] He tells us that the brāhmaṇas used to eat the flesh of the cow in ancient times, though he was not satisfied with different explanations offered to him regarding the disappearance of the practice.[35] In any case Alberuni's informants evidently retained the memory of the old custom of slaughtering the cow and eating its flesh. Thus while non-vegetarian diet continued in Brāhmaṇical circles, the commentaries and religious digests that forbid the killing of the cow speak of it as an earlier practice. Aparārka (twelfth century) cites Purāṇic and Smṛti passages, which clearly prohibit the killing of the cow.[36] On the basis of a verse from the *Mārkaṇḍeya Purāṇa*, he recommends the offering of a golden vessel in lieu of a cow to the guest and states that according to Bhṛgu no animal is to be sacrificed in the *kaliyuga*.[37] Yet he quotes a passage from Śaṅkha to the effect that the flesh of buffaloes, goats, rams, *ruru* deer, ordinary deer and spotted deer are edible.[38] Devaṇṇabhaṭṭa (thirteenth century) quotes a passage from Kratu, which prohibits ritual killing of cows in the kali age[39] and supports it with a Purāṇic authority.[40] Similarly Hemādri (AD 1260-70) disallows the killing of cows and the offering of meat in *śrāddha*.[41] His position, however, appears contradictory. For he allows cow slaughter on the occasions of *gosava* and *madhuparka* but treats it as a heinous act on other occasions in the *kaliyuga*.[42] A little later Caṇḍeśvara (AD 1310-60) in his *Gṛhastharatnākara* quotes approvingly a passage from Hārīta who allows consumption of the flesh of goats, rams, buffaloes, deer, rhinoceros, and large forest boars,[43] without mentioning the cow, though Narasiṃha/ Nṛsiṃha (1360-1435) in his *Prayogapārijāta* reproduces Āśvalāyana's dictum making it obligatory to eat beef at the *madhuparka* ceremony but also lifts a passage from the *Ādityapurāṇa* according to which in the *kaliyuga* a guest should be welcomed without killing a cow.[44] Kamalākarabhaṭṭa, in his *Nirṇayasindhu* (AD 1612), repeats the opinion of Vijñāneśvara and states, on the basis of an unknown authority, that although the rule of killing a cow fit for Mitra and Varuṇa, or a barren cow, or one that has ceased to bear after first calving is duly ordained, such sacrifice, being opposed to public feeling, should not be performed.[45] The works of medieval commentators abound in references to the rejection of cow slaughter, though many of them do not treat the ritual killing of animals, including the domesticated ones, with contempt.[46] The *Parāśaramādhavīya*, a commentary on the *Pārāśarasmṛti* by Madhvācārya (fourteenth century), the *Madanapārijāta* of Madanapāla (fourteenth century), the *Madanaratna* of Madanasiṃha (late fifteenth century), the *Udvāhatattva* of Raghunandana (sixteenth century), the *Samayamayūkha* of Nīlakaṇṭha (seventeenth century), the *Samayaprakāśa* of Mitra Miśra (early seventeenth century), and the *Nirṇayasindhu* of Kamalākarabhaṭṭa (1612) disapprove of cow killing.[47] This sentiment seems to have been indeed strong in the Brāhmaṇical circles and Dāmodara, probably the elder brother of Nīlakaṇṭha, is even credited with persuading the yavanas of Mūlasthāna (Multan) to give up cow slaughter.[48]

Recurrent references to the rejection of cow slaughter in the medieval period does imply that it was not uncommon and that this fact was recognized by the medieval Dharmaśāstra writers. For this reason the condemnation of cow killing as a *kalivarjya* became an idèe fixe, even though the brāhmaṇas do not seem to have forgotten the ancient practice of sacrificing cattle and eating their flesh. As recently as the early twentieth century Mahāmahopādhyāya Madana Upadhyaya, a Maithila brāhmaṇa, recalls several passages from earlier texts indicating that cows and buffaloes were done to death on ritual occasions in the past and refers to the contemporary Nepalese practice of eating buffalo meat (*nepālaeva mahiṣābhakṣyaḥ*). Like other Dharmaśāstra writers, however, he too describes the cow as unslayable in the kali age.[49] Despite the Dharmaśāstric prohibition of cow slaughter, however, instances of cow sacrifice are documented even in recent times. Sacrificial killing of cows and buffaloes, for example, was practised at Todgarh in Merwara (Rajasthan) until 1874 when the local Rawats entered into an agreement to abstain from beef eating.[50] In our own times the killing of cow for rituals and sacrifices has fallen in disuse and its slaughter for food is viewed with aversion, though brāhmaṇas and members of other castes sell the decrepit ones to butchers and abattoirs without qualms.

The buffalo, another beef animal, despite its greater utility in traction and, in dairy and meat products than the cow has, however, failed to achieve exemption from being killed. Although most Indians of high caste do not generally eat buffalo flesh today, there are several places where buffalo sacrifice has continued till recently. In south India, for example, buffaloes were sacrificed by the hundreds at the Athanuramman temple in Salem district (Tamilnadu) until the Hindu Religious Charities and Endowments Board took over the administration of scores of village goddess temples in the middle of the twentieth century.[51] Buffaloes continue to be offered to the three main goddesses at Cenci (Tamilnadu) during the annual festival in *caitra* month.[52] At Sonepur and Baud in Orissa the Dumbals/Dumals are known to have sacrificed buffaloes till the 1970s.[53] In the village of Bangaọn Mahisi in north-eastern Bihar, the tradition of buffalo sacrifice has remained fairly strong till today. Buffaloes are sacrificed at the temple of Kāmākhyā in Guwahati (Assam), and that of Kālī in Calcutta (West Bengal) where a slaughterhouse was advertised as the temple of goddess Kālī so that the credulous could purchase meat from there thinking it to be the *prasāda* of the deity. The continuation of ritual slaughter of the buffalo at different places may partly be attributed to the Dharmaśāstric sanction for eating its flesh, though the extent of direct brāhmaṇa participation in the killing of buffalo and eating its flesh may have varied from region to region.[54] Outside Brāhmaṇical society, there are many tribes, who continue to kill cattle and eat their flesh. For example, the Dire of Hyderabad eat beef openly at feasts,[55] and the tribes of eastern India sacrifice the mithan (also called gayal, a species of cattle) and eat its flesh with relish.[56]

The extent to which such practices as these may be treated as survivals of ancient tradition attested in the texts is difficult to say. But there is reason to believe that the Brāhmaṇical ideas have shaped the attitude of some tribal groups, among whom beef was a respectable and fairly common food item in earlier times.[57] For example, the Saoras (Śabaras) of Orissa, who are known to have formerly sacrificed cows and bullocks and to have eaten their flesh, under Brāhmaṇical influence almost gave up the practice by the 1950s. This may indicate the general pattern of acculturation in India.[58]

NOTES

1. B.N.S. Yadava, *Society and Culture in Northern India in the Twelfth Century*, Central Book Depot, Allahabad, 1973, p. 260.
2. Despite substantial earlier evidence for plough agriculture and cattle rearing, there is no doubt that the codification of knowledge about agriculture and related matters began only in early medieval times. This is evident from such early medieval works as the *Bṛhatsaṃhitā*, *Agni Purāṇa*, *Kṛṣiparāśara*, *Kāśyapīyakṛṣisūkti* and *Upavanavinoda* of Sārṅgadhara (thirteenth century). The agricultural maxims and pithy sayings of Dāka and Khanā, still current in eastern India, go back to the tenth century (B.N.S. Yadava, op. cit., p. 257). These works, containing systematic information on agricultural operations and animal husbandry, indicate the pre-eminent position that these occupations came to occupy from around the middle of the first millennium AD. Also see D.M. Bose et al., A *Concise History of Science in India*, Indian National Science Academy, Delhi, 1971, Chap. 6.
3. V. Nath has discussed how the Vedic sacrifices gave way to the

Purāṇic gift-giving in early medieval times. See her '*Mahādāna*: The Dynamics of Gift-Economy and the Feudal Milieu', in D.N. Jha, ed., *The Feudal Order: State, Society and Ideology in Early Medieval India*, Manohar, Delhi, 2000, pp. 411-40.

4. For a detailed discussion of the development of the idea of *Kaliyuga* and its relationship with social and economic transformation see R.S. Sharma, 'The Kali Age: A Period of Social Crisis', in D.N. Jha, ed., *The Feudal Order*, pp. 61-77; B.N.S. Yadava, 'The Accounts of the Kali Age and the Social Transition from Antiquity to the Middle Ages', ibid., pp. 79-120; D.N. Jha, Editor's Introduction, ibid., pp. 6-10.
5. The number of practices forbidden in the *kaliyuga* increased to more than fifty and came to be consolidated in the seventeenth century by Dāmodara in his *Kalivarjyavinirṇaya*. According to the theory of incarnations (*avatāras*) contained in the Dharmaśāstra and the Purāṇa texts, the *kaliyuga*, the last of the four *yugas* (eons) of progressive degeneration of mankind, is believed to come to an end with the appearance of Viṣṇu as Kalki on a horseback to uproot the mlecchas and restore *dharma*. It is interesting that Shivaji was lionized as 'the first harbinger' of Kalki and as a protector of cows and brāhmaṇas in some texts whose composition broadly coincides with that of the *Kalivarjyavinirṇaya* [Jayarāma's *Parṇālaparvata-grahaṇākhyāna* (1673) cited in P.V. Kane, *History of Dharmaśāstra*, III, Bhandarkar Oriental Research Institute, Poona, 1973, pp. 925-6; *Śiva Digvijaya* cited in L.L. Sundara Ram, *Cow Protection in India*, The South Indian Humanitarian Layers, Madras, 1927, p. 192. Cf. Deryck O. Lodrick, *Sacred Cows, Sacred Places*, University of California Press, 1981, p. 65.] Mercifully, neither Shivaji nor his recent 'incarnation', Bal Thackeray, can be credited with any success in exterminating mlecchas (Muslims/Christians/Sikhs) or 'restoring' *dharma* of the VHP/ Bajrang Dal brand.
6. *eten'tyajāḥ samākhyātā ye cānye cā gavāśanāḥ/*
eṣāṃ saṃbhāṣanātsnānaṃ darśanādarkavīkṣaṇaṃ// Vyāsasmṛti, I.12. Cf. V. Jha who cites an identical passage from the *Vedavyāsasmṛti* ('Stages in the History of Untouchables', *IHR*, II, no. 1, 1975, p. 31).
7. *amedhyareto gomāṃsaṃ cāṇḍālānnamathāpi vā/*
yadi bhuktantu vipreṇa kṛcccraṃ cāndrāyaṇaṃ caret//Parāśara, XI.1.
8. Ibid., IX. 61-2.

9. Ibid., XI.1; VIII.43-50.
10. *balāddāsīkṛtā ye ca mlecchacāṇḍāladasyubhiḥ/ aśubhaṃ kāritāḥ karma gavādiprāṇihiṃsanam/ /Devala,* 17.
11. *Atri,* 218, 315; *Yama,* 30; *Āṅgirasa,* 25-34; *Saṃvartta,* 132-7, 198; *Pārāsara,* IX. 36-9. The list of references is illustrative and cannot claim to be exhaustive.
12. In a story related by Somadeva (eleventh century) a cāṇḍāla is described as carrying a load of the flesh of cows which are the object of veneration of the three worlds; Vindumatī, beloved of Saktideva, is said to have been reborn as a fisherwoman for the minor offence of repairing with her teeth the broken strings (of cow hide?) of a vīṇā (*Kathāsaritasāgara* of Somadeva, text with Hindi translation by Pandit Kedarnath Sharma, Bihar Rashtrabhasha Parisad, Patna, 1960, pt. I, pp. 577-9.)
13. *Śātātapa,* II. 13.
14. *Brāhmaṇasarvasva* of Halāyudha, ed. Tejascandra Vidyananda, 2nd edn., Calcutta, BS 1299, p. 174 cited in Taponath Chakravarty, *Food and Drink in Ancient Bengal,* Firma K.L. Mukhopadhyaya, Calcutta, 1959, p. 50.
15. For example *Yama,* 45-7, 50-3.
16. *Śaṅkha,* VII. 29-30.
17. K.R. Malkani's Editorial in *Organiser,* 11 November 1966 rpt. in *Seminar,* no. 93 (special issue on the Cow), May 1967.
18. *EI,* XXI, no. 35, p. 207.
19. *SII,* VIII, no. 54 cited in *EI,* XXIV, no. 22, p. 159.
20. *EI,* IV, no. 27B, p. 203.
21. Deryck O. Lodrick, op. cit., has made a useful study of the origins and survivals of animal homes but presents inadequate historical data pertaining to the precolonial period.
22. According to the *Tantrasāra* (eleventh century), *and Śyāmārahasya* (sixteenth century) the *mahāmāṃsa* includes the flesh of the cow, man, ram, horse, buffalo, boar, goat and deer (N.N. Bhattacharyya, *History of the Tantric Religion,* Manohar, Delhi, 1982, p. 445).
23. Trivikrama (early tenth century) describes a marriage feast in which purely vegetararian food was offered to the army, much to the chagrin of northerners (*Nalacampū,* Nirnaya Sagar Press, p. 251 cited in P.K. Gode, *Studies in Indian Cultural History,* vol. III, Bhandarkar Oriental Research Institute, Poona, 1969, p. 76, fn. 4). Dhuṇḍirāja (*c.* 1700) describes meat eating in north India, especially Bengal, as an evil custom (*durācāra*) in

his Sanskrit grammatical work *Gīravāṇapadamañjarī* (see P.K. Gode, op. cit., pp. 61-77).

24. *tadyathaivādo manuṣyarāja āgate'nyasminvārhati ukṣāṇaṃ vā vehataṃ vā kṣadante, Aitareya Brāhmaṇa,* III.4 cited in Kane, op. cit., II, pt. 1, p. 542, n. 1254.
25. . . . *govyajamāṃsamaprokṣitaṃbhakṣayet.* . . . Medhātithi on Manu, V.27. . . .*madhuparkovyākhyātaḥ tatra govadovihitaḥ* . . . Medhātithi on Manu, V.41. See *Mānava-Dharma-Śāstra* (with the commentaries of Medhātithi, Sarvajñanārāyaṇa, Kullūka, Nandana and Rāmacandra), ed. V.N. Mandalīka, Ganpat Krishnaji's Press, Bombay, 1886, pp. 604, 613.
26. . . . *upakalpanavacanāt tadanujñāpekṣo mahokṣādivadhaḥ* . . . Viśvarūpa on *Yājñavalkyasmṛti,* I.108. *The Yājñavalkyasmṛti with the Commentary Bālakrīḍā of Viśvarūpācārya,* ed. T. Ganapati Sastri, 2nd edn., Munshiram Manoharlal, Delhi, 1982, p. 97. It may be noted that Yaj. I.109 occurs in this edn. as I.108.
27. *Yājñavalkyasmṛti with Vijñāneṣvara's Mitākśarā,* ed. Gangasagar Rai, Chowkhamba Sanskrit Pratisthan, Delhi, 1998, p. 54.
28. *mahokṣaṃ vā mahājaṃ vā śrotriyāyopakalpayet (Yāj. I.109) iti vidhāne'pi lokavidviṣṭvādananuṣṭhānaṃ/. . . maitrāvaruṇīṃ gāṃ vaśāmanubandhyāmālabhet iti gavālambhanavidhāne'pi lokavidviṣṭvādananuṣṭhānaṃ/ Yājñavalkyasmṛti with Vijñaneśvara's Mitākṣarā,* ibid., p. 258.
29. *atra yadyapi gṛhāgataśrotriyatṛptyarthaṃ govadhaḥ kartavya iti pratīyate, tathāpi kaliyuge nāyaṃ dharmaḥ/ kiṃtu yugāntare/ Kṛtyakalpataru* of Lakṣmīdhara, Niyatakālakāṇḍaṃ, tṛtīyabhagaṃ, ed. K.V. Rangaswami Aiyangar, Gackwad Oriental Series, Baroda, 1950, p. 190.
30. *dīrghakālaṃ brahmacaryaṃ dhāraṇaṃ ca kamaṇḍaluḥ/*
gotrānmatṛsapindādvā vivāho govadhastathā//
*narāśvamedhau madyaṃ ca kalau varjyaṃ dvijātibhiḥ//*ibid., p. 190.
31. *Kṛtyakalpataru* of Bhaṭṭa Lakṣmīdhara, vol. IV, *Śrāddhakāṇḍa,* ed. K.V. Rangaswami Aiyangar, Gackwad Oriental Series, Baroda, 1950, p. 192.
32. Ibid., Introduction, p. 13.
33. J.R. Gharpure, ed., *Yājñavalkyasmṛti with the commentaries of Mitākṣarā and Vīramitrodaya, Acāradhyāya,* The Collection of Hindu Law Texts, Bombay, 1936, p. 303.
34. Edward C. Sachau, *Alberuni's India,* Low Price Publications, Delhi, rpt. 1996, Chap. LXVIII.

35. Ibid.
36. Kane, op. cit., III, p. 928, fn. 1799.
37. Ibid., p. 929.
38. Ibid., II, pt. 2, p. 781.
39. *devarācca sutotpattiḥ dattā kanyā na dīyate/ na yajñe govadhaḥ kāryaḥ kalau ca na kamaṇḍaluḥ* cited in Kane, op. cit., III, p. 928.
40. Ibid., p. 929.
41. Ibid.
42. *gosava eva kāraṇaṃ hanane madhuparkaśca/tayorabhāvād gohiṃsanaṃ garhitameva kaliyuge, Caturvagacintāmaṇi*, IV, *Prāyaścittakhaṇḍam*, ed. Paṇḍit Pramatha Nātha Tarkabhūṣana, Asiatic Society, Calcutta, 1911, p. 80.
43. Kane, op. cit., II, pt. 2, p. 781.
44. R.L. Mitra, *Indo-Aryans*, p. 384.
45. *asvargyaṃ lokavidviṣṭaṃ dharmmapyācarennatviti niṣedhāt/yathā, mahokṣaṃ vā mahājaṃ vā śrotriyāya prakalpayediti vidhāne'pi lokavidviṣṭatvādananuṣṭhānaṃ/yathā vā maitrāvaruṇīṃ gāṃ vaśāmanubandhyāmālabhet iti gavālambhanavidhāne'pi lokavidviṣṭatvādananuṣṭhānaṃ/ Nirṇayasindhu* quoted by R.L. Mitra, op. cit., p. 387.
46. Laxmanshastri Joshi, 'Was the cow killed in Ancient India?', *Quest*, 75 (1972), p. 83.
47. For references see Kane, op. cit., III, pp. 927-8, 946-7.
48. Ibid., I, pt. 2, p. 806.
49. *Palapiyūṣalatā* by Mahāmahopādhyāya Madana Upadhyaya, Gourīśayantrālaya, Darbhanga, Saṃvat, 1951. There are several texts from Mithilā which deal with meat eating: e.g. *Ācāracintāmaṇi* of Vācaspati Miśra (around AD 1500), *Nityakṛtyaratnamālā* of Mukunda Jha Bakshi and *Maṃsāśanavyavasthā* of Mahāmahopādhyāya Citradhara Miśra, may all contain similar information, though, despite my best efforts, I could not access these texts.
50. J. Digges La Touche, *The Rajputana Gazetteer*, II, Ajmer-Merwara, p. 48.
51. It is interesting to note that the Pallava, Coḷa and Pāṇḍya temples are never without a Durgā standing on a severed buffalo head. An analysis of south Indian toponyms also indicates that buffaloes were sacrificed at certain places. For example, Mysore is named after Mahiṣāsura.
52. I owe this information to Dr. Ulrike Niklas.
53. For references to buffalo sacrifice see A. Eschmann, Hermann

Kulke and G.C. Tripathi, eds., *The Cult of Jagannath and the Regional Tradition of Orissa*, Manohar, Delhi, 1978, pp. 267n, 271, 278, 281.

54. Dr. N. Ganesan informs me that in South India the brāhmaṇa priests bless the buffalo before the animal is killed but do not eat its flesh. For a brief description of buffalo sacrifice see Alf Hiltebeitel, 'Sexuality and Sacrifice: Convergent Subcurrents in the Firewalking Cult of Draupadī', in Fred W. Clothey, ed., *Images of Man: Religion and Historical Process in South Asia*, New Era, Madras, 1982, pp. 72-111.
55. Christoph von Furer-Haimendorf, *The Aboriginal Tribes of Hyderabad*, II, Macmillan, London, 1943, p. 239.
56. Frederick J. Simoons and Elizabeth S. Simoons, *A Ceremonial Ox of India: The Mithan in Nature, Culture and History*, University of Wisconsin Press, Madison, 1968, pp. 194-6.
57. For references see Frederick J. Simoons, *Eat Not This Flesh*, pp. 113-19.
58. Ibid., p. 117. Simoons mentions several other tribes like the Reddis of Hyderabad, Kharias of Chota Nagpur and Central India and the Kamars of Chhatisgarh who reject cow slaughter and the eating of beef.

5

A Paradoxical Sin and the Paradox of the Cow

Most of the legal texts and religious digests accord to the cow a status higher than they do to other cattle and say it is not to be killed in the *kaliyuga*. The intention of their authors may have been to discourage a practice they saw prevailing around them. Perhaps this may partially explain why the killing of the cow or ox figures as a sin in religious texts even when the Vedas, Brāhmaṇas and Upaniṣads do not include cattle killing in the list of sins or moral transgressions.[1] Yāska explains a Ṛgvedic passage (X.5.6) by enumerating seven sins, but this list does not include cattle killing. Similarly the Brāhmaṇa texts and the Upaniṣads do not mention the killing of the kine as a sin. Although the killing of a brāhmaṇa (*brahmahatyā*), theft (*steya*), drinking of liquor (*surāpāna*), sexual intercourse with a teacher's wife (*gurvaṅganāgama*) and association with those guilty of these offences are listed as the gravest sins (*mahāpātaka*), the killing of the cow, despite the high status it is said to have enjoyed, is not mentioned as a major offence.[2] The slaying of kine has been viewed as a minor sin (*upapātaka*) by almost all the lawgivers. It is first mentioned as a minor sin (*upapātaka*) in the Dharmasūtras[3] but more frequently in the Smṛtis and later commentaries, which also lay down rules and procedures for its atonement. Manu[4] and Yājñavalkya,[5] despite their approval of ritual slaughter of cattle lay down elaborate penances for the killer of the cow, and the term *goghna* used by Pāṇini in the sense of an honoured guest now came to acquire the pejorative meaning of a cow killer. Yet, paradoxical though it may seem, the lawgivers do not classify slaying of cow as a major offence (*mahāpātaka*).

Lawgivers from Manu onwards are generally unanimous in describing cow killing as a minor sin, but do not lay down a uniform penalty for the cow killer. Parāśara, who belongs to the early medieval period, prescribes the *prājāpatya* penance (*govadhasyā'nurūpeṇa prājāpatyaṃ vinirdiśet*),[6] and assures us that by feeding brāhmaṇas a killer of cattle is bound to become pure (*brāhmaṇān bhojayitvā tu goghnaḥ suddhyenna saṃśayaḥ*).[7] According to a passage of the *Śaṅkhalikhitasmṛti*, another later legal work, the killer of the cow should fast for twenty-five days and nights, subsisting on the five products of the cow (*pañcagavya*),[8] tonsure his head and wear a top-knot, wear cow-hide as an upper garment, follow cows, lie down in a cow-pen and donate a cow.[9] Attention has also been drawn to the fact that the penance for cow killing (*govadha*) differed according to the caste of the owner of the cow, especially in the later law books and digests.[10] If the cow belonged to a brāhmaṇa, its killer would incur greater sin than if it were possessed by a non-brāhmaṇa. Later exegetical writings, in fact, emphasize the superiority of the brāhmaṇa's cow. Vijñāneśvara (AD 1100) raises this question in interpreting Yājñavalkya (III. 263) and explains it by arguing that since, according to Nārada, the property of the brāhmaṇas is the highest, a heavy punishment is necessary for killing a brāhmaṇa's cow[11]—a view which also finds support in the early seveteenth century from Mitra Miśra.[12] Although this reminds us of the Vedic period when the brāhmaṇa's cow may have achieved a certain degree of inviolability on account of the animal being the ideal *dakṣinā*, the Dharmaśāstric texts do not look on cow killing as a major sin even when the victim belonged to a brāhmaṇa. On the contrary some texts consider it no more than a minor indecorous act. For example Atri, an early medieval lawgiver, equates beef eating with such acts as cleaning one's teeth with one's fingers and eating only salt or soil[13] and with drinking water from the *aṣṭaśallī*(?) with one's hand.[14] Several other early medieval lawgivers like Śātātapa and Vṛddha-vasiṣṭha quoted by Devaṇṇabhaṭṭa (early thirteenth century)[15] expressed more or less similar views. Thus even within brāhmaṇa circles there is divergence of attitudes towards cow slaughter and, despite the ban on it during the kali age, the offence was not considered serious enough to be classed among the major sins.

The Paradox of Purification

No one would question the fact that practice of eating animal food has continued to our own times and that the memory of the ancient tradition of cow killing persisted till very late in the minds of people, so much so that it is reflected as late as the eighteenth and nineteenth centuries in religious digests and commentaries on

Dharmasāstra texts as well as on some classical Sanskrit literary works. But it is equally true that the cow has played a purificatory role in Brāhmaṇical society from very early times.

As early as the *Ṛgveda*, cow's milk and milk products appear to have been used in rituals and ceremonies[16] and the use of the term *kāmadugha* for cow in the sense of 'milking desires' or 'yielding objects of desire like milk' or 'yielding what one wishes' in the *Atharvaveda*, *Taittirīya Saṃhitā*, and *Śatapatha Brāhmaṇa* may imply a tendency to look upon the animal as a giver of plenty.[17] Although the cow of plenty had not achieved the sanctity assigned to it in modern times, the literature of the post-Vedic period provides clearer indications of the purificatory role of the products of the cow. Apart from textual references to the ritual use of cow's milk and milk products, we now come across the use of other derivatives either for purification or for the expiation of a sin. For instance, cow dung was smeared on the sacrificial altar[18] and ghee was used to purify men.[19] According to Baudhāyana, the land becomes pure when cows walk on it[20] and drinking gruel of barley that has passed through a cow is a meritorious act.[21] Baudhāyana treats cowpens as sacred places[22] and cow dung as effective in removing defilement.[23] A mere touch of cow dung, he tells us, cleanses a man[24] and metal objects can be cleaned by smearing with cow dung or by immersing in cow's urine.[25] The dung and urine of the cow along with milk, curds and clarified butter, which seem to have acquired significance from the Vedic period onwards owing to their use in rituals and sacrifice, figure as *pañcagavya* (five products of the cow) first in the *Dharmasūtra* of Baudhāyana[26] and continue to find mention in subsequent legal texts in various contexts.[27] References to the purifying abilities of the cow and its derivatives, however, multiply in subsequent times. The *Vasiṣṭha Dharmasūtra* makes several references to the purificatory use of the products of the cow (separately as well as in mixture), the *pañcagavya*, sometimes also called *brahmakūrca*.[28] Manu recommends the swallowing of *pañcagavya* as atonement for stealing food, a vehicle, a bed, a seat, flowers, roots, or fruit[29] and refers to a penance called *saṃtāpanakṛcchra* in which subsistence on the five products of the cow and a decoction of *kuśa* grass was prescribed.[30] His near contemporary, Viṣṇu, mentions *pañcagavya* more frequently,[31] though he also adds another derivative of the cow and calls it *gorocanā*,[32] which is taken to mean a yellow pigment prepared from the urine or bile of the cow.[33] Yājñavalkya refers to the products of the cow (*pañcagavya*) as having purificatory powers[34] and Nārada mentions the cow among eight sacred objects.[35] The law books, especially the later ones,[36] lay down different rules for the preparation of the *pañcagavya*, but are unanimous about its role in purification and in the expiation of sin. However, some lawgivers do not permit its use by members of lower castes. Viṣṇu clearly states that if a śūdra drinks *pañcagavya* he goes to hell.[37] The lawgiver Atri[38] repeats this view in the early medieval period, though according to Devala[39] and Parāśara,[40] śūdras and women may take it without Vedic *mantras*. Nandapaṇḍita, a seventeenth-century commentator on the law book of Viṣṇu, however, quotes an anonymous Smṛti passage to justify the exclusion of śūdras and women from its use.[41] The divergence of opinion on the minor details about the use of *pañcagavya* by different castes indicates a linkage between the highly stratified social structure and the idea of purification. But the fact remains that the Dharmaśāstras unanimously recognize the indispensability of the five products of the cow for purification and expiation and accord them a place of importance in the ritual arena.

Mention of the five products of the cow (*pañcagavya*) as well as its sixth derivative, *gorocanā*, is also found in the classical Indian medical treatises of Caraka, Suśruta and

Vāgbhaṭa. Caraka, for example, recommends the use of *pañcagavya*, among other things, in high fever[42] and advises that *pañcagavyaghṛta*[43] and *mahāpañcagavyaghṛta*[44] should be used in fever and several other ailments. He also speaks of the curative powers of the urine (*gomūtra*)[45] and bile (*gorocanā*)[46] of the cow just as Vāgbhaṭa mentions them much later in the seventh century.[47] Despite this textual evidence, it nevertheless remains arguable if the *pañcagavya* gained importance as a ritual purificant on account of its supposed medicinal properties.

Equally doubtful is the suggestion of some scholars that *pañcāmṛta* is a modern substitute for *pañcagavya*.[48] The *pañcāmṛta* (five nectars) is a mixture of milk, curds, clarified butter, sugar and honey and is often used for bathing the idol, the leftovers of the material being used as an offering to the deity.[49] The earliest reference to it is found in the *Baudhāyanagṛhyaśeṣasūtra*,[50] which may belong to the early centuries of the Christian era when sacrifice was gradually being replaced by deity worship (*pūjā*). Scholars have also noted the occurrence of *pañcāmṛta* in later texts.[51] It appears therefore that the idea of *pañcāmṛta* developed independently of that of the *pañcagavya*, and the one cannot be treated as a substitute for the other.

Whatever be the history of the concept of *pañcagavya*, there is no doubt that it has continued to play an important role in both purificatory and expiatory rites, even if some law books do not permit śūdras and women to use it. But the Dharmaśāstras also provide enough evidence, to disprove the purity of the cow. Manu states that food smelt by a cow has to be purified by putting earth on it[52]—a statement repeated by Viṣṇu[53] and indirectly supported by Vasiṣṭha who states that the back of a cow is pure.[54] According to Yājñavalkya also, the food smelt by the cow has to be purified.[55] He adds that the mouths of goats and horses are pure but that of a cow is not; nor is human excrement.[56] Among the later lawgivers Aṅgīrasa categorically asserts that bronze vessels smelt by the cow or touched by a crow and those in which a śudra has eaten, are to be purified by rubbing them with ashes for ten days[57]—a view repeated by Parāśara[58] and Vyāsa.[59] Śaṅkha goes to the extent of saying that all the limbs of the cow are pure except her mouth.[60] The Dharmaśāstra view of the impurity of the mouth of a cow is also reflected in commentaries of the early medieval period and subsequent times. Medhātithi (AD 900), for example, commenting on the crucial passage of Manu, repeats the view that a cow is holy in all limbs except her mouth *(gāvo medhyā mukhād-ṛte)*.[61] Similarly Vijñāneśvara (AD 1100) and Mitra Miśra (seventeenth century) state that all eatables smelt by the cow need to be purified.[62] In fact there is no lawgiver who describes the mouth of the cow as pure, though, like several other domesticated animals, the cow is a herbivore.

It appears therefore that the idea of the impurity of the cow's mouth developed from the post-Vedic period onwards and is found in almost all the law books. It finds an echo in the popular Purāṇic legend about the god Viṣṇu who cursed Kāmadhenu so that her mouth should be impure and her tail held holy forever.[63] Although a Brāhmaṇical concoction, this myth was intended to rationalize the Dharmaśāstric view for which there appears no logical basis. A late nineteenth-century account, in fact, refers to a brāhmaṇa priest waving a wild cow's tail over his clients to scare away demons while they were bathing in the sacred pool at Hardwar,[64] and it is difficult to imagine how one could get the tail of the animal without killing it. It appears from all this that the notion of purity of the products of the cow goes hand in hand with that of the impurity of its mouth. This contradiction, deeply rooted in the Dharmaśāstric portrayal of the cow, is irreconcilable.

NOTES

1. P.V. Kane, *History of Dharmaśāstra*, Bhandarkar Oriental Institute, Poona, 1973, III, p. 613.
2. For a discussion of *mahāpātaka* see ibid., Bhandarkar Oriental Institute, Poona, 1973, IV, section I.
3. S.C. Banerji, *Dharma-Sūtras: A Study in their Origin and Development*, Punthi Pustak, Calcutta, p. 96; P.V. Kane, op. cit., IV, p. 32.
4. *Manu*, XI.108-16.
5. *Yāj.*, III.263-4.
6. *Pārāśara*, VIII.44.
7. Ibid., VIII.49-50.
8. These are milk, curds, ghee, urine and dung.
9. Kane, op. cit., IV, p. 108.
10. Ibid., pp. 107-10.
11. *kathaṃ punarbrāhmaṇagavīnāṃ gurutvaṃ? 'devabrāhmaṇarājñāṃ tu vijñeyaṃ dravyamuttamaṃ' iti nāradena taddravyasyottamatvābhidhānāt, goṣu brāhmaṇasaṅsthāsviti daṇḍabhūyastvadarśanācca/ Mitākṣarā* on *Yāj.* III.263, see *Yājñavalkyasmṛti*, ed. Gagasagar Rai, Chowkhambha Sanskrit Pratisthan, Delhi, 1998, p. 518.
12. *Yājñavalkyasmṛti*, English tr. With notes, J.R. Gharpure, Bombay, 1936, p. 1825.
13. *aṅgulyā dantakāṣṭhaṃ ca pratyakṣaṃ lavaṇaṃ tathā/*
    mṛttikābhakṣaṇaṃ caiva tulyaṃ gomāṃsabhakṣaṇam//Atri, 314.
    Also see *Attri*, 315.
14. *aṣṭaśalyāgato nīraṃ pāṇinā pibate dvijaḥ/*
    surāpānena tattulyaṃ tulyaṃ gomāṃsabhakṣaṇam//Atri, 388.
15. *hastadattāni cānnāni pratyakṣalavaṇaṃ tathā/*
    mṛttikābhakṣaṇaṃ caiva gomāṃsāśanavatsmṛtam//Sātātapa
    ghṛtaṃ vā yadi vā tailaṃ vipro nādyānnakhcyutam/
    yamastamasucim prāha tulyaṃ gomāṃsabhakṣaṇe//Vṛddhavasiṣṭha.
    Devaṇṇabhaṭṭa in his *Smṛticandrikā* (*Āhnikakāṇḍa*, ed. L. Srinivasacharya, Mysore, Government Oriental Library Series, 1914, p. 604) quotes both the passages. Also see *Śrāddhakāṇḍa*, p. 224.
16. Frederick J. Simoons, 'The Purificatory Role of the Five Products of the Cow in Hinduism', *Ecology of Food and Nutrition*, 3 (1974), p. 29.
17. For early occurrences of *kāmadugha* and *kāmaduḥ* see Otto Böthlink and Rudolph Roth, *Sanskrit-Wörterbuch*, rpt. Meicho-Fukyu-Kai, Tokyo, 1976 and M. Monier-Williams, *Sanskrit-English*

Dictionary, new edn., Indian rpt., Motilal Banarsidass, 1963. In later texts, however, the two terms are often used for the desire-fulfilling cow or celestial cow.

18. *ŚB*, XII.4.4.1.
19. *ŚB*, III.1.2.11.
20. *BaudhDS*, I.6.19.
21. Ibid., III.13.
22. Ibid., II.5.8.; III.10.12. Also *VasiṣthaDS*, XXII.12.
23. Ibid., I.5.8.52.
24. Ibid., I.5.10.17.
25. Ibid., I.6.14.5,7.
26. Ibid., I.5.11.38; IV.5.11-25.
27. The word *pañcagavya* is usually interpreted to mean the five products of the cow, listed above (n. 8). See the Sanskrit dictionaries of Böthlink-Roth, M. Monier-Williams, V.S. Apte and K. Mylius, s.v. *pañcagavya*; also *Śabdakalpadruma*, s.v. *pañcagavya*. *Atri*, 115 and 296, *Mitākṣarā* on *Yāj*. III.263. Some law books add *kuśodaka* (*kuśa* water) to this list of five products. According to one interpretation the term means a decoction of *kuśa* grass and according to another, it stands for 'water mixed with *kuśa* grass'. Shingo Einoo agrees with the second interpretation. He also suggests that despite the inclusion of *kuśa* water in the *pañcagavya* as its sixth ingredient, the term came to denote only the five products of the cow in course of time (Shingo Einoo, 'Notes on the Initiation Rites in the Gṛhyapariśiṣṭas', unpublished manuscript, n. 19).
28. *VasiṣthaDS*, III.56; XIII.12; XXVII.13-14. For a discussion of *brahmakūrca* see Kane, op. cit., IV, pp. 146-7.
29. *Manu*, XI.166.
30. Ibid., XI.213.
31. *Viṣṇu*, XXII.18, 79, 88; XXIII.45; XLVI.19; LI.47; LIV.6-7, etc.
32. Ibid., XXIII.58-9.
33. V.S. Apte, *The Practical Sanskrit-English Dictionary*, s.v. *gorocanā*.
34. *Yāj*. III.263.
35. *Nārada*, XVIII.54.
36. E.g., *Pārāśara*, XI.28-34; *Devala*, 62-5, *Laghuśātātapa*, 158-62, etc., cited in Kane, op. cit., II, pt. 2, pp. 773-4.
37. *Viṣṇu*, LIV.7.
38. *pañcagavyaṃ pibet śūdro brāhmaṇastu surāṃ pibet/*
    ubhau tau tulyadoṣau ca vasato narake ciraṃ/ *Atri*, 297.
39. *strīṇāṃ caiva tu surāṇāṃ patitānāṃ tathaiva ca/*

pañcagavyaṃ na dātavyaṃ dātavyaṃ mantravarjitam//Devala, 61.
40. *Pārāśara,* XI.7, 28.
41. SBE II, p. 175 n. 7.
42. *pañcagavyasya payasaḥ prayogo viṣamajvare, Caraka, cikitsā,* III. 303; *pañcagavyaṃ mahātiktaṃ kalyāṇakamathāpi vā/ snehanārthaṃ ghṛtaṃ dadyāt kāmalāpāṇḍurogiṇe//*Ibid., XVI. 43.
43. Ibid., X.17.
44. Ibid., X.18-24
45. Ibid., V.96, 178; VII.87. The text refers to the therapeutic use of the urine of several other animals like buffalo, goat and sheep (*Caraka, vimāna,* VIII. 136).
46. *Caraka, cikitsā,* VII. 87.
47. *Aṣṭāṅga Hṛdayam* of Vāgbhaṭa, text, Eng. tr. notes, appendix and indices by K.R. Srikantha Murthy, vol. I, 3rd edn., Krishnadas Academy, Varanasi, 1996, Appendix, p. 476.
48. S. Stevenson, *The Rites of the Twice-Born,* Oxford University Press, London, 1920, p. 166; L.S.S. O'Malley, *Indian Caste Customs,* Cambridge University Press, Cambridge, 1932, p. 75; J.H. Hutton, *Caste in India,* 4th edn., Oxford University Press, London, 1963, p. 108. For a more recent statement on the point see Frederick J. Simoons, 'The Purificatory Role of the Five Products of the Cow in Hinduism', op. cit., p. 30.
49. P.V. Kane, op. cit., II, pt. 2, p. 731; Gudrun Bühnemann, *Pūjā: A Study in Smārta Ritual,* Gerald & Co., Vienna, 1988, p. 139f.
50. *Bodhāyanagṛhyaśeṣasūtra,* II.20.11. in *Bodhāyanagṛhyasūtram* of Bodhāyana Maharṣi, ed. L. Srinivasachar and R. Shama Sastri, 3rd edn., Oriental Research Institute, Mysore, 1983 (1st edn., Mysore, 1904).
51. *Saurapurāṇa* by Srimat Vyāsa, ed. Pandita Kasinatha Sastri, Anandasrama Sanskrit Series, Poona, 1889, p. 156.
52. *pakṣijagdhaṃ gavāghrātamavadhūtamavakṣutaṃ/ dūṣitaṃ keśakīṭaiśca mṛtprakṣepeṇa śuddhyati//Manu,* V.125.
53. *ViṣṇuDS,* XXIII.38.
54. *VasiṣṭhaDS,* XXVII.9.
55. *goghrāte'nne tathā keśamakṣikākīṭadūṣite, Yāj,* I.189.
56. *ajāśvayormukhaṃ medhyaṃ na gorṇa narajā malāḥ. Yāj,* I.194.
57. *gavāghrātāni kāṅsyāni śūdrocchiṣṭāni yāni tu/ bhasmanā daśabhiḥ śuddhyetkākenopahate tathā//Āṅgirasa,* 43.
58. *Pārāśara,* VII.25.
59. *Vyāsa,* III.53.
60. *Śaṅkha,* XVI.14. Cf. ibid., XVII.45.

61. P.V. Kane, op. cit., II, pt. 2, p. 775.
62. See *Mitākṣarā* and *Vīramitrodaya* on *Yāj.* I.189.
63. William Crooke (*The Popular Religion and Folklore of Northern India*, II, 2nd edn., 4th Indian rpt., Munshiram Manoharlal, Delhi, 1974, p. 233). But the *Skanda Purāṇa* provides a different version of the story: Once Śiva's fiery liṅga grew speedily. Curious, Brahmā tried to ascend to the top of it, but without success. While coming down he saw Surabhi (the divine cow) standing in the shade of the ketakī tree on Mt. Meru. On her advice Brahmā told a lie to the gods that he saw the top of the liṅga and produced Surabhi and Ketakī as witnesses. Thereupon a voice from the sky cursed Brahmā, Ketakī and Surabhi that they would not be worshipped. A variation of the legend occurs in the *Brahma Purāṇa* (S.A. Dange, *Encyclopaedia of Purāṇic Beliefs and Practices*, I, Navrang, Delhi, 1986, p. 201). The name Kāmadhenu, also known as Surabhi and Nandinī, does not occur in the Vedic texts but is mentioned in various contexts in later works especially the epics and the Purāṇas (Vettam Mani, *Puranic Encyclopedia*, Motilal Banarsidass, Delhi, 1984, s.v. Kāmadhenu.
64. William Crooke, *The Popular Religion and Folklore of Northern India*, II, pp. 232-3.

6

Resume: The Elusive 'Holy Cow'

Several points emerge from our limited survey of the textual evidence, mostly drawn from Brāhmaṇical sources from the *Ṛgveda* onwards. In the first place, it is clear that the early Aryans, who migrated to India from outside, brought along with them certain cultural elements. After their migration into the Indian subcontinent pastoralism, nomadism and animal sacrifice remained characteristic features of their life for several centuries until sedentary field agriculture became the mainstay of their livelihood. Animal sacrifices were very common, the most important of them being the famous *aśvamedha* and *rājasūya.* These and several other major sacrifices involved the killing of animals including cattle, which constituted the chief form of the wealth of the early Aryans. Not surprisingly, they prayed for cattle and sacrificed them to propitiate their gods. The Vedic gods had no marked dietary preferences. Milk, butter, barley, oxen, goats and sheep were their usual food, though some of them seem to have had their special preferences. Indra had a special liking for bulls. Agni was not a tippler like Indra, but was fond of the flesh of horses, bulls and cows. The toothless Pūṣan, the guardian of the roads, ate mush as a Hobson's choice. Soma was the name of an intoxicant but, equally important, of a god, and killing animals (including cattle) for him was basic to most of the Ṛgvedic *yajñas*. The Maruts and the Aśvins were also offered cows. The Vedas mention about 250 animals out of which at least 50 were deemed fit for sacrifice, by implication for divine as well as human consumption. The *Taittirīya Brāhmaṇa* categorically tells us: 'Verily the cow is food' (*atho annaṃ vai gauḥ*) and Yājñavalkya's insistence on eating the tender (*aṃsala*) flesh of the cow is well known. Although there is reason to believe that a brāhmaṇa's cow may not have been killed, that is no index of its inherent sanctity in the Vedic period or even later.

The subsequent Brāhmaṇical texts (e.g. Gṛhyasūtras and Dharmasūtras) provide ample evidence of the eating of flesh including beef. Domestic rites and rituals associated with agricultural and other activities involved the killing of cattle. The ceremonial welcome of guests (sometimes known as *arghya* but generally as *madhuparka*) consisted not only of a meal of a mixture of curds and honey but also of the flesh of a cow or bull. Early lawgivers go to the extent of making meat mandatory in the *madhuparka*—an injunction more or less dittoed by several later legal texts. The sacred thread ceremony for its part was not all that sacred; for it was necessary for a *snātaka* to wear an upper garment of cowhide.

The slaughter of animals formed an important component of the cult of the dead in the Vedic texts. The thick fat of the cow was used to cover the corpse and a bull was burnt along with it to enable the departed to ride in the nether world. Funerary rites include the feeding of brāhmaṇas after the prescribed period and quite often the flesh of the cow or ox was offered to the dead. The textual prescriptions indicate the degree of satisfaction obtained by the ancestors' souls according to the animal offered—cow meat could keep them content for at least a year! The Vedic and the post-Vedic texts often mention the killing of animals including the kine in the ritual context. There was, therefore, a relationship between the sacrifice and sustenance. But this need not necessarily mean that different types of meat were eaten only if offered in sacrifice. Archaeological evidence, in fact, suggests non-ritual killing of cattle. This is indicative of the fact that beef and other animal flesh formed part of the dietary culture of people and that edible flesh was not always ritually consecrated.

The idea of *ahiṃsā* seems to have made its first appearance in the Upaniṣadic thought and literature. There is no doubt that Gautama Buddha and Mahāvīra vehemently challenged the efficacy of the Vedic animal sacrifice, although a general aversion to beef and other kinds of animal flesh is not borne out by Buddhist and Jaina texts. Despite the fact that the Buddha espoused the cause of *ahiṃsā*, he is said to have died after eating a meal of pork (*sūkaramaddava*). Aśoka's compassion for animals is undeniable, though cattle were killed for food during the Mauryan period as is evident from the *Arthaśāstra* of Kauṭilya and Aśoka's own list of animals exempt from slaughter, which, significantly, does not include the cow. The Buddhists in India and outside continued to eat various types of meat including beef even in later times, often inviting unsavoury criticism from the Jainas. In Lahul, for example, Buddhists eat beef, albeit secretly, and in Tibet they eat cows, sheep, pigs and yak.

Like Buddhism, Jainism also questioned the efficacy of animal sacrifice and enthusiastically took up the cause of non-violence. But meat eating was so common in Vedic and post-Vedic times that even Mahāvīra, the founder of Jainism, is said to have eaten poultry. Perhaps the early Jainas were not strict vegetarians. A great Jaina logician of the eighth century tells us that monks did not have objection to eating flesh or fish given to them by the laity. In spite of all this, there is no doubt that meat became a strong taboo among the followers of Jainism. Its canonical and non-canonical literature provides overwhelming evidence on the subject. The inflexibility of the Jaina attitude is deeply rooted in the basic tenets of Jaina philosophy, which, at least in theory, is impartial in its respect for all forms of life without according any special status to the cow. Thus, although both Buddhism, and, to a greater extent, Jainism contributed to the growth of *ahiṃsā* doctrine, neither seems to have developed the sacred cow concept independently.

Despite the Upaniṣadic, Buddhist and Jaina advocacy of *ahiṃsā*, the practice of ritual and random killing of animals including cattle continued in the post-Mauryan centuries. Although Manu (200 BC-AD 200) extols the virtue of *ahiṃsā*, he provides a list of creatures whose flesh was edible. He exempts the camel from being killed for food, but does not grant this privilege to the cow. On the contrary, he opines that animal slaughter in accordance with Vedic practice does not amount to killing, thus giving sanction to the ritual slaughter of cattle. He further recommends meat eating on occasions like *madhuparka* and *śrāddha*. One may not be far from the truth if one interprets Manu's injunctions as a justification for ritual cattle slaughter and beef eating, as indeed a later commentator does.

Next in point of time is the law book of Yājñavalkya (AD 100–300) who not only enumerates the kosher animals and fish but also states that a learned brāhmaṇa (*śrotriya*) should be welcomed with a big ox or goat, delicious food and sweet words. That the practice of flesh eating and killing cattle for food was customary right through the Gupta period and later is sufficiently borne out by references to it found in the Purāṇas and the Epics. Several Purāṇic texts, we are told, bear testimony to the feeding of brāhmaṇas with beef at the funeral ceremony, though some of them prohibit the killing of a cow in honour of the guest and others recommend buffalo sacrifice for the goddess at Durgā Pūjā, Navarātri, or Dasara.

The evidence from the epics is quite eloquent. Most of the characters in the *Mahābhārata* are meat eaters. Draupadī promises to Jayadratha and his retinue that Yudhiṣṭhira would provide them with a variety of game including gayal, śambara and buffalo. The Pāṇḍavas seem to have survived on meat during their exile. The *Mahābhārata* also makes a laudatory reference to the king Rantideva in whose kitchen two thousand cows were butchered each day, their flesh, along with grain, being distributed among the brāhmaṇas. Similarly the *Rāmāyaṇa* of Vālmīki makes frequent reference to the killing of animals including the cow for sacrifice and for food. Rāma was born after his father Daśaratha performed a big sacrifice involving the slaughter of a large number of animals declared edible by the Dharmaśāstras. Sītā, assures the Yamunā, while crossing it that she would worship the river with a thousand cows and a hundred jars of wine when Rāma accomplishes his vow. Her fondness for deer meat drives her husband crazy enough to kill Mārīca, a deer in disguise. Bharadvāja welcomes Rāma by slaughtering a fatted calf in his honour.

Non-vegetarian dietary practices find an important place in the early Indian medical treatises, whose chronology broadly coincides with that of the law books of Manu and Yājñavalkya, the early Purāṇas and the two epics. Caraka, Suśruta and Vagbhaṭa provide an impressive list of fish and animals and all three speak of the therapeutic uses of beef. The continuity of the tradition of eating beef is also echoed in early Indian secular literature till late times. In the Gupta period, Kālidāsa alludes to the story of Rantideva who killed numerous cows every day in his kitchen. More than two centuries later, Bhavabhūti refers to two instances of guest reception, which included the killing of a heifer. In the tenth century Rājaśekhara mentions the practice of killing an ox or a goat in honour of a guest. Later Śrīharṣa mentions a variety of non-vegetarian delicacies served at a dazzling marriage feast and refers to two interesting instances of cow killing. At that time, however, Someśvara shows clear preference for pork over other meats and does not mention beef at all.

While the above references, albeit limited in number, indicate that the ancient practice of killing the kine for food continued till about the twelfth century, there is considerable evidence in the commentaries on the *Kavya* literature and the earlier Dharmaśāstra texts to show that the Brāhmaṇical writers retained its memory till very late times. Among the commentators on the secular literature, Cāṇḍupaṇḍita from Gujarat, Narahari from Telengana in Andhra Pradesh, and Mallinātha who is associated with the king Devarāya II of Vidyānagara (Vijayanagara), clearly indicate that, in earlier times, the cow was done to death for rituals and hence for food. As late as the eighteenth century Ghanaśyāma, a minister of a Tanjore ruler, states that the killing of cow in honour of a guest was the ancient rule.

Similarly the authors of Dharmaśāstra commentaries and religious digests from the ninth century onwards keep alive the memory of the archaic practice of beef eating and some of them even go so far as to permit beef in specific circumstances. For example, Medhātithi, probably a Kashmiri brāhmaṇa, says that a bull or ox was killed in honour of a ruler or anyone deserving to be honoured, and unambiguously allows eating the flesh of cow (*govyajamāṃsam*) on ritual occasions. Several other writers of exegetical works seem to lend support to this view, though sometimes indirectly. Viśvarūpa of Malwa, probably a pupil of Śaṅkara, Vijñāneśvara who may have lived not far from Kalyāṇa in modern Karnataka, Haradatta, also a southerner (*dākṣinātya*), Lakṣmīdhara, a minister of the Gāhaḍwāla king Hemādri, Narasiṃha a minister of the Yādavas of Devagiri, and Mitra Miśra from Gopācala (Gwalior) support the practice of killing a cow on special occasions. Thus even when the Dharmaśāstra commentators view cow killing with disfavour, they generally admit that it was an ancient practice but to be avoided in the kali age.

While the above evidence is indicative of the continuity of the practice of beef eating, the lawgivers had already begun to discourage it around the middle of the first millennium when society began to be gradually feudalized, leading to major socio-cultural transformation. This phase of transition, first described in the epic and Purāṇic passages as the *kaliyuga*, saw many changes and modifications of social norms and customs. The Brāhmaṇical religious texts now begin to speak of many earlier practices as forbidden in the *kaliyuga*, i.e. *kalivarjyas*. While the list of *kalivarjyas*, swelled up over time, most of the relevant texts mention cow slaughter as forbidden in the *kaliyuga*. According to some early medieval lawgivers a cow killer was an untouchable and one incurred sin even by talking to him. They increasingly associated cow killing and beef eating with the proliferating number of untouchable castes. It is, however, interesting that some of them consider these acts as no more than minor behavioural aberrations.

Equally interesting is the fact that almost all the prescriptive texts enumerate cow killing as a minor sin (*upapātaka*), not a major offence (*mahāpātaka*). Moreover, the Smṛti texts provide easy escape routes by laying down expiatory procedures for intentional as well as inadvertent killing of the cow. This may imply that cattle slaughter may not have been uncommon in society, and the atonements were prescribed merely to discourage eating of beef. To what extent the Dharmaśāstric injunctions were effective, however, remains a matter of speculation; for the possibility of at least some people eating beef on the sly cannot be ruled out. As recently as the late nineteenth century it was alleged that Swami Vivekananda ate beef during his stay in America, though he vehemently defended his action.[1] Also, Mahatma Gandhi spoke of the hypocrisy of the orthodox Hindus who 'do not so much as hesitate or inquire when during illness the doctor . . . prescribes them beef tea'.[2] Even today 72 communities in Kerala—not all of them untouchable perhaps—prefer beef to the expensive mutton and the Hindutva forces are persuading them to go easy on it.[3]

Although cow slaughter and the eating of beef gradually came to be viewed as a sin and a source of pollution from the early medieval period, the cow and its products (milk, curds, clarified butter, dung and urine) or their mixture called *pañcagavya* had assumed a purificatory role much earlier. Vedic texts attest to the ritual use of cow's milk and milk products, but the term *pañcagavya* occurs for the first time in the *Baudhāyana Dharmasūtra.* Manu, Viṣṇu, Vasiṣṭha, Yājñavalkya and several later lawgivers like Atri, Devala and Parāśara mention the use of the mixture of the five products of the cow for both purification and expiation. The commentaries and religious digests, most of which belong to the medieval period, abound in references to the purificatory role of the *pañcagavya.* It is interesting that the medical treatises of Caraka, Suśruta and Vāgbhaṭa speak of its medicinal uses. The underlying assumption in all these cases is that the *pañcagavya* is pure. But several Dharmaśāstra texts forbid its use by women and the lower castes. If a sūdra drinks *pañcagavya*, we are told, he goes to hell.

It is curious that prescriptive texts that repeatedly refer to the purificatory role of the cow, also provide much evidence of the notion of pollution and impurity associated with this animal. According to Manu, the food smelt by a cow has to be purified. Other early lawgivers like Viṣṇu and Yājñavalkya also express similar views. The latter in fact says that while the mouth of the goat and horse is pure that of the cow is not. Among the later juridical texts, those of Aṅgīrasa, Parāśara, Vyāsa and so on, support the idea of the cow's mouth being impure. The lawgiver Śaṅkha categorically states that all limbs of the cow are pure except her mouth. The commentaries on different Dharmaśāstra texts reinforce the notion of impurity of the cow's mouth. All this runs counter to the idea of the purificatory role of the cow.

Needless to say, then, that the image of the cow projected by Indian textual traditions, especially the Brāhmaṇical-Dharmaśāstric works, over the centuries is polymorphic. Its story through the millennia is full of inconsistencies and has not always been in conformity with dietary practices current in society. It was killed but the killing was not killing. When it was not slain, mere remembering the old practice of butchery satisfied the brāhmaṇas. Its five products including faeces and urine have been considered pure but not its mouth. Yet through these incongruous attitudes the Indian cow has struggled its way to sanctity.

But the holiness of the cow is elusive. For there has never been a cow-goddess, nor any temple in her honour.[4] Nevertheless the veneration of this animal has come to be viewed as a characteristic trait of modern day non-existent monolithic 'Hinduism' bandied about by the Hindutva forces.

NOTES

1. Romain Rolland, *The Life of Vivekananda and the Universal Gospel*, Advaita Ashrama, Calcutta, 11th Impression, August 1988, p. 44, n. 3.
2. M.K. Gandhi, *An Autobiography or The Story of My Experiments with Truth,* Navajivan Trust, Ahmedabad, 1927, rpt. 2000, p. 324. Gandhi saw a five-footed 'miraculous' cow at the Kumbhmela at Allahabad in 1915, the fifth foot being nothing but 'a foot cut off from a live calf and grafted upon the shoulder of the cow' which attracted the lavish charity of the ignorant Hindu (p. 325).
3. *India Today,* 15 April 1993, p. 72.
4. A.L. Basham, *The Wonder That Was India,* 27th Impression, Rupa & Co., 1996, p. 319.

Bibliography

Ācārāṅga Cūrṇi of Jinadāsagaṇi, Ṛsabhadeva Kesharimalji Śvetāmbara Sansthā, Ratlam, 1941.

Ācārāṅga Sūtra, ed. W.S. Schubring, Leipzig, 1910; Eng. tr. H. Jacobi, SBE XXII, Oxford, 1884.

Achaya, K.T., *Indian Food: A Historical Companion*, Oxford University Press, New Delhi, 1998.

———, *A Historical Dictionary of Indian Food*, Oxford University Press, New Delhi, 1999.

Adhyātma Rāmāyaṇa, Eng. tr. Lala Baij Nath, Pāṇini Office, Allahabad, 1913.

Agnipurāṇam, Nag Publishers, Delhi, 1985.

Agniveśya Gṛhyasūtra, ed. L.A. Ravi Varma, Trivandrum Sanskrit Series, Trivandrum University Press, Trivandrum, 1940.

Agrawala, V.S., *India as Known to Pāṇini*, revd. and enl. edn., Prithvi Prakashan, Varanasi, 1963.

———, *Harṣacarita: Ek Sāmskritik Adhyayana*, Bihar Rashtrabhasha Parishad, Patna, 1964.

Aitareya Āraṇyaka, ed. A.B. Keith, Anecdota Oxoniensia, Aryan Series, vol. I, Oxford, 1909.

Aitreya Brāhmaṇa, ed. Theodor Aufrecht, *Das Aitreya Brāhmaṇa*, Bonn, 1879; Eng. tr. A.B. Keith, *Rigveda Brāhmaṇas: The Aitareya and Kauṣītaki Brāhmaṇas of the Rigveda*, Harvard University Press; 1st Indian rpt. edn., Motilal Banarsidass, Delhi, 1971.

Alsdorf, Ludwig, *Beiträge zur Geschichte von Vegetarianismus und Rinderverehrung in Indien*, Akademie der Wissenschaften und der Literatur, Wiesbaden, 1962.

Aṅgutta Nikāya, ed. Bhikkhu J. Kashyap, Nalanda, 4 vols., Devanagari Pali Series, Pali Publication Board, Bihar Government, 1960.

Āṅgīrasasmṛti, in *Aṣṭādaśasmṛtyaḥ* (Hindi tr. Sundarlal Tripathi, Khemraj Shrikrishnadas), Venkateshwar Steam Press, Bombay, Ṡaka 1846.

Āpastamba Dharmasūtra, ed. G. Buhler, Bombay, 1932; Eng. tr. G. Bühler, SBE II, Oxford, 1879.

Āpastamba Gṛhyasūtra, ed. Umesh Chandra Pandey, 2nd edn., Varanasi, 1971. Eng. tr. H. Oldenberg, SBE XXIX, Oxford, 1886.

Āpastamba Śrautasūtra, ed. Richard Garbe, 3 vols., Bibliotheca Indica, Calcutta, 1882, 1885, 1902.

Apte, V.M., *Social and Religious Life in the Gṛhyasūtras*, Popular Book Depot, Bombay, 1939.

Apte, V.S., *The Practical Sanskrit-English Dictionary*, revd. and enl. edn., Kyoto, 1998.

Arthaśāstra of Kauṭilya, ed. and tr. R.P. Kangle, *The Kauṭilīya Arthaśāstra*, 3 parts, 2nd edn., rpt., Motilal Banarsidass, Delhi, 1997. *Kauṭilya's Arthaśāstra*, tr. R. Shamasastry, 7th edn., Mysore, 1961.

Aṣṭāṅga Hṛdayam, ed. and tr. K.R. Srikantha Murthy, Krishnadas Academy, Varanasi, 1996.

Āśvalāyana Gṛhyasūtra, Ānandāśramasamskṛtagranthāvaliḥ 105, new edn., Poona, 1978; Eng. tr. H. Oldenberg, SBE XXIX, Oxford, 1886.

Āśvalāyana Śrautasūtra, Ānandāśramasamskṛtagranthāvaliḥ 81, Poona, 1917.

Atharvaveda, ed. R. Roth, W.D. Whitney and Max Lindenau, *Atharva Veda Saṅhita*, Berlin, 1924, tr. M. Bloomfield, *Hymns of the Atharvaveda*, SBE XLII, Oxford, 1897.

Atrismṛti in *Aṣṭādasasmṛtyaḥ* Hindi tr. Sundarlal Tripathi, Khemraj Shrikrishnadas, Venkateshwar Steam Press, Bombay, Ṡaka 1846.

Āvaśyakacūrṇi of Jinadāsagaṇi, 2 vols., Ratlam, 1928.

Azzi, Corry, 'More on India's Sacred Cattle', *Current Anthropology*, 15 (1974), pp. 317-24.

Babb, Lawrence A., *Ascetics and Kings in a Jain Ritual Culture*, Motilal Banarsidass, Delhi, 1998.

Bālarāmāyaṇa of Rājaśekhara, ed. Ganagasagar Rai, Chowkhamba, Varanasi, 1984.

Bandhu, Vishva, *A Vedic Word-Concordance*, Vishveshvaranand Vedic Research Institute, Hoshiarpur, I, pt. 1 (1976) and II, pt. 1 (1973).

Banerjea, J.C., 'Social Life in the Pouranic Age', *Hindustan Times*, vol. 38, no. 227, July 1918.

Banerji, S.C., *Dharma-Sūtras: A Study in Their Origin and Development*, Punthi Pustak, Calcutta, 1962.

———, *A Glossary of Smṛti Literature*, Punthi Pustak, Calcutta, 1963.

Basham, A.L., *History and Doctrines of the Ājīvikas*, Luzac & Company, London, 1951.

———, *The Wonder that was India*, 27th impression, Rupa & Co., Delhi, 1996.

———, 'The Practice of Medicine in Ancient and Medieval India', in Charles Leslie, ed., *Asian Medical Systems: A Comparative Study*, Motilal Banarsidass, Delhi, 1998, pp. 18-43.

Basu, Jogiraj, *India of the Age of the Brāhmaṇas*, Sanskrit Pustak Bhandar, Calcutta, 1969.

Beal, Samuel, *Si-Yu Ki: Buddhist Records of the Western World*, London, 1884, Indian rpt., Motilal Banarsidass, Delhi, 1981.

Baudhāyana Dharmasūtra, ed. E. Hultzsch, Leipzig, 1884; Eng. tr. G. Bühler, SBE XIV, Oxford, 1882.

Baudhāyana Gṛhyasūtra, ed. R. Shama Sastri, 2nd edn., Oriental Library Publications, Mysore, 1920.

Baudhāyana Śrautasūtra belonging to the Taittirīya Saṃhitā, ed. W. Caland, 3 vols., Bibliotheca Indica, Calcutta, 1904-24.

Bell, Charles, *Tibet Past and Present*, Oxford, 1924, rpt., Delhi, 1990.

Bennett, John W., 'Comment on: An Approach to the Sacred Cow of India by Alan Heston', *Current Anthropology*, 12 (1971).

Berkson, Carmel, *The Divine and Demoniac: Mahiṣa's Heroic Struggle with Durgā*, Oxford University Press, Delhi-New York, 1995.

Bhāradvāja Gṛhyasūtra (The Domestic Ritual according to the School of Bhāradvāja), ed. J.W. Henriette Salomons, Leiden, 1913.

Bhāradvāja Śrautasūtra, ed. and tr. C.G. Kashikar, 2 pts., Vaidik Samshodhana Mandala, Poona, 1964.

Bhāṣā-Paricched with Siddhānta-Muktāvali by Viśvanātha Nyāya-Pañcānana, tr. Swami Madhvananda with an Introduction by Satkari Mookerjee, Advaita Ashrama, Calcutta, 1977.

Bhattacharyya, N.N., *History of Tantric Religion*, Manohar, Delhi, 1982.

Bhaviṣyapurāṇa, Nag Publishers, Delhi, 1984.

Biddulph, J., *Tribes of the Hindoo Koosh*, Calcutta, 1880.

Bloomfield, M., *Religion of the Veda*, New York, 1908.

Bodhāyanagṛhyaśeṣasūtra in *Bodhāyanagṛhyasūtram* of Bodhāyana Maharṣi, ed. L. Srinivasachar and R. Shama Sastri, 3rd edn., Oriental Research Institute, Mysore, 1983 (1st edn., Mysore, 1904), pp. 187-400.

Bolling, George von Melville, and Julius von Negelein, eds., *The Pariśiṣṭas of the Atharvaveda* with Hindi notes by Ram Kumar Rai, Chowkhamba Orientalia, Varanasi, 1976.

Bose, D.M., S.N. Sen and B.V. Subbarayappa, eds., *A Concise History of Science in India*, Indian National Science Academy, Delhi, 1971.

Böthtlingk, Otto, und Roth Rudolph, *Sanskrit-Wörterbuch*, St. Petersburg, 1855-75, rpt., Tokyo, 1976.

Brāhmaṇasarvasva of Halāyudha, ed. Tejascandra Vidyananda, 2nd edn., Calcutta, BS 1299.

Brahmapurāṇa, ed. Pañcānana Tarkaratna, Vangavasi Press, Calcutta, BS 1316.

Brahmavaivartapurāṇa, ed. with introduction in Sanskrit and English, pt. 1, J.L. Shastri, Motilal Banarsidass, Delhi, 1984.

Bṛhadāraṇyaka Upaniṣad, in S. Radhakrishnan, *The Principal Upaniṣads*, Centenary Edn., Oxford University Press, Delhi, 1989, 4th Impression, 1991.

Bṛhadharmapurāṇa, ed. Haraprasad Shastri, Krishnadas Academy, 2nd edn., Varanasi, 1974.

Bṛhaspatismṛti, Gaekwad Oriental Series, Baroda, 1941. Eng. tr. J. Jolly, Minor Law-Books, SBE XXXIII, Oxford, 1889.

Bṛhatkalpa Bhāṣya of Saṅghadāsagaṇi with commentary by Malayagiri and Kṣemakīrti, Atmananda Jaina Sabha, Bhavnagar, 1933-8.

Bṛhatsaṃhitā of Varāhamihira (with Bhaṭṭotpala's commentary), ed. Sudhakara Dvivedi, The Vizianagaraṁ Sanskrit Series, X, 2 pts., Banaras, 1895-7; Eng. tr. V. Subrahmanya Sastri and M. Ramakrishna Bhat, 2 vols., Bangalore, 1947.

Brockington, John, *The Righteous Rāma*, Oxford University Press, Delhi, 1984.

———, *The Sanskrit Epics*, E.J. Brill, Leiden, 1998.

Brown, W. Norman, 'The Sanctity of the Cow in Hinduism', *Madras University Journal*, XXVIII, no. 2, 1957, pp. 29-49.

———, *Man in the Universe*, University of California Press, Berkeley, 1966.

Bühnemann, Gudrun, *Pūjā: A Study in Smārta Ritual*, Publications of the De Nobili Research Library, Gerold & Co., Vienna, 1988.

Caland, W., 'Eine dritte Mitteilung uber das Vādhūlasūtra', *Acta Orientalia*, vol. 6 (1928), pp. 97-241.

Caraka Saṃhitā, ed. Brahmanand Tripathi, Chowkhamba Surabharati Prakashan, Varanasi, 4th edn., 1996; *Caraka-Saṃhitā*, text and tr., Priyavrat Sharma, Chowkhamba Orientalia, Delhi/ Varanasi, 1981.

Caturvargacintāmaṇi of Hemādri, vol. III (Pariśeṣakhaṇḍa), pt. 2 (Śrāddhakalpa-2), ed. Pandit Yajñeśvara Smṛtiratna and Pandit Kāmākhyānātha Tarkavāgīśa, Chowkhamba Sanskrit Sansthan, Varanasi, 1985; vol. IV, Prāyaścittakhaṇḍam, ed. Pandit Pramatha Nātha Tarkabhūṣaṇa, Asiatic Society, Calcutta, 1911.

Chakravarty, Taponath, *Food and Drink in Ancient Bengal*, Firma K.L. Mukhopadhyaya, Calcutta, 1959.

Chāndogya Upaniṣad, in S. Radhakrishnan, *The Principal Upaniṣads*, Centenary edn., Oxford University Press, Delhi, 1989.

Chapple, Christopher Key, *Nonviolence to Animals, Earth, and Self in Asian Traditions*, State University of New York Press, Albany, 1993.

———, 'Ahiṃsā in the Mahābhārata: a story, a philosophical perspective, and an admonishment', *Journal of Vaiṣṇava Studies*, 4.3 (1996), pp. 109-25.

Chattopadhyaya, Brajadulal, *Representing the Other?: Sanskrit Sources and Muslims*, Manohar, Delhi, 1998.

Choudhary, Gulabchandra, *Jain Sāhitya kā Bṛhad Itihās*, 6 pts., Parshvanath Vidyashram Shodh Sansthan, Varanasi, 1966-73.

Crooke, W., *The Popular Religion and Folklore of Northern India*, 2 vols., 2nd edn., 1896, Indian rpt., Munshiram Manoharlal, Delhi, 1974.

———, 'The Veneration of the Cow in India', *Folklore*, XXIII, 1912, pp. 275-306.

———, *A Glossary of North Indian Peasant Life*, ed. with an introduction by Shahid Amin, Oxford University Press, Delhi, 1989.

Chattopadhyay, Aparna, 'A Note on Beef-Eating in Mauryan Times', *Indo-Asian Culture*, vol. XVII, no. 2 (April 1968), pp. 49-51.

Dākavacanāmṛta, pts. 1-2, Kanhaiyalal Krishnadas, Shri Rameshwar Press, Darbhanga, 1924, pt. III, n.d..

Dandekar, R.N., *Vedic Bibliography*, vol. I, Karnataka Publishing House, Bombay, 1946; vols. 2-5, Bhandarkar Oriental Research Institute, Poona, 1973-93.

Dandekar, V.M., 'Cow Dung Models', *Economic and Political Weekly*, 4 (1969), pp. 1267-9.

———, 'India's Sacred Cattle and Cultural Ecology', *Economic and Political Weekly*, 4 (1969), 1559-67.

———, 'Sacred Cattle and More Sacred Production Functions', *Economic and Political Weekly*, 5 (1970), pp. 527, 529-31.

Dange, S.A., *Encyclopaedia of Puranic Beliefs and Religious Practices*, Navrang, New Delhi, 1986.

Dani, A.H. and V.M. Masson, eds., *History of Civilizations of Central Asia*, I, UNESCO Publishing, Paris, 1992.

Dargyay, Eva K., 'Buddhism in Adaptation: Ancestor Gods and Their Tantric Counterparts in the Religious Life of Zanskar', *History of Religion*, vol. 28, no. 2 (November 1988), pp. 123-34.

Daśavaikālika Sūtra, Nirnaya Sagar Press, Bombay, 1918.

Dasgupta, R.K., 'Spirit of India-I', *Statesman*, 15 March 2001.

Deo, S.B., *History of Jaina Monachism*, Deccan College Research Institute, Poona, 1956.

Deussen, P., *The Philosophy of the Upaniṣads*, London, 1906.

Devahuti, D., *Harsha: A Political Study*, 2nd edn., Oxford University Press Delhi, 1983.

Devalasmṛti in *Bīs Smṛtiyān* (Twenty Smrtis with Hindi tr.), ed. Shriram Sharma Acharya, Sanskriti Sansthana, Bareli, 1966.

Devībhāgavatapurāṇa, Nag Publishers, Delhi, 1986.

Devī Purāṇa, ed. Pushpendra Kumara Sharma, Shri Lal Bahadur Sastri Kendriya Sanskrit Vidyapeeth, Delhi, 1976.

Dhammapadam (with a gloss), ed. Shri Satkari Sharma Vangiya and Hindi tr. Kancchedilal Gupta, Chowkhamba Vidyabhavan, 4th edn., Varanasi, 1960.

Diakonov, I.M., 'On the Original Home of the speakers of Indo-European', *Journal of Indo-European Studies*, XIII (1985), pp. 92-174.

Diener, Paul and Eugene E. Robkin, 'Ecology, Evolution, and the Search for Origins: The Question of Islamic Pig Prohibition', *Current Anthropology*, vol. 19, no. 3 (September 1978), pp. 493-540.

Dīgha Nikāya, 3 vols., ed. Bhikhhu Jagdish Kassapa, Nalanda-Devanagari-Pali Series, Pali Publication Board, Bihar Government, 1958. *Dīgha Nikaya*, ed. T.W. Rhys Davids and J.E. Carpenter, 3 vols., London, 1890-1911; tr. T.W. Rhys Davids, 3 vols., London, 1889-1921.

Divanji, P.C., '*Laṅkāvatārasūtra* on Non-Vegetarian Diets', *Annals of the Bhandarkar Oriental Research Institute*, vol. 18 (1940), pp. 317-22.

Drew, Frederic, *The Jammoo and Kashmir Territories: A Geographical Account*, Edward Stanford, London, 1875.

Dixit, K.K., *Ślokavārttika: A Study*, L.D. Institute of Indology, Ahmedabad, 1983.

Dugar, Pandit Hiralal Jain, *Shramaṇa Bhagavān Mahāvira tathā Māmsāhāra Parihāra*, Shri Atmanand Jain Mahasabha (Panjab), Shri Jainendra Press, Delhi, 1964.

Dumont, Louis, *Homo Hierachicus*, Oxford University Press, Delhi, 1988.

Dundas, Paul, *The Jains*, Routledge, London and New York, 1992.

———, 'Food and Freedom: The Jaina Sectarian Debate on the Nature of the Kevalin', *Religion*, XV (1985), pp. 161-98.

Einoo, Shingo, *Die Cāturmāsya oder die altindischen Tertialopfer dargestellt nach den Vorschriften der Brāhmaṇas und der Śrautasūtras*, Monumenta Serindica no. 18, Tokyo, 1988.

———, 'The Formation of the Pūjā Ceremony', in Hanns-Peter Schmidt and Albrecht Wezler, eds., *Veda-Vyākaraṇa-Vyākhyāna: Festschrift Paul Thieme zum 90*, Verlag fur Orientalistische Fachpublikationen, Reinbek, 1996, pp. 73-87.

———, 'The Autumn Goddess Festival described in the Purāṇas', in Masakazu Tanaka and Musashi Tachikawa, eds., *Living With Śakti: Gender, Sexuality and Religion in South Asia*, National Museum of Ethnology, Osaka, 1999, pp. 33-70.

———, 'Is the Sārasvatasattra the Vedic Pilgrimage?', in K. Kimura, F. Sueeki, A. Saito, H. Marui and M. Shimoda, eds., *Sūnyatā and Reality: Volume in Memory of Professor Ejima Yasunori* (CD-Rom Book), Shunjusha Co., Tokyo, 2000.

———, 'Notes on the Initiation Rites in the Gṛhyapariśiṣṭas', unpublished manuscript.

Elmore, Theodore, *Dravidian Gods in Modern Hinduism*, University of Nebraska Press, Lincoln, 1915.

Epigraphia Indica, vols. IV, XXI, XXIV.

Erdosy, George, ed., *The Indo-Aryans of Ancient South Asia*, Munshiram Manoharlal, Delhi, 1997.

Eschman, A., Hermann Kulke and G.C. Tripathi, eds., *The Cult of Jagannatha and the Regional Tradition of Orissa*, Manohar, Delhi, 1978.

Falk, Harry, 'Soma I and II', *BSOAS*, 52, pt. 1 (1989), pp. 77-90.

Falk, Harry, 'Zur Tierzucht im Alten Indien', *Indo-Iranian Journal*, 24 (1982), pp. 169-80.

Freitag, Sandria, 'Sacred Symbol as Mobilizing Ideology: The North Indian Search for a "Hindu" Community', *Comparative Studies in Society and History*, vol. 22 (1980), pp. 597-625.

———, *Collective Action and Community: Public Arena and the Emergence of Communalism in North India*, Oxford University Press, Delhi, 1990.

———, 'Contesting in Public: Colonial Legacies and Contemporary Communalism', in David Ludden, ed., *Making India Hindu*, Oxford University Press, Delhi, 1996.

Frontline, 13 April 2001.

Furer-Haimendorf, Christoph von, *The Aboriginal Tribes of Hyderabad*, 2 vols., Macmillan, London, 1943.

Gandhi, M.K., *How to Serve the Cow*, Navjivan, Ahmedabad, 1954.

———, *An Autobiography or The Story of My Experiments with Truth*, Navjivan Trust, Ahmedabad, 1927, rpt. October 2000.

Ganguli, R., 'Cattle and Cattle-Rearing in Ancient India', *Annals of the Bhandarkar Oriental Research Institute*, vol. XII (1931), pp. 216-30.

Garuḍapurāṇa, Nag Publishers, Delhi, 1984.

Gaur, R.C., *Excavations at Atranjikhera*, Motilal Banarsidass, Delhi, 1983.

Gautama Dharmasūtra, ed. Adolf Friedrich Stenzler, Sanskrit Text Society, London, 1876; Eng. tr. G. Buhler, SBE II, Oxford, 1879.

Gobhila Gṛhyasūtra, ed. Chintamani Bhattacharya, Calcutta Sanskrit Series no. 17, Calcutta, 1936. Eng. tr. H. Oldenberg, SBE XXIX, Oxford, 1886; text with Hindi translation, Thakur Udaya Narain Singh, Chowkhamba Sanskrit Pratisthan, Delhi, 1992.

Gode, P.K., *Studies in Indian Cultural History*, vol. III, Bhandarkar Oriental Institute, Poona, 1969.

Gombrich, Richard, *Theravāda Buddhism: A Social History from Ancient Benares to Modern Colombo*, Routledge & Kegan Paul Ltd., London-New York, 1988.

Gonda, J., *The Savayajñas*, Amsterdam, 1965.

———, *Vedic Literature*, Otto Harrassowitz, Wiesbaden, 1975.

———, *Change and Continuity in Indian Religion*, Munshiram Manoharlal, Delhi, 1997.

———, *Vedic Ritual: The Non-Solemn Rites*, E.J. Brill, Leiden, 1980.

Gopal, Ram, *India of Vedic Kalpasūtras*, National Publishing House, Delhi, 1959.

Gopatha Brāhmaṇa, ed. Rajendra Lal Mitra, rpt., Indological Book House, Delhi, 1972; ed. Dieuke Gaastra, *Das Gopatha Brāhmaṇa*, Leiden, 1919.

Teun Goudriaan and Sanjukta Gupta, *Hindu Tantric and Śakta Literature*, Otto, Harrassowitz, Wiesbaden, 1981.

Gunasekara, V.A., 'Buddhism and Vegetarianism, The Rationale for the Buddha's Views on the Consumption of Meat', *Buddhasasana Home Page* (English Section). *http://www.uq.net.au/slsoc/budsoc.html*

Gṛhastharatnākara of Caṇḍeśvara, Bibliotheca Indica, Calcutta, 1928.

Halāyudhakośaḥ (*Abhidhānaratnamālā*), ed. Jaishankar Joshi, Uttar Pradesh Hindi Sansthan, 3rd edn., Lucknow, 1993.

Halbfass, Wilhelm, *Tradition and Reflection: Explorations In Indian Thought*, Sri Satguru Publications, Delhi, 1992.

Handiqui, K.K., *Yaśastilaka and Indian Culture*, Jaina Samskriti Samrakshaka Mandala, Sholapur, 1949.

Harcourt, A.F.P., *The Himalyan Districts of Kooloo, Lahoul and Spiti* (Selections from the Records of the Government of the Punjab, New Series no. X), rpt., Vivek Publishing Company, Kamla Nagar, Delhi, 1982.

Harijan, 15 September 1940.

Hārītasmṛti, in *Aṣṭādaśasmṛtyaḥ* (Hindi tr. Sundarlal Tripathi, Khemraj Shrikrishnadas) Venkateshwar Steam Press, Bombay, Śaka 1846.

Harris, Marvin, 'The Cultural Ecology of India's Sacred Cattle', *Current Anthropology*, 7, 1966, pp. 51-66.

———, *Cows, Pigs, Wars and Witches*, Random House, New York, 1974.

Harṣacarita (with the commentary of Śaṅkara), ed. K.P. Parab, 5th edn., Nirnaya Sagar Press, Bombay, 1925; tr. E.B. Cowell and F.W. Thomas, London, 1929.

Hazra, R.C., *Studies in the Purāṇic Records on Hindu Rites and Customs*, 2nd edn., Motilal Banarsidass, Delhi, 1975.

Heston, Alan, 'An Approach to the Sacred Cow of India', *Current Anthropology*, 12(1971), pp. 191-209.

Heesterman, J.C., *The Ancient Indian Royal Consecration*, Mouton & Co., The Hague, 1957.

———, 'Vrātya and Sacrifice', *Indo-Iranian Journal*, VI (1962), pp. 1-37.

———, Review of Alsdof, Beiträge zur Geschichte von Vegetarismus in *Indo-Iranian Journal*, IX (1966), pp. 147-9.

———, 'Non-Violence and Sacrifice', *Indologica Taurinensia*, XII (1984), pp. 119-27.

———, *The Inner Conflict of Tradition*, Oxford University Press, Delhi, 1985.

———, *The Broken World of Sacrifice: An Essay in Ancient Indian Ritual*, The University of Chicago Press, Chicago, 1993.

Hiltebeitel, Alf, 'On the Handling of the Meat, and Related matters, in Two South Indian Buffalo sacrifices', *L'Uomo*, 9, pp. 171-99.

———, 'Sexuality and Sacrifice: Convergent Subcurrents in the Firewalking Cult of Draupadī', in Fred W. Clothey, ed., *Images of Man: Religion and Historical Process in South Asia*, New Era, Madras, 1982, pp. 72-111.

———, ed., *Criminal Gods and Demon Devotees: Essays on the Gods of Popular Hinduism*, Manohar, Delhi, 1990.

Hiraṇyakeśī Gṛhyasūtra, Ānandaśramasamskṛtagranthāvaliḥ 53, pt. 8, 1929; Eng. tr. H. Oldenberg, SBE XXIX, Oxford, 1886.

Hiraṇyakeśī Śrautasūtra, Ānandāśramasamskṛtagranthāvaliḥ 53, 10 vols., 1907-32.

Hopkins, E. Washburn, 'The Buddhist Rule Against Eating Meat', *Journal of American Oriental Society*, XXVII (1907), pp. 455-64.

Hutton, J.H., *Caste in India*, 4th edn., Oxford University Press, London, 1963.

Imperial Gazetteer of India, Provincial Series, Kashmir and Jammu, Calcutta, 1909.

India Today, 15 April 1993.

Jaiminīya-Brāhmaṇa of the Sāma Veda, ed. Raghu Vira and Lokesh Chandra, Sarasvatī-Vihāra Series 31, Nagpur, 1954.

Jaiminīya Gṛhyasūtra, ed. W. Caland, *De literatuur van den Sāmaveda en het Jaiminīyagṛhyasūtra*, Amsterdam, 1906; Eng. tr. W. Caland, Punjab Sanskrit Series 2, Lahore, 1922.

Jaiminīya Upaniṣad Brāhmaṇa, ed. Hanns Oertel, *Journal of American Oriental Society*, 16 (1893-6), pp. 72-260.

Jain, D.C., *Economic Life As Depicted in Jaina Canonical Literature*, Research Institute of Prakrit, Jainology and Ahiṃsā, Vaishali, 1980.

Jain, Jagdish Chandra, *Prākrit Sāhitya Kā Itihās*, Chowkhamba Vidya Bhavan, Varanasi, 1961.

———, *Jaina Āgama Sāhitya men Bhāratīya Samāja*, Chowkhamba Vidya Bhavan, Varanasi, 1965.

———, *Prākrit Narrative Literature: Origin and Growth*, Munshiram Manoharlal, Delhi, 1981.

———, *Life in Ancient India as Depicited in the Jain Canom and Commentaries*, 2nd edn. Munshiram Manoharlal, Delhi, 1984.

Jain, Jyoti Prasad, *The Jaina Sources of the History of Ancient India*, Munshiram Manoharlal, Delhi, 1964.

Jain, Prem Suman, *Kuvalayamālākahā Kā Sāmskritik Adhyayana*, Institute of Prakrit, Jainology and Ahiṃsā, Vaishali, 1975.

Jaini, P.S., *Collected Papers on Jaina Studies*, Motilal Banarsidass, Delhi, 2000.

Jamison, Stephanie W., *The Ravenous Hyenas and the Wounded Sun: Myth and Ritual in Ancient India*, Cornell University Press, Ithaca and London, 1991.

Jātaka with commentary ed. V. Fausböll, 7 vols., London, 1877-97; Hindi tr., Bhadanta Ananda Kausalyayana, Hindi Sahitya Sammelan, Prayag, Saṃvat 2008-14.

Jha, D.N., *Ancient India in Historical Outline*, Manohar, Delhi, 1998, rpt. March 2001.

Jha, Vivekanand, 'Stages in the History of Untouchables', *Indian Historical Review*, II, 1 (July 1975), pp. 14-31.

Joshi, Laxmansastri, 'Was the Cow Killed in Ancient India?', *Quest*, 75(March-April 1972), pp. 83-7.

Jolly, Julius, *Hindu Law and Custom*, First published in German, 1896; Eng. tr. Batakrishna Ghosh, Bhartiya Publishing House, Delhi, 1975.

Joshi, J.P. 'A Note on the Excavation at Bhagwanpura', *Purātattva*, no. 8 (1975-6).

———, *Excavation at Bhagwanpura 1975-76*, Archacological Survey of India, Delhi, 1993.

Kālikāpurāṇa, pts. 1-2, ed. B.N. Shastri, Nag Publishers, Delhi, 1991.

Kalpa Sūtra, Eng. tr., H. Jacobi, SBE XXII, Oxford, 1884.

Kane, P.V., *History of Dharmaśāstra*, 5 vols., 2nd edn., Bhandarkar Oriental Research Institute, Poona, 1968-77.

Kapadia, H.R., 'Prohibition of Flesh Eating in Jainism', *Review of Philosophy and Religion*, IV (1933), pp. 232-9.

———, *A History of the Canonical Literature of the Jainas*, Surat, 1941.

Kapiṣṭhala-Kaṭha-Saṃhitā, ed. Raghu Vira, 2nd edn., Delhi, 1968.

Kāśyapīyakṛsisūkti, ed. G. Wojtilla, *Acta Orientalia Academial Saentianum Hung*, XXXIII, no. 2 (1979).

Kaṭhaka Gṛhyasūtra, ed. W. Caland, Research Department, D.A.V. College, Lahore, 1925; *Dās Kāṭhaka-Gṛhya-Sūtra*, ed. Caren Dreyer, Stuttgart, 1986.

Kaṭhaka Saṃhitā, ed. Leopold von Schroeder, *Kāṭhakam. Die Saṃhitā der Kaṭha Śākhā*, 3 Bde, Leipzig, 1900-10.

Kathāsaritasāgara of Somadeva, ed. with Hindi tr. Pandit Kedarnath Sharma, Bihar Rashtrabhasha Parisad, Patna, 1960.

Kaṭhopaniṣad in S. Radhakrishnan, *The Principal Upaniṣads*, Centenary Edn., Oxford University Press, Delhi, 1989, 4th Impression, 1991.

Kātyāyána Śrautasūtra, ed. Albrecht Weber, Berlin-London, 1859, rpt., Chowkhamba Sanskrit Series, Varanasi, 1972; ed. W. Caland, Bibliotheca Indica, Calcutta, 1941; Eng. tr., H.G. Ranade, Deccan College, Poona, 1978.

Kauṣika-sūtra of the Atharvaveda with extracts from the commentaries of Dārila and Keśava, ed. M. Bloomfield, *Journal of American Oriental Society*, 14 (1890).

Kauṣītaki Brāhmaṇa, ed. B. Lindner, Jena, 1887; Eng. tr., A.B. Keith, *Rigveda Brāhmaṇas: The Aitareya and Kauṣītaki Brāhmaṇas of the Rigveda*, Harvard University Press; 1st Indian rpt. edn., Motilal Banarsidass, Delhi, 1971.

Keith, A.B., *The Religion and Philosophy of the Veda and Upanishads*, Harvard Oriental Series 31, Cambridge, Massachusetts, 1925; Indian rpt., Motilal Banarsidass, Delhi, 1970.

Khādira Gṛhyasūtra (with the commentary of Rudraskanda) ed. tr. and published by Thakur Udaya Narayana Singh, Muzaffarpur, 1934: Eng. tr. H. Oldenberg, SBE XXIX, Oxford, 1886.

Kochhar, Rajesh, *The Vedic People: Their History and Geography*, Orient Longman, Delhi, 1999.

Kolhatkar, M.B., *Surā: The Liquor and the Vedic Sacrifice*, D.K Printworld, Delhi, 1999.

Kosambi, D.D., *Introduction to the Study of Indian History*, Popular Prakashan, Bombay, 1956.

Kṛtyakalpataru of Lakṣmīdhara, ed. K.V. Rangaswami Aiyangar, Gaekwad Oriental Series, Baroda, 1950.

Kṛsiparāśara, ed. and tr. G.P. Majumdar and S.C. Banerji, Bibliotheca Indica, Calcutta, 1960.

Kūrmapurāṇa, ed. PancananaTarkaratna, Vangavasi Press, Calcutta, 1332 BS.

Kuvalayamālā of Uddyotanasūri, 2 pts., ed. A.N. Upadhye, Singhi Jain Series, Bombay, 1959, 1970.

Lal, B.B., 'Excavations at Hastinapur and other Explorations in the Upper Ganga and Satlej Basins 1950-52', *Ancient India,* nos. 10-11 (1954-5), pp. 5-151.

Laṅkāvatārasūtra, ed. Bunyiu Nanjio, Kyoto, 1923; tr. D.T. Suzuki, Routledge, 1932.

Lāṭyāyana Śrautasūtra, ed. Anandachandra Vedantavagisa, Bibliotheca Indica, Calcutta, 1870-2; new edn. with appendix containing corrections and emendations to the text, C.G. Kasikar, Delhi, 1982.

Legge, James, *Fahien's Record of the Buddhistic Kingdoms,* Oxford, 1886.

Lincoln, Bruce, *Priests, Warriors and Cattle,* University of California Press, Berkeley and Los Angeles, 1982.

Lodrick, Deryck O., *Sacred Cows and Sacred Places: Origins and Survivals of Animal Homes in India,* University of California Press, Berkeley, 1981.

Ludden, David, *Making India Hindu,* Oxford University Press, Delhi, 1996.

Macdonell, A.A., *Vedic Mythology,* Strassburg, 1897; Indian rpt., Indological Book House, Varanasi, 1963.

Macdonell, A.A. and A.B. Keith, *Vedic Index of Names and Subjects,* 2 vols., Indian rpt., Motilal Banarsidass, Delhi-Varanasi-Patna, 1958 [Unless otherwise specified this edn. has been used], Macdonell and Keith, *Vedic Index,* I, pp. 580-2 (Hindi translation by Ramkumar Rai, Chowkhamba Vidyabhavan, Varanasi, 1962).

Maitrāyaṇī Saṃhitā, ed. Leopold von Schroeder, 4 Bde, Leipzig, 1881-6.

Maitrāyaṇīya Upaniṣad, in S. Radhakrishnan, *The Principal Upanisads,* Centenary Edn., Oxford University Press, Delhi, 1989.

Majjhima Nikāya, ed. P.V. Bapat (vol. I); Rahul Sanskrityayana (vols. 2-3). Nalanda Devanagari Pali Series, Bihar Government, 1958. Hindi tr. Rahul Sanskrityayana, Mahabodhi Sabha, Varanasi, 2nd edn., 1964.

Mahābhārata, 19 vols., Critical edn., Bhandarkar Oriental Research Institute, Poona, 1933-59.

Mahāvīracarita, ed. with Hindi tr. Rampratap Tripathi Shastri, Lok Bharati Prakashan, Allahabad, 1973.

Malalasekera, G.P., *Dictionary of Pāli Proper Names*, 2 vols., 1st edn., Pali Text Series, 1937, 1st Indian edn., Munshiram Manoharlal, Delhi, 1983.

Malamoud, Charles, *Cooking the World: Ritual and Thought in Ancient India*, Oxford University Press, Delhi, 1996.

Mallory, J.P., *In Search of the Indo-European Language, Archaeology and Myth*, London, 1991.

Malvaniya, Dalsukh, *Niśītha: Ek Adhyayana*, Sanmati Jñana Pīth, Agra, n.d.

Māṃsatattvaviveka of Viśvanātha Nyāya Pañcānana, Sarasvatibhavan Series, Benaras, 1927.

Mānasollāsa of Someśvara, 2 vols., Gaekwad Oriental Series, Baroda, 1925, 1939.

Mānavagṛhyasūtra of the Maitrāyaṇīya Śākhā (with the commentary of Aṣṭāvakra), ed. Ramakrishna Harshaji, Delhi, 1982.

Mānavaśrautasūtra belonging to the Maitrāyaṇī Śākhā, ed. J.M. van Geldner, Satapitaka Series 17, Delhi, 1961.

Vettam Mani, *Purāṇic Encyclopedia*, rpt., Motilal Banarsidass, Delhi, 1984.

Manusmṛti or *Manava Dharmaśāstra* (with the commentaries of Medhātithi, Sarvajñanārāyaṇa, Kullūka, Rāghavānanda, Nandana, and Rāmacandra) ed. V.N. Mandalika, Ganpat Krishnaji's Press, Bombay, 1886; Eng. tr., G. Bühler, SBE XXV, Oxford, 1921.

Mārkaṇḍeya Purāṇa, ed. K.M. Banerjee, Bibliotheca Indica, Calcutta, 1862; Eng. tr. F.E. Pargiter, Bibliotheca Indica, Calcutta, 1904.

Daigan and Alicia Matsunaga, *The Buddhist Concept of Hell*, Philosophical Library, New York, 1972.

Matsyapurāṇa (=*Srimaddvaipāyanamunipraṇītam Matsyapurānam*), Ānandāshrama Sanskrit Series, Poona, 1981.

Mayrhofer, Manfred, *A Concise Etymological Dictionary*, 4 vols., Carl Winter, Universitatsverlag, Hiedelberg, 1956-80. Revised edition as *Etymologisches Wörterbuch des Altindoarischen*, 3 Baender, Carl Winter, Universitaetsverlag, Heidelberg, 1986-98.

McDermott, James P., 'Animals and Humans in Early Buddhism', *Indo-Iranian Journal*, 32 (1989), pp. 269-80.

Meghadūta (with the commentary of Mallināthа), ed. and tr. M.R. Kale, 8th edn., Motilal Banarsidass, Delhi, rpt., 1979.

Meulenbeld, G. Jan, *A History of Indian Medical Literature*, vols. IA and IB, Egbert Forsten, Groningen, 1999.

Milindapañho, ed. V. Trenckner, London, 1928; Eng. tr. T.W. Rhys Davids, *The Questions of King Milinda,* SBE XXXV-XXXVI, Oxford, 1890-4.

Mishra, Shivashekhar, *Mānasollāsa: Ek Sānskritik, Adhyayana,* Chowkhamba Vidyabhavan, Varanasi, 1966.

Mitra, R.L., *Indo-Aryans: Contributions to the Elucidation of Ancient and Medieval History,* 2 vols., rpt., Indological Book House, Varanasi, 1969.

Rajendralal Mitra: 150th Anniversary Lectures, The Asiatic Society, Calcutta, 1978.

Modak, B.R., *The Ancillary Literature of the Atharvaveda: A Study with special reference to the Pariśiṣṭas,* Rashtriya Veda Vidya Pratishthan, New Delhi, 1993.

Moharājaprājaya of Yaśahpāla, Gaekwad Oriental Series 9, Baroda, 1918.

Monier-Williams, M., *Sanskrit-English Dictionary,* new edn., Motilal Banarsidass, Delhi, 1963.

Mylius, Klaus, *Wörterbuch des Altindischen Rituals,* Institute fur Indologie, Wichtrach, 1995.

Naiṣadhamahākāvyam (with the commentary of Mallinātha), ed. Haragovind Shastri, Chowkhamba, Varanasi, 1981; Eng. tr. *Naiṣadhacarita of Śrīharṣa* (with commentaries), K.K. Handiqui, Deccan College, Poona, 1965.

Nalacampū of Trivikrama, eds., Durgaprasad and Sivadatta, Nirnaya Sagara Press, Bombay, 1885, 3rd edn., Bombay, 1921; also ed. Chowkhamba Sanskrit Series, Benaras, 1932.

Nāradasmṛti, ed. Julius Jolly, Calcutta, 1885; Eng. tr., Julius Jolly, *The Minor Law-Books,* SBE XXXIII, Oxford, 1889.

Nāradīyamahāpurāṇa, Nag Publishers, Delhi, 1984.

Nariman, J.K., *Literary History of Sanskrit Buddhism,* 2nd edn., rpt., Pilgrims Book Pvt. Ltd., Delhi, 1972.

Nath, B., 'Animal Remains from Hastinapur', *Ancient India,* nos. 10-11 (1954-5), pp. 107-20.

Nath, B., 'Animal Remains from Rupar and Bara Sites, Ambala district, E. India', *Indian Museum Bulletin,* 3, nos. 1-2, pp. 69-116.

Vijay, Nath, '*Mahadana*: The Dynamics of Gift-economy and the Feudal Milieu', in D.N. Jha, ed., *The Feudal Order: State, Society and Ideology in Early Medieval India,* Manohar, Delhi, 2000, pp. 411-40.

Niśītha Cūrni (*Niśītha Viśeṣa Cūrṇi*) of Jinadāsagaṇi (with commentary), ed. Kavi Amar Muni Upadhyaya and Muni Kanhaiyalal, Agra, 1957-60.

Nyberg, Harri, 'The Problem of the Aryans and the Soma: The Botanical Evidence', in George Erdosy, ed., *The Indo-Aryans of Ancient South Asia*, Munshiram Manoharlal, New Delhi, 1997.

O'Flaherty, W.D., *Asceticism and Eroticism in the Mythology of Śiva*, Oxford University Press, London, 1973.

Oldenberg, Herman, *The Gṛhyasūtras*, SBE XXIX, Oxford, 1886.

———, *Ṛgveda: Textkritische und exegetische Noten*, Weidmannsche Buchhandlung, Berlin, 1912.

O'Malley, L.S.S., *Indian Caste Customs*, Cambridge University Press, 1932.

Palapiyūṣalatā of Madana Upādhyāya, Gourīśayantrālaya, Darbhanga, Saṃvat 1951.

Pañcaviṃśa Brāhmaṇa, ed. A Chinnaswami Sastri, *Tāṇḍyamahābrāhmaṇa belonging to the Sāma Veda with the commentary of Sāyanācārya*, 2 vols., Kashi Sanskrit Series, Haridas Sanskrit Granthamala 105, Benaras, 1935-6; Eng. tr. Caland, Asiatic Society, Calcutta, 1931.

Pandey, Gyan, 'Rallying round the Cow', in Ranajit Guha, ed., *Subaltern Studies*, II, Oxford University Press, Delhi, 1983.

Paramatthajotikā, Colombo, 1920.

Pārāśarasmṛti, ed. Daivajñavācaspati Śrīvāsudeva, Chowkhamba Sanskrit Series, Varanasi, 1968; ed. with Hindi tr. Shriguruprasad Sharma, Chowkhamba Vidya Bhavan, Varanasi, 1998; *Aṣṭādaśasmṛtyaḥ* (with Hindi tr. by Sundarlal Tripathi, Khemraj Shrikrishnadas, Venkateshwar Steam Press, Bombay, Śaka 1846.

Pāraskara Gṛhyasūtra, ed. Mahadeva Gangadhar Bakre, Bombay, 1917. Ed. Jagdish Chandra Mishra, Chowkhamba, Varanasi, 1991; Eng. tr. H. Oldenberg, SBE XXIX, Oxford, 1886.

Parpola, Asko, 'The Problem of the Aryans and the Soma: Textual-linguistic and Archaeological Evidence', George Erdosy, ed., *The Indo-Aryans of Ancient South Asia*, Munshiram Manoharlal, Delhi, 1997.

Pillay, K.K., *A Social History of Tamils*, I, University of Madras, 1975.

Prabandhacintāmaṇi of Merutuṅgasūri, ed. Muni Jinavijaya, Singhi Jain Series, I, Santiniketan, 1933; Eng. tr. C.H. Tawney, rpt., Indian Book Gallery, Delhi, 1982.

Prabha, Chandra, *Historical Mahākāvyas in Sanskrit (Eleventh to Fifteenth Century)*, Delhi, 1976.

Prabhāvakacarita of Prabhācandra, ed. H.M. Sharma, Nirnaya Sagar Press, Bombay, 1909; ed. Jinavijaya, Singhi Jain Series, Ahmedabad, 1940.

Prāchīn Bhārat men Gomāmsa: Ek Samīkshā (author not mentioned), published by Motilal Jalan, Gita Press, Gorakhpur, n.d.

Prakash, Om, *Food and Drinks in Ancient India*, Munshiram Manoharlal, Delhi, 1961.

Prasad, Chandra Shekhar, 'Meat-Eating and the Rule of Tikoṭiparisuddha', in A.K. Narain, ed., *Studies in Pāli and Buddhism*, B.R. Publishing Corporation, Delhi, 1979.

Prayogapārijata of Nṛsiṃha, Nirnaya Sagar Press, Bombay, 1916.

Proudfoot, I., *Ahiṃsā and A Mahābhārata Story*, Australian National University, Canberra, 1987.

Radhakrishnan, S., *The Principal Upaniṣads*, Centenary Edn., Oxford University Press, Delhi, 1989.

Rahula, Walpola, *History of Buddhism in Ceylon*, M.D. Gunasena, 2nd edn., Colombo, 1966.

Rahula, Walpola, 'Memorandum by Walpola Rahula of the Early Sources For the Meaning of *Sūkaramaddava*', *Journal of American Oriental Society*, 102.4 (1982), pp. 602-3.

Raj, K.N., 'India's Sacred Cattle: Theories and Empirical Findings', *Economic and Political Weekly*, 6 (1971), pp. 717-22.

Sundara Ram, L.L., *Cow Protection in India*, The South Indian Humanitarian League, Madras, 1927.

Ramachandran, Rajesh, 'A Crisis of Identity', *The Hindustan Times*, 7 May 2000.

Rāmāyaṇa, critical edn., 7 vols., Oriental Institute, Baroda, 1960-75; *The Vālmīki Rāmāyaṇa according to southern recension*, 2 vols., ed. T.R. Krishnacharya, 1st edn., Kumbakonam, 1905, rpt., Sri Satguru Publications, Delhi, 1982.

Rasavāhinī, ed. Saranatissa Thera, Colombo, 1920.

Renfrew, Colin, *Archaeology and Language: The Puzzle of Indo-European Origins*, Penguin, Harmondsworth, 1989.

Renou, Louis, *Bibliographie Védique*, Librairie D'amerique et D'Orient, Paris, 1931.

Renou, Louis, *Études Védiques et Pāṇinéennes*, Éditions E. de Boccard, Paris, 1966.

Renou, Louis, *Vedic India*, Indological Book House, Varanasi, 1971.

Ṛgveda, ed. Theodor Aufrecht, *Die Hymnen des Rigveda*, 2 Bde. 2. Auflge Bonn, 1877; German tr. K. Fiedrich Geldner, *Der Rig-Veda*, Harvard Oriental Series XXXIII-XXXVI, Cambridge, Massachusetts, 1951-7.

Rhys Davids, T.W., *Buddhist India*, 1st edn., T. Fisher Unwin, London, 1911; Indian rpt., Motilal Banarsidass, Delhi, 1971.

Rolland, Romain, *The Life of Vivekananda and the Universal Gospel*, Advaita Ashrama, Calcutta, Eleventh Impression, August 1988.

Ronnow, K., 'Zur Erklärung des Pravargya, des Agnicayana und Sautrāmaṇi', *Le Monde Oriental*, 23 (1929), pp. 113-73.

Roy, Pradipto, 'The Sacred Cow in India', *Rural Sociology*, 20 (1955), pp. 8-15.

———, 'Social Background', *Seminar No. 93: The Cow* (May 1967), pp. 17-23.

Śabdakalpadruma by Rājā Rādhākānt Deva, vols. 1-5, rpt., Nag Publishers, Delhi, 1987.

Sachau, Edward C., *Alberuni's India*, 1st published 1910, rpt., Low Price Publications, Delhi, 1996.

Saḍviṃśabrāhmaṇa, ed. Herman Frederick Eelsingh, Leiden, 1908.

Sahu, B.P., *From Hunters to Breeders*, Anamika Prakashan, Delhi, 1988.

———, 'Patterns of Animal Use in Ancient India', *Proceedings*, Indian History Congress, 48th Session, Goa, 1987.

Samaraiccakahā of Haribhadrasūri, ed. H. Jacobi, Calcutta, 1926.

Saṃvarttasmṛti, *Aṣṭādaśasmṛtyaḥ* (Hindi tr. Sundarlal Tripathi, Khemraj Shrikrishnadas), Venkateshwar Steam Press, Bombay, Śaka 1846.

Saṃyutta Nikāya, ed. Bhikkhu J. Kashyap, Nalanda Devanagari Pali Series, Pali Publication Board, Bihar Government, 1959, 4 vols. Hindi tr. Bhikkhu Jagdish Kashyap, 2 pts., Mahabodhi Sabha, Varanasi, 1954.

H.D. Sankalia, '(The Cow) In History', *Seminar* no. 93, May 1967.

———, *Prehistory and Protohistory of India and Pakistan*, 2nd edn., Deccan College, Poona, 1974.

Śaṅkhasmṛti in *Aṣṭādaśasmṛtyaḥ* (Hindi tr. Sundarlal Tripathi, Khemraj Shrikrishnadas), Venkateshwar Steam Press, Bombay, Śaka 1846.

Śāṅkhyāyana Gṛhyasūtra, ed. S.R. Sehgal, Delhi, 1960; Eng. tr., H. Oldenberg, SBE XXIX, Oxford, 1886.

Śāṅkhyāyana Śrautasūtra, ed. Alfred Hillebrandt, Bibliotheca Indica, Calcutta, 1888.

Śatapatha Brāhmaṇa, ed. Albrecht Weber, Berlin-London, 1855; Eng. tr., Julius Eggeling, 5 vols., SBE XII, XXVI, XLI, XLIII, XLIV, Oxford, 1882, 1885, 1894, 1885, 1900.

Śātātapasmṛti in *Aṣṭādaśasmṛtyaḥ* (Hindi tr. Sundarlal Tripathi, Khemraj Shrikrishnadas), Venkateshwar Steam Press, Bombay, Śaka 1846.

Saurapurāṇa by Srimat Vyas, ed. Pandit Kashinath Sastri, Ānandāśrama Sanskrit Series no. 18, Poona, 1889.

Schmidt, Hanns-Peter 'The Origin of Ahiṃsā', in *Mélanges d'Indianisme a la memoire de Louis Renou*, Éditions E. de Boccard, Paris, 1968.

———, 'Ahiṃsā and Rebirth', in Michael Witzel, ed., *Inside the Texts Beyond the Texts: New Approaches to the Study of the Vedas*, Harvard Oriental Series, Opera Minora 2, Cambridge, 1997.

———, *The Cow in the Pasture*, Leiden, 1976.

Schmithausen, Lambert, *Buddhism and Nature*, Lecture delivered on the Occasion of the Expo 1990, The International Institute for Buddhist Studies, Tokyo, 1991.

———, 'The Early Buddhist Tradition and Ecological Ethics', *Journal of Buddhist Ethics*, 4 (1997), *http://jbe.la.psu.edu/4/4cont. html.*

Seminar, no. 93 (May 1967).

Sen, Madhu, *A Cultural Study of the Niśītha Cūrṇi*, Sohanlal Jaindharma Pracharak Samiti (Amritsar) available at P.V. Research Institute, Varanasi, 1975.

Seneviratne, H.L., 'Food Essence and the Essence of Experience', in R.S. Khare, ed., *The Eternal Food: Gastronomic Ideas and Experiences of Hindus and Buddhists*, State University of New York Press, Albany, 1992, pp. 179-200.

Sharma, A.K., 'Faunal Remains from Mathura', in J.P. Joshi et al., eds., *Facets of Indian Civilization–Recent Perspectives: Essays in Honour of Prof. B.B. Lal*, Aryan Books International, Delhi, 1997.

Sharma, R.S., *Material Culture and Social Formations in Ancient India*, Macmillan, Delhi, 1983.

———, *Looking for the Aryans*, Orient Longman, Chennai, 1994.

———, *Advent of the Aryans in India*, Manohar, Delhi, 1999.

Sharma, Shanta Rani, *Society and Culture in Rajasthan c. AD 700-900*, Pragati Prakashan, Delhi, 1996.

Shastri, A.M., *India As Seen in the Bṛhatsaṃhitā*, Motilal Banarsidass, Delhi, 1969.

Shastri, Nemichandra, *Prākrit Bhāshā aur Sāhitya ka Ālochanātmak Itihās*, Tara Publications, Varanasi, 1966.

Shastri, Rajnikant, *Hindu Jati Kā Utthān aur Patan*, Kitab Mahal, Allahabad, 1988.

Shende, N.J., *The Religion and Philosophy of the Atharvaveda*, rpt., Bhandarkar Oriental Research Institute, Poona, 1985.

Shrivastava, Kumud Bala, '*Prabandhacintāmaṇi Ka Sāṃskritik Adhyayana*', Ph.D. thesis, Banaras Hindu University, 1985.

Simoons, Frederick J., 'Contemporary Research Themes in Cultural Geography of Domesticated Animals', *Geographical Review*, 64 (1974), pp. 557-76.

———, 'The Purificatory Role of the Five Products of the Cow in Hinduism', *Ecology of Food and Nutrition*, 3 (1974), pp. 21-34.

———, 'Questions in the sacred-cow controversy', *Current Anthropology*, 20. 3 (1979), pp. 467-76.

———, *Eat Not This Flesh*, The University of Wisconsin Press, Madison, 2nd edn., 1994.

——— and Elizabeth S. Simoons, *A Ceremonial Ox of India: The Mithan in Nature, Culture and History*, University of Wisconsin Press, Madison, 1968.

Singh, S.D., *Ancient Indian Warfare with special reference to the Vedic Period*, E.J. Brill, Leiden, 1965.

Sircar, D.C., *Select Inscriptions Bearing on Indian History and Civilization*, I, 2nd edn., University of Calcutta, 1965.

Sircar, D.C., *The Śākta Pīṭhas*, 2nd rev. edn., Motilal Banarsidass, Delhi, 1973.

Skandapurāṇa, 7 vols., Nag Publishers, Delhi, 1986-7.

Ślokavārttika of Śrī Kumārila Bhaṭṭa, ed. and rev. Svami Dvarikadasa Sastri, Tara Publications, Varanasi, 1978; Eng. tr. Ganga Nath Jha, Sri Satguru Publications, Delhi, 1983.

Slater, Gilbert, *The Dravidian Element in Indian Culture*, London, 1924.

Smith, Brian K., *Reflections on Resemblance, Ritual, and Religion*, Oxford University Press, New York, 1989.

———, 'Eaters, Food, and Social Hierarchy in Ancient India', *Journal of the Academy of Religion*, LVIII, no. 2 (1990), pp. 177-202.

———and Wendy Doniger, 'Sacrifice and Substitution: Ritual Mystification and Mythical Demystification', *Numen*, XXXVI (1989), pp. 189-223.

Smṛticandrikā of Devaṇṇabhaṭṭa, Āhnikakāṇḍa, ed. L. Srinivasacharya, Government Oriental Library Series, Mysore, 1914; *Smṛticandrikā* of Devaṇṇabhaṭṭa, Śrāddhakāṇḍa, Government Oriental Library Series, Mysore, 1918.

Sorensen, S., *An Index to the Names in the Mahābhārata*, Motilal Banarsidass, Delhi, 1963.

South Indian Inscriptions, VIII.

Spera, Guiseppe, *Notes on Ahiṃsā*, Torino, 1982.

Śrautakośa, vols. I and II (English Section), Vaidik Samsodhna Mandala, Poona, 1962.

Srinivasan, Doris, *Concept of Cow in the Ṛgveda*, Motilal Banarsidass, Delhi, 1979.

Staal, Fritz, *Agni: The Vedic Ritual of the Fire Altar*, 2 vols., Asian Humanities Press, Berkeley, 1983.

Stevenson, Sinclair, *The Rites of the Twice-Born*, Oxford University Press, London, 1920.

———, *The Heart of Jainism*, 1st edn., Oxford University Press, 1915; 1st Indian edn., Munshiram Manoharlal, Delhi, 1970.

Stietencron Heinrich von, et al., eds., *Epic and Purāṇic Bibliography*, part I, Otto Harrassowitz, Wiesbaden, 1992.

Subhāṣitasandoha of Amitagati, Bombay, 1932.

Sumaṅgalavilāsinī of Buddhaghoṣa, II, Pali Text Society, London, 1971.

Sūryaprajñapti with the commentary of Malayagiri, Agamodaya Samiti, Nirnaya Sagar Press, Bombay, 1919.

Suśruta Saṃhitā, ed. Nripendranath Sengupta and Balai Chandra Sengupta, 2 pts., Calcutta, 1938; Eng. tr. Kunjalal Bhisagratna, 3 vols., Calcutta, 1907-15; *Suśruta Saṃhitā* (Scientific Synopsis), P. Ray, H.N. Gupta and M. Roy, Indian National Science Academy, New Delhi, 1980.

Sutta Nipāta, text and Hindi tr. Bhikkhu Dharmaratna, Mahabodhi Sabha, Varanasi, 1960.

Sūtrakṛtāṅga Sūtra, Eng. tr., H. Jacobi, SBE XLV, Oxford, 1895.

Śvetāśvara Upaniṣad, in S. Radhakrishnan, *The Principal Upaniṣads*, Centenary Edn., Oxford University Press, Delhi, 1989.

Śyāmārahasya of Purnānanda Giri, ed. R.M. Chattopadhyaya in *Vividhatantrasaṃgraha*, Calcutta, 1877-80; ed. with Bengali tr., Prasanna Kumara Sastri, BS 1317.

Tāṇḍyabrāhmaṇa belonging to the Sama Veda with the commentary of Sāyanācārya, 2 vols., Kashi Sanskrit Series, Haridas Sanskrit Granthmala, Benaras, 1935-6.

Tachikawa, Musashi, 'Homa in the Vedic Ritual: The Structure of the Darśa-pūrṇamāsa', in Yasuhiko Nagano and Yasuke Ikari, eds., *From Vedic Altar to Village Shrine*, National Museum of Ethnology, Osaka, 1993.

Taittirīya Āraṇyaka of the Black Yajur Veda with the commentary of Sāyanācārya, ed. R.L. Mitra, Bibliotheca Indica, Calcutta, 1872.

Taittirīya Brāhmaṇa with the commentary of Sāyanācārya, Ānandāśramagranthavali 37, 3 vols., 3rd edn., Poona, 1979.

Taittirīya Saṃhitā, ed. Albrecht Weber, *Die Taittirīya-Saṃhitā*, 2 Bde, Leipzig, 1871-2; Eng. tr., A.B. Keith, *The Veda of the Black Yajus*

School entitled Taittirīya Sanhitā, Harvard Oriental Series, XVIII and XIX, rpt., Motilal Banarsidass, Delhi, 1967.

Tahtinen, Unto, *Ahiṃsā: Non-Violence in Indian Tradition*, Rider and Company, London, 1976.

Tantrasāra of Abhinavagupta, ed. M.K. Shastri, Bombay, 1918.

Thapar, Romila, 'The Theory of Aryan Race and Politics', *Transactions of the International Conference of Eastern Studies*, no. XL, pp. 41-66.

Thieme, Paul, *Der Fremdling im Ṛgveda*, Deutsche Morgenlandische Gesellschaft, Leipzig, 1938, Kraus Ṙeprint Ltd., Nendeln, Liechtenstein, 1966.

Thite, G.U., *Sacrifice in the Brāhmaṇa Texts*, University of Poona, 1975.

Times of India, 28 May 1999.

Tod, James, *Annals and Antiquities of Rajasthan*, 2 vols., rpt., Oriental Books Reprint Corporation, New Delhi, 1983.

Touche, J. Digges La, *The Rajputana Gazetteer*, vol. II.

Trautmann, Thomas R., *Aryans and the British India*, Vistaar Publications, Delhi, 1997.

Tripathi, Vibha, *Painted Grey Ware: An Iron Age Culture of Northern India*, Concept Publishing Company, Delhi, 1976.

Tsuji, Naoshiro (alias Fukushima), *On the Relation of Brāhmaṇas and Śrautasūtras*, The Tôyô Bunko Ronsô, Series A, XXXIII, (English Summary), The Tôyô Bunko, Tokyo, 1952.

Tull, Herman W., 'The Killing That is not Killing: Men, Cattle and the Origins of Non-violence (*Ahiṃsā*) in the Vedic Sacrifice', *Indo-Iranian Journal*, 39 (1996), pp. 223-44.

Upavanavinod of Śārṅgadhara, ed. G.P. Majumdar, Calcutta, 1935.

Uttarādhyayana Sūtra, Eng. tr. H. Jacobi, SBE XLV, Oxford, 1895.

Uttararāmacarita (with notes and the commentary of Ghanaśyāma), ed. and tr. P.V. Kane and C.N. Joshi, Motilal Banarsidass, Delhi, 1962.

Uvāsagadasāo, Eng. tr. A.F. Rudolph Hoernle, Asiatic Society, Calcutta, 1989.

Vādhūlasūtra, ed. and German tr. W. Caland, *Acta Orientalia*, vol. 1 (1923), 2 (1924), 4 (1926), 6 (1928); M. Sparreboom and J.C. Heesterman, *The Ritual of Setting up the Sacrificial Fires According to the Vādhūla School, Vādhūlaśrautasūtra*, Verlag der Osterreichischen Akademie der Wissenschaften, Wien, 1989.

Vaikhānasa Gṛhyasūtra, ed. W. Caland, Bibliotheca Indica, Calcutta, 1927; text and tr. Asiatic Society, Calcutta, 1927-9.

Vaikhānasa Śrautasūtra, ed. W. Caland, Bibliotheca Indica, Calcutta, 1941.

Vaitāna Śrautasūtra, ed. Vishwa Bandhu, Woolner Sanskrit Series 13, Hoshiarpur, 1967.

Vasiṣṭha Dharmasūtra (*Śrīvāsiṣṭhadharmaśāstram*), ed. Alois Anton Führer, Bombay Sanskrit and Prakrit Series 23, Bombay, 1883: Eng. tr. G. Buhler, SBE XIV, Oxford, 1882.

Vasudevahiṇḍī of Saṅghadāsagaṇi, ed. with introduction and Hindi tr. Dr. Shreeranjan Sūrideva, Pandit Rampratap Charitable Trust, Beawar, Rajasthan, 1989.

Vibhaṅgaṭṭhakathā, Simon Hewavitarne Bequest Series, Colombo.

Vinaya Piṭaka, Eng tr. T.W. Rhys Davids and H. Oldenberg, *Vinaya Texts*, SBE XIII, XVII, XX, Oxford, 1882-5; Hindi tr., Rahul Sankrityayana, Mahabodhi Sabha, Sarnath, Benaras, 1935.

Vipākasūtra, ed. P.L. Vaidya, Poona, 1933.

Viṣṇudharmottarapurāṇa, Nag Publishers, Delhi, 1985.

Viṣṇusmṛti, ed. Julius Jolly, Bibliotheca Indica, Calcutta, 1881; Eng. tr. as *The Institutes of Viṣṇu*, SBE VII, Oxford, 1880.

Vyāsasmṛti in Aṣṭādaśasmṛtyaḥ (Hindi tr. Sundarlal Tripathi, Khemraj Shrikrishnadas, Venkateshwar Steam Press, Bombay, Śaka 1846.

Vyavahārabhaṣya, ed. W. Schubring, Leipzig, 1918.

Wackernagel, Jacob, *Altindische Grammatik*, vol. II, pt. 2, Vandenhoeck & Ruprecht, Gottingen, 1954.

Waddell, L.A., *The Buddhism of Tibet or Lamaism*, 2nd edn., Cambridge, 1939.

Waley, Arthur, 'Did Buddha die of eating pork?: With a note on Buddha's image', *Mélanges Chinois et bouddhiques*, vol. 1931-2, Juliet, 1932, pp. 343-53.

Warder, A.K., *Indian Buddhism*, Motilal Banarsidass, Delhi, 1970.

Wasson, R. Gordon, 'The Last Meal of the Buddha with Memorandum by Walpola Rahula of the Early Sources for the Meaning of *Sūkaramaddava*', *Journal of American Oriental Society*, 102.4 (1982), pp. 591-603.

Watters, Thomas, *On Yuan Chwang's Travels in India*, London, 1904-5, 2nd Indian edn., Munshiram Manoharlal, Delhi, 1973.

Welch, Holmes, *The Practice of Chinese Buddhism*, Harvard University Press, 1967.

Whitehead, Henry, *The Village Gods of South India*, Association Press, Calcutta, 1921.

Wijesekera, N.D., *The People of Ceylon*, 2nd edn., M.D. Gunasena, Colombo, 1965.

Winternitz, Maurice, *A History of Indian Literature*, 2 vols., 2nd edn., rpt., Munshiram Manoharlal, Delhi, 1977.

Witzel, Michael, 'On the Sacredness of the Cow', unpublished manuscript, abbreviated version published as *Ushi.wo meguru Indojin no kagae* (in Japanese), The Association of Humanities and Sciences, Kobe Gakuin University, no. 1, 1991.

———, ed., *Inside the Texys Beyond the Texts*, Harvard Oriental Series, Opera Minora, 2, Cambridge, 1997.

Wood, Roy C., *The Sociology of the Meal*, Edinburgh University Press, 1995.

Wujastyk, Dominik, *The Roots of Ayurveda*, Penguin India, 1998.

Yadava, B.N.S., *Society and Culture in Northern India in the Twelfth Century*, Central Book Depot, Allahabad, 1973.

Yājñavalkyasmṛti, ed. with the *Mitākṣarā* commentary of Vijñāneśvara and Hindi tr. Ganga Sagar Rai, Chowkhamba Sanskrit Pratisthan, Delhi, 1998; ed. with the commentary *Bālakrīḍā* of Viśvarūpācārya, Mahamahopadhyaya T. Ganapati Sastri, 1st edn., Trivandrum, 1921-2, 2nd edn., Munshiram Manoharlal, Delhi, 1982; ed. with commentaries of Vijñāneśvara, Mitramiśra, and Śūlapāṇi, ed. J.R. Gharpure, 2 vols., The Collection of Hindu Law Texts, Bombay, 1936-43.

Yamasmṛti in *Aṣṭādaśasmṛtyaḥ* (Hindi tr. Sundarlal Tripathi, Khemraj Shrikrishnadas) Venkateshwar Steam Press, Bombay, Śaka 1846.

Yaśastilakacampū of Somadeva, ed. Sivadutt and Parab, Bombay, 1901-3.

Zend Avesta, Eng. tr. by James Darmesteter and L.H. Mills, 3 vols., SBE, Oxford, 1883-7.

Zimmermann, Francis, *The Jungle and the Aroma of Meats*, University of California Press, Berkeley, 1987.

Index

Untouchability, the Dead Cow and the Brahmin

B.R. Ambedkar[1]

Beef-eating as the root of untouchability

The Census Returns [of 1910] show that the meat of the dead cow forms the chief item of food consumed by communities which are generally classified as untouchable communities. No Hindu community, however low, will touch cow's flesh. On the other hand, there is no community which is really an Untouchable community which has not something to do with the dead cow. Some eat her flesh, some remove the skin, some manufacture articles out of her skin and bones.

---

[1] Excerpted from Chapters 10 to 14 of B.R. Ambedkar's 1948 work *The Untouchables: Who Were They and Why They Became Untouchables?* as reprinted in Volume 7 of *Dr. Babasaheb Ambedkar Writings and Speeches*, published by Government of Maharashtra, 1990. Major deletions of sentences and paragraphs are indicated with ellipses. Explanatory insertions appear in square parentheses. All footnotes are from the original text by Ambedkar unless otherwise indicated.—Publisher

From the survey of the Census Commissioner, it is well established that Untouchables eat beef. The question however is: Has beef-eating any relation to the origin of untouchability? Or is it merely an incident in the economic life of the Untouchables? Can we say that the Broken Men[2] came to be treated as Untouchables because they ate beef? There need be no hesitation in returning an affirmative answer to this question. No other answer is consistent with facts as we know them.

In the first place, we have the fact that the Untouchables, or the main communities which compose them, eat the dead cow and those who eat the dead cow are tainted with untouchability and no others. The corelation between untouchability and the use of the dead cow is so great and so close that the thesis that it is the root of untouchability seems to be incontrovertible. In the second place, if there is anything that separates the Untouchables from the Hindus, it is beef-eating. Even a superficial view of the food taboos of the Hindus will show that there are two taboos regarding food which serve as dividing lines. There is one taboo against meat-eating. It divides Hindus into vegetarians and flesh-eaters. There is another taboo which is against beef-eating. It divides Hindus into those who eat cow's flesh and those who do not. From the point of view of untouchability the first dividing line is of no importance. But the second is. For it completely marks off the Touchables from the Untouchables. The Touchables, whether they are vegetarians or flesh-eaters, are united in their objection to eating cow's flesh. As against them stand the Untouchables who eat cow's flesh without

---

[2] Earlier in the same text, Ambedkar proposes that owing to continuous tribal warfare in primitive society, some of the defeated weaker tribes that were "completely annihilated, defeated and routed" came to be regarded as "Broken Men". He argues that in "primitive Hindu society" too, there must have been Settled Tribes and Broken Men—the latter forced to live outside the village. Following the intense struggle between Buddhism and Brahmanism, the Buddhists who retained the practice of beef-eating became the Broken Men and came to be treated as Untouchables, says Ambedkar.—Publisher

compunction and as a matter of course and habit.[3]

In this context it is not far-fetched to suggest that those who have a nausea against beef-eating should treat those who eat beef as Untouchables.

There is really no necessity to enter upon any speculation as to whether beef-eating was or was not the principal reason for the rise of Untouchability. This new theory receives support from the Hindu Shastras. The Veda Vyas Smriti contains the following verse which specifies the communities which are included in the category of Antyajas and the reasons why they were so included.[4]

> L.12–13: The *Charmakars* (Cobbler), the *Bhatta* (Soldier), the *Bhilla*, the *Rajaka* (washerman), the *Puskara*, the *Nata* (actor), the *Vrata*, the *Meda*, the *Chandala*, the *Dasa*, the *Svapaka*, and the *Kolika*—these are known as Antyajas as well as others who eat cow's flesh.

Generally speaking, the Smritikars never care to explain the why and the how of their dogmas. But this case is an exception. For in this case, Veda Vyas does explain the cause of untouchability. The clause "as well as others who eat cow's flesh" is very important. It shows that the Smritikars knew that the origin of untouchability is to be found in the eating of beef. The dictum of Veda Vyas must close the argument. It comes, so to say, straight from the horse's mouth; and what is important is that it is also rational, for it accords with facts as we know them.

The new approach in the search for the origin of untouchability has brought to the surface two sources of the origin of untouchability. One is the general atmosphere of scorn and contempt spread by the Brahmins against those who were Buddhists, and the second is the habit of beef-eating kept on by the Broken Men. As has been said, the first circumstance could not be sufficient to account for stigma of untouchability attaching itself to the Broken Men. For the scorn and contempt for Buddhists spread by the Brahmins was too general and

[3] The Untouchables have felt the force of the accusation levelled against them by the Hindus for eating beef. Instead of giving up the habit the Untouchables have invented a philosophy which justifies eating the beef of the dead cow. The gist of the philosophy is that eating the flesh of the dead cow is a better way of showing respect to the cow than throwing her carcass to the wind.

[4] Quoted in Kane's *History of Dharma Shastra*, Vol. II, Part I, p. 71.

affected all Buddhists and not merely the Broken Men. The reason why Broken Men only became Untouchables was because in addition to being Buddhists they retained their habit of beef-eating which gave additional ground for offence to the Brahmins to carry their new-found love and reverence to the cow to its logical conclusion. We may therefore conclude that the Broken Men were exposed to scorn and contempt on the ground that they were Buddhists, and the main cause of their untouchability was beef-eating.

The theory of beef-eating as the cause of untouchability also gives rise to many questions. Critics are sure to ask: What is the cause of the nausea which the Hindus have against beef-eating? Were the Hindus always opposed to beef-eating? If not, why did they develop such a nausea against it? Were the Untouchables given to beef-eating from the very start? Why did they not give up beef-eating when it was abandoned by the Hindus? Were the Untouchables always Untouchables? If there was a time when the Untouchables were not Untouchables even though they ate beef why should beef-eating give rise to untouchability at a later stage? If the Hindus were eating beef, when did they give it up? If untouchability is a reflex of the nausea of the Hindus against beef-eating, how long after the Hindus had given up beef-eating did Untouchability come into being? ....

Did the Hindus never eat beef?

To the question whether the Hindus ever ate beef, every Touchable Hindu, whether he is a Brahmin or a non-Brahmin, will say 'no, never'. In a certain sense, he is right. From times no Hindu has eaten beef. If this is all that the Touchable Hindu wants to convey by his answer there need be no quarrel over it. But when the learned Brahmins argue that the Hindus not only never ate beef but they always held the cow to be sacred and were always opposed to the killing of the cow, it is impossible to accept their view....

That the Aryans of the Rig Veda did kill cows for

purposes of food and ate beef is abundantly clear from the Rig Veda itself. In Rig Veda (X. 86.14) Indra says: "They cook for one 15 plus twenty oxen." The Rig Veda (X. 91.14) says that for Agni were sacrificed horses, bulls, oxen, barren cows and rams. From the Rig Veda (X. 72.6) it appears that the cow was killed with a sword or an axe....

Among the Kamyashtis set forth in the Taittiriya Bramhana, not only is the sacrifice of oxen and cows laid down, we are even told what kind and description of oxen and cows are to be offered to what deities. Thus, a dwarf ox is to be chosen for sacrifice to Vishnu; a drooping horned bull with a blaze on the forehead to Indra as the destroyer of Vritra; a black cow to Pushan; a red cow to Rudra; and so on. The Taittiriya Brahmana notes another sacrifice called *Panchasaradiya-seva*, the most important element of which was the immolation of seventeen five-year old humpless, dwarf bulls, and as many dwarf heifers under three years old....

The killing of cow for the guest had grown to such an extent that the guest came to be called 'Go-ghna', which means the killer of the cow. To avoid this slaughter of the cows the Ashvalayana Grahya Sutra (I. 24.25) suggests that the cow should be let loose when the guest comes so as to escape the rule of etiquette....

Such is the state of the evidence on the subject of cow-killing and beef-eating. Which part of it is to be accepted as true? The correct view is that the testimonies of the Satapatha Brahmana and the Apastamba Dharma Sutra, in so far as they support the view that Hindus were against cow-killing and beef-eating, are merely exhortations against the excesses of cow-killing and not prohibitions against cow-killing. Indeed the exhortations prove that cow-killing and eating of beef had become a common practice. And that, notwithstanding these exhortations, cow-killing and beef-eating continued. That most often they fell on deaf ears is proved by the conduct of Yajnavalkya, the great Rishi of the Aryans... [who once] said:

"I, for one, eat it, provided that it is tender."

That the Hindus at one time did kill cows and did eat beef is proved abundantly by the description of the Yajnas given in the Buddhist Sutras which relate to periods much later than the Vedas and the Brahmanas. The scale on which the slaughter of cows and animals took place was colossal. It is not possible to give a total of such slaughter on all accounts committed by the Brahmins in the name of religion. Some idea of the extent of this slaughter can however be had from references to it in the Buddhist literature. As an illustration reference may be made to the Kutadanta Sutta in which Buddha preached against the performance of animal sacrifices to Brahmin Kutadanta. Buddha, though speaking in a tone of sarcastic travesty, gives a good idea of the practices and rituals of the Vedic sacrifices when he said:

> And further, O Brahmin, at that sacrifice neither were any oxen slain, neither goats, nor fowls, nor fatted pigs, nor were any kind of living creatures put to death. No trees were cut down to be used as posts, no Darbha grasses mown to stress around the sacrificial spot. And the slaves and messengers and workmen there employed were driven neither by rods nor fear, nor carried on their work weeping with tears upon their faces.

Kutadanta, on the other hand, in thanking Buddha for his conversion gives an idea of the magnitude of the slaughter of animals which took place at such sacrifices when he says:

> I, even I betake myself to the venerable Gotama as my guide, to the Doctrine and the Order. May the Venerable One accept me as a disciple, as one who, from this day forth, as long as life endures, has taken him as his guide. And I myself, O, Gotama, will have the seven hundred bulls, and the seven hundred steers, and the seven hundred heifers, and the seven hundred goats, and the seven hundred rams set free. To them I grant their life. Let them eat grass and drink fresh water and may cool breezes waft around them.

In the Samyuta Nikaya (III, 1–9) we have another description of a Yajna performed by Pasenadi, king of Kosala. It is said that five hundred bulls, five hundred calves and many heifers, goats and rams were led to the pillar to be sacrificed.

With this evidence no one can doubt that there was a time when Hindus – both Brahmins and non-Brahmins – ate not only flesh but also beef.

Why did non-Brahmins give up beef-eating?

The food habits of the different classes of Hindus have been as fixed and stratified as their cults. Just as Hindus can be classified on their basis of their cults so also they can be classified on the basis of their habits of food. On the basis of their cults, Hindus are either Saivites (followers of Siva) or Vaishnavites (followers of Vishnu). Similarly, Hindus are either *Mansahari* (those who eat flesh) or *Shakahari* (those who are vegetarians).

For ordinary purposes the division of Hindus into two classes *Mansahari* and *Shakahari* may be enough. But it must be admitted that it is not exhaustive and does not take account of all the classes which exist in Hindu society. For an exhaustive classification, the class of Hindus called *Mansahari* shall have to be further divided into two sub-classes: (i) Those who eat flesh but do not eat cow's flesh; and (ii) Those who eat flesh including cow's flesh. In other words, on the basis of food taboos, Hindu society falls into three classes: (i) Those who are vegetarians; (ii) Those who eat flesh but do not eat cow's flesh; and (iii) Those who eat flesh including cow's flesh. Corresponding to this classification, we have in Hindu society three classes: (1) Brahmins; (2) Non-Brahmins; and (3) Untouchables. This division, though not in accord with the fourfold division of society called Chaturvarna, is yet in accord with facts as they exist. For, in the Brahmins[5] we have a class which is vegetarian, in the non-Brahmins the class which eats flesh but does not eat

---

[5] The Brahmins of India fall into two divisions (1) Pancha Dravid and (2) Pancha Gauda. The former are vegetarians, the latter are not.

cow's flesh, and in the Untouchables a class which eats flesh including cow's flesh....

Anyone who stops to turn over this classification in his mind is bound to be struck by the position of the non-Brahmins. One can quite understand vegetarianism. One can quite understand meat-eating. But it is difficult to understand why a person who is a flesh-eater should object to one kind of flesh, namely cow's flesh. This is an anomaly which calls for an explanation. Why did the non-Brahmin give up beef-eating? For this purpose it is necessary to examine laws on the subject. The relevant legislation must be found either in the Law of Asoka or the Law of Manu....

Examining the legislation [Edicts] of Asoka the question is: Did he prohibit the killing of the cow? On this issue there seem to be a difference of opinion. Prof. Vincent Smith is of the opinion that Asoka did not prohibit the killing of the cow. Commenting on the legislation of Asoka on the subject, Prof. Smith says: "It is noteworthy that Asoka's rules do not forbid the slaughter of cow, which, apparently, continued to be lawful."[6]

Prof. Radhakumud Mookerji joins issue with Prof. Smith and says[7] that Asoka did prohibit the slaughter of the cow. Prof. Mookerji relies upon the reference in Pillar Edict V to the rule of exemption which was made applicable to all four-footed animals and argues that under this rule cow was exempted from killing. This is not a correct reading of the statement in the Edict. The statement in the Edict is a qualified statement. It does not refer to all four-footed animals but only to four-footed animals which are not utilised or eaten. A cow cannot be said to be a four-footed animal which was not utilised or eaten. Prof. Vincent Smith seems to be correct in saying that Asoka did not prohibit the slaughter of the cow. Prof. Mookerji tries to get out of the difficulty by saying that at the time of Asoka the cow

---

[6] Smith, *Asoka*, p. 58.

[7] Mookerji, *Asoka*, pp. 21, 181, 184.

was not eaten and therefore came within the prohibition. His statement is simply absurd for the cow was an animal which was very much eaten by all classes.

It is quite unnecessary to resort, as does Prof. Mookerji, to a forced construction of the Edict and to make Asoka prohibit the slaughter of the cow as though it was his duty to do so. Asoka had no particular interest in the cow and owed no special duty to protect her against killing. Asoka was interested in the sanctity of all life—human as well as animal. He felt his duty to prohibit the taking of life where taking of life was not necessary. That is why he prohibited slaughtering animals for sacrifice[8] which he regarded as unnecessary and of animals which are not utilised nor eaten which again would be wanton and unnecessary. That he did not prohibit the slaughter of the cow in specie may well be taken as a fact, which for having regard to the Buddhist attitude in the matter, cannot be used against Asoka as a ground for casting blame.

Coming to Manu there is no doubt that he too did not prohibit the slaughter of the cow. On the other hand he made the eating of cow's flesh on certain occasions obligatory.

Why then did the non-Brahmins give up eating beef? There appears to be no apparent reason for this departure on their part. But there must be some reason behind it. The reason I like to suggest is that it was due to their desire to imitate the Brahmins that the non-Brahmins gave up beef-eating. This may be a novel theory but it is not an impossible theory. As the French author Gabriel Tarde has explained, culture within a society spreads by imitation of the ways and manners of the superior classes by the inferior classes. This imitation is so regular in its flow that its working is as mechanical as the working of a natural law. Gabriel Tarde speaks of the laws of imitation. One of these laws is that the lower classes always imitate the higher classes. This is a matter of such common knowledge that hardly any individual can be found to question its validity.

---

[8] See Rock Edict No. 1.

That the spread of cow-worship among and cessation of beef-eating by the non-Brahmins has taken place by reason of the habit of the non-Brahmins to imitate the Brahmins who were undoubtedly their superiors is beyond dispute. Of course there was an extensive propaganda in favour of cow-worship by the Brahmins. The Gayatri Purana is a piece of this propaganda. But initially it is the result of the natural law of imitation. This, of course, raises another question: Why did the Brahmins give up beef-eating?

What made the Brahmins become vegetarians?

The non-Brahmins have evidently undergone a revolution. From being beef-eaters to have become non-beef-eaters was indeed a revolution. But if the non-Brahmins underwent one revolution, the Brahmins had undergone two. They gave up beef-eating which was one revolution. To have given up meat-eating altogether and become vegetarians was another revolution.

That this was a revolution is beyond question. For... there was a time when the Brahmins were the greatest beef-eaters. Although the non-Brahmins did eat beef they could not have had it every day. The cow was a costly animal and the non-Brahmin could ill afford to slaughter it just for food. He only did it on special occasion when his religious duty or personal interest to propitiate a deity compelled him to do. But the case with the Brahmin was different. He was a priest. In a period overridden by ritualism there was hardly a day on which there was no cow sacrifice to which the Brahmin was not invited by some non-Brahmin. For the Brahmin every day was a beef-steak day. The Brahmins were therefore the greatest beef-eaters. The Yajna of the Brahmins was nothing but the killing of innocent animals carried on in the name of religion with pomp and ceremony with an attempt to enshroud it in mystery with a view to conceal their appetite for beef. Some idea of this mystery pomp and ceremony can be had from the directions contained in the Atreya Brahmana touching on the killing of animals in a Yajna.

The actual killing of the animal is preceded by certain initiatory rites accompanied by incantations too long and too many to be detailed here. It is enough to give an idea of the main features of the sacrifice. The sacrifice commences with the erection of the sacrificial post called the Yupa to which the animal is tied before it is slaughtered. After setting out why the Yupa is necessary the Atreya Brahmana proceeds to state what it stands for. It says:[9]

> This Yupa is a weapon. Its point must have eight edges. For a weapon (or iron club) has eight edges. Whenever he strikes with it an enemy or adversary, he kills him. (This weapon serves) to put down him (every one) who is to be put down by him (the sacrificer). The Yupa is a weapon which stands erected (being ready) to slay an enemy. Thence an enemy (of the sacrificer) who might be present (at the sacrifice) comes of all ill after having seen the Yupa of such or such one.

The selection of the wood to be used for the Yupa is made to vary with the purposes which the sacrificer wishes to achieve by the sacrifice. The Atreya Brahmana says:

> He who desires heaven, ought to make his Yupa of Khadira wood. For the gods conquered the celestial world by means of a Yupa, made of Khadira wood. In the same way the sacrificer conquers the celestial world by means of a Yupa, made of Khadira wood.
>
> He who desires food and wishes to grow fat ought to make his Yupa of Bilva wood. For the Bilva tree bears fruits every year; it is the symbol of fertility; for it increases (every year) in size from the roots up to the branches, therefore it is a symbol of fatness. He who having such a knowledge makes his Yupa of Bilva wood, makes fat his children and cattle....
>
> He who desires beauty and sacred knowledge ought to make his Yupa of Palasa wood. For the Palasa is among the trees of beauty and sacred knowledge.... the Palasa is the womb of all trees....

This is followed by the ceremony of anointing the sacrificial

[9] Atreya Brahmana (Martin Haug) II, pp. 72–74.

post.[10] .... Then comes the ceremony of actually killing the animal. The Atreya Brahmana gives the details of the mode and manner of killing the animal. Its directions are:[11]

> Turn its feet northwards! Make its eye to go to the sun, dismiss its breath to the wind, its life to the air, its hearing to the directions, its body to the earth. In this way he (the Hotar [chief priest]) places it (connects it) with these worlds.
>
> Take off the skin entire (without cutting it). Before operating the naval, tear out omentum. Stop its breathing within (by stopping its mouth). Thus he (the Hotar) puts its breath in the animals.
>
> Make of its breast a piece like an eagle, of its arms (two pieces like) two hatchets, of its forearms (two pieces like) two spikes, of its shoulders (two pieces like) two Kashyapas, its loins should be unbroken (entire); (make of) its thighs (two pieces like) two shields, of the two kneepans (two pieces like) two oleander leaves; take out its twentysix ribs according to their order; preserve every limb of it in its integrity. Thus he benefits all its limbs....

Given these facts, no further evidence seems to be necessary to support the statement that the Brahmins were not merely beef-eaters but they were also butchers. Why then did the Brahmins change front? Let us deal with their change of front in two stages. First, why did they give up beef-eating?

As has already been shown cow-killing was not legally prohibited by Asoka. Even if it had been prohibited, a law made by the Buddhist Emperor could never have been accepted by the Brahmins as binding upon them.

Did Manu prohibit beef-eating? If he did, then that would be binding on the Brahmins and would afford an adequate explanation of their change of front. Looking into the Manu Smriti one does find the following verses:

> V. 46. He who does not seek to cause the sufferings of bonds and death to living creatures, (but) desires the good of all (beings), obtains endless bliss.

---

[10] *Atreya Brahmana* (Martin Haug) II, pp. 74–78.

[11] *Atreya Brahmana* (Martin Haug) II, pp. 86–87.

> V. 47. He who does not injure any (creature), attains without an effort what he thinks of, what he undertakes, and what he fixes his mind on.
> V. 48. Meat can never be obtained without injury to living creatures, and injury to sentient beings is detrimental to (the attainment of) heavenly bliss; let him therefore shun (the use of) meat.
> V. 49. Having well considered the (disgusting) origin of flesh and the (cruelty of) fettering and slaying corporeal beings, let him entirely abstain from eating flesh.

If these verses can be treated as containing positive injunctions they would be sufficient to explain why the Brahmins gave up meat-eating and became vegetarians. But it is impossible to treat these verses as positive injunctions, carrying the force of law. They are either exhortations or interpolations introduced after the Brahmins had become vegetarians in praise of the change....

That Manu did not prohibit meat-eating is evident enough. That Manu Smriti did not prohibit cow-killing can also be proved from the Smriti itself. In the first place, the only references to cow in the Manu Smriti are to be found in the catalogue of rules which are made applicable by Manu to the Snataka [brahmin student-scholar]. They are set out below:

> 1. A Snataka should not eat food which a cow has smelt.[12]
> 2. A Snataka should not step over a rope to which a calf is tied.[13]
> 3. A Snataka should not urinate in a cowpan.[14]
> 4. A Snataka should not answer call of nature facing a cow.[15]
> 5. A Snataka should not keep his right arm uncovered when he enters a cowpan.[16]
> 6. A Snataka should not interrupt a cow which is sucking her calf, nor tell anybody of it.[17]

---

[12] Manu, 209.

[13] Ibid., 38.

[14] Ibid., 45.

[15] Ibid., 48.

[16] Ibid., 58.

[17] Ibid., 59.

7. A Snataka should not ride on the back of the cow.[18]

8. A Snataka should not offend the cow.[19]

9. A Snataka who is impure must not touch a cow with his hand.[20]

From these references it will be seen that Manu did not regard the cow as a sacred animal. On the other hand, he regarded it as an impure animal whose touch caused ceremonial pollution.

There are verses in Manu which show that he did not prohibit the eating of beef. In this connection, reference may be made to Chapter III. 3. It says: "He (Snataka) who is famous (for the strict performance of) his duties and has received his heritage, the Veda from his father, shall be honoured, sitting on couch and adorned with a garland with the present of a cow (the honey-mixture)." ....

[A]ccording to Manu cow-killing was only a minor sin. It was reprehensible only if the cow was killed without good and sufficient reason. Even if it was otherwise, it was not heinous or inexplicable. The same was the attitude of Yajnavalkya.[21]

All this proves that for generations the Brahmins had been eating beef. Why did they give up beef-eating? Why did they, as an extreme step, give up meat-eating altogether and become vegetarians? It is two revolutions rolled into one. As has been shown, it has not been done as a result of the preachings of Manu, their Divine Law-maker. The revolution has taken place in spite of Manu and contrary to his directions. What made the Brahmins take this step? Was philosophy responsible for it? Or was it dictated by strategy?

Two explanations are offered. One explanation is that this deification of the cow was a manifestation of the Advaita philosophy that one supreme entity pervaded the whole universe, that on that account all life human as well as animal was sacred.

---

[18] Ibid., 70.

[19] Ibid., 162.

[20] Ibid., 142.

[21] Yaj. III. 227 and III. 234.

This explanation is obviously unsatisfactory. In the first place, it does not fit in with facts. The Vedanta Sutra which proclaims the doctrine of oneness of life does not prohibit the killing of animals for sacrificial purposes as is evident from II.1.28. In the second place, if the transformation was due to the desire to realise the ideal of Advaita then there is no reason why it should have stopped with the cow. It should have extended to all other animals.

Another explanation,[22] more ingenious than the first, is that this transformation in the life of the Brahmin was due to the rise of the doctrine of the Transmigration of the Soul. Even this explanation does not fit in with facts. The Brahadamyaka Upanishad upholds the doctrine of transmigration (vi.2) and yet recommends that if a man desires to have a learned son born to him he should prepare a mass of the flesh of the bull or ox or of other flesh with rice and ghee. Again, how is it that this doctrine which is propounded in the Upanishads did not have any effect on the Brahmins up to the time of the Manu Smriti, a period of at least 400 years. Obviously, this explanation is no explanation. Thirdly, if Brahmins became vegetarians by reason of the doctrine of Transmigration of the Soul how is it, it did not make the non-Brahmins take to vegetarianism?

To my mind, it was strategy which made the Brahmins give up beef-eating and start worshipping the cow. The clue to the worship of the cow is to be found in the struggle between Buddhism and Brahmanism and the means adopted by Brahmanism to establish its supremacy over Buddhism. The strife between Buddhism and Brahmanism is a crucial fact in Indian history. Without the realisation of this fact, it is impossible to explain some of the features of Hinduism. Unfortunately students of Indian history have entirely missed the importance of this strife. They knew there was Brahmanism. But they seem to be entirely unaware of the struggle for supremacy in which these creeds were engaged and that their struggle, which

---

[22] Kane's *Dharma Shastra* II, Part II. p. 776.

extended for 400 years has left some indelible marks on religion, society and politics of India.

This is not the place for describing the full story of the struggle. All one can do is to mention a few salient points. Buddhism was at one time the religion of the majority of the people of India. It continued to be the religion of the masses for hundreds of years. It attacked Brahmanism on all sides as no religion had done before.

Brahmanism was on the wane and if not on the wane, it was certainly on the defensive. As a result of the spread of Buddhism, the Brahmins had lost all power and prestige at the Royal Court and among the people. They were smarting under the defeat they had suffered at the hands of Buddhism and were making all possible efforts to regain their power and prestige. Buddhism had made so deep an impression on the minds of the masses and had taken such a hold of them that it was absolutely impossible for the Brahmins to fight the Buddhists except by accepting their ways and means and practising the Buddhist creed in its extreme form. After the death of Buddha his followers started setting up the images of the Buddha and building stupas. The Brahmins followed it. They, in their turn, built temples and installed in them images of Shiva, Vishnu and Ram and Krishna etc—all with the object of drawing away the crowd that was attracted by the image worship of Buddha. That is how temples and images which had no place in Brahmanism came into Hinduism. The Buddhists rejected the Brahmanic religion which consisted of Yajna and animal sacrifice, particularly of the cow. The objection to the sacrifice of the cow had taken a strong hold of the minds of the masses especially as they were an agricultural population and the cow was a very useful animal. The Brahmins in all probability had come to be hated as the killer of cows in the same way as the guest had come to be hated as Gognha, the killer of the cow by the householder, because whenever he came a cow had to be killed in his honour. That being the case, the Brahmins could do nothing to improve their position against the Buddhists except by giving up the Yajna as a form of worship and the sacrifice of the cow.

That the object of the Brahmins in giving up beef-eating was to snatch away from the Buddhist Bhikshus the supremacy they had acquired is evidenced by the adoption of vegetarianism by Brahmins. Why did the Brahmins become vegetarian? The answer is that without becoming vegetarian the Brahmins could not have recovered the ground they had lost to their rival, namely Buddhism. In this connection it must be remembered that there was one aspect in which Brahmanism suffered in public esteem as compared to Buddhism. That was the practice of animal sacrifice which was the essence of Brahmanism and to which Buddhism was deadly opposed. That in an agricultural population there should be respect for Buddhism and revulsion against Brahmanism which involved slaughter of animals including cows and bullocks is only natural. What could the Brahmins do to recover the lost ground? To go one better than the Buddhist Bhikshus not only to give up meat-eating but to become vegetarians—which they did. That this was the object of the Brahmins in becoming vegetarians can be proved in various ways.

If the Brahmins had acted from conviction that animal sacrifice was bad, all that was necessary for them to do was to give up killing animals for sacrifice. It was unnecessary for them to be vegetarians. That they did go in for vegetarianism makes it obvious that their motive was far-reaching. Secondly, it was unnecessary for them to become vegetarians. For the Buddhist Bhikshus were not vegetarians. This statement might surprise many people owing to the popular belief that the connection between Ahimsa and Buddhism was immediate and essential. It is generally believed that the Buddhist Bhikshus eschewed animal food. This is an error. The fact is that the Buddhist Bhikshus were permitted to eat three kinds of flesh that were deemed pure. Later on they were extended to five classes.

Yuan Chwang, the Chinese traveller was aware of this and spoke of the pure kinds of flesh as San-Ching. The origin of this practice among the Bhikshus is explained by Mr. Thomas Walters. According to the story told by him:[23]

> In the time of Buddha there was in Vaisali a wealthy general named Siha who was a convert to Buddhism. He became a liberal supporter of the Brethren and kept them constantly supplied with good flesh-food. When it was noticed abroad that the Bhikshus were in the habit of eating such food specially provided for them, the Tirthikas made the practice a matter of angry reproach. Then the abstemious ascetic Brethren, learning this, reported the circumstances to the Master, who thereupon called the Brethren together. When they assembled, he announced to them the law that they were not to eat the flesh of any animal which they had seen put to death for them, or about which they had been told that it had been slain for them. But he permitted to the Brethren as 'pure' (that is, lawful) food the flesh of animals the slaughter of which had not been seen by the Bhikshus, not heard of by them, and not suspected by them to have been on their account. In the Pali and *Ssu-fen* Vinaya it was after a breakfast given by Siha to the Buddha and some of the Brethren, for which the carcass of a large ox was procured, that the Nirgranthas reviled the Bhikshus and Buddha instituted this new rule declaring fish and flesh 'pure' in the three conditions. The animal food now permitted to the Bhikshus came to be known as the 'three pures' or 'three pure kinds of flesh', and it was tersely described as 'unseen, unheard, unsuspected', or as the Chinese translations sometimes have it 'not seen, not heard nor suspected to be on my account'. Then two more kinds of animal food were declared 'lawful for the Brethren' viz., the flesh of animals which had died a natural death, and that of animals which had been killed by a bird of prey or other savage creature. So there came to be five classes or descriptions of flesh which the professed Buddhist was at liberty to use as food. Then the 'unseen, unheard, unsuspected' came to be treated as one class, and this together with the 'natural death' and 'bird killed' made a *san-ching*.

As the Buddhist Bhikshus did eat meat the Brahmins had no reason to give it up. Why then did the Brahmins give up

---

[23] Yuan Chwang (1904) Vol. 1. p. 55.

meat-eating and become vegetarians? It was because they did not want to put themselves merely on the same footing in the eyes of the public as the Buddhist Bhikshus.

The giving up of the Yajna system and abandonment of the sacrifice of the cow could have had only a limited effect. At the most it would have put the Brahmins on the same footing as the Buddhists. The same would have been the case if they had followed the rules observed by the Buddhist Bhikshus in the matter of meat-eating. It could not have given the Brahmins the means of achieving supremacy over the Buddhists which was their ambition. They wanted to oust the Buddhists from the place of honour and respect which they had acquired in the minds of the masses by their opposition to the killing of the cow for sacrificial purposes. To achieve their purpose the Brahmins had to adopt the usual tactics of a reckless adventurer. It is to beat extremism with extremism. It is the strategy which all rightists use to overcome the leftists. The only way to beat the Buddhists was to go a step further and be vegetarians.

There is another reason which can be relied upon to support the thesis that the Brahmins started cow-worship, gave up beef-eating and became vegetarians in order to vanquish Buddhism. It is the date when cow-killing became a mortal sin. It is well-known that cow-killing was not made an offence by Asoka. Many people expect him to have come forward to prohibit the killing of the cow. Prof. Vincent Smith regards it as surprising. But there is nothing surprising in it.

Buddhism was against animal sacrifice in general. It had no particular affection for the cow. Asoka had therefore no particular reason to make a law to save the cow. What is more astonishing is the fact that cow-killing was made a *Mahapataka*, a mortal sin or a capital offence by the Gupta Kings who were champions of Hinduism which recognised and sanctioned the killing of the cow for sacrificial purposes. As pointed out by Mr. D. R. Bhandarkar:[24]

---

[24] *Some Aspects of Ancient Indian Culture*, (1940), pp. 78–79.

We have got the incontrovertible evidence of inscriptions to show that early in the 5th century A. D. killing a cow was looked upon as an offence of the deepest turpitude, turpitude as deep as that involved in murdering a Brahman. We have thus a copper-plate inscription dated 465 A.D. and referring itself to the reign of Skandagupta of the Imperial Gupta dynasty. It registers a grant and ends with a verse saying : 'Whosoever will transgress this grant that has been assigned (shall become as guilty as) the slayer of a cow, the slayer of a spiritual preceptor (or) the slayer of a Brahman. A still earlier record placing *go-hatya* on the same footing as *brahma-hatya* is that of Chandragupta II, grandfather of Skandagupta just mentioned. It bears the Gupta date 93, which is equivalent to 412 A.D. It is engraved on the railing which surrounds the celebrated Buddhist stupa at Sanchi, in Central India. This also speaks of a benefaction made by an officer of Chandragupta and ends as follows: "Whosoever shall interfere with this arrangement ... he shall become invested with (the guilt of) the slaughter of a cow or of a Brahman, and with (the guilt of) the five *anantarya*." Here the object of this statement is to threaten the resumer of the grant, be he a Brahminist or a Buddhist, with the sins regarded as mortal by each community. The *anantaryas* are the five *mahapatakas* according to Buddhist theology. They are: matricide, patricide, killing an Arhat, shedding the blood of a Buddha, and causing a split among the priesthood. The *mahapatakas* with which a Brahminist is here threatened are only two: viz., the killing of a cow and the murdering of a Brahman. The latter is obviously a *mahapataka* as it is mentioned as such in all the Smritis, but the former has been specified only an *upapataka* by Apastamba, Manu, Yajnavalkya and so forth. But the very fact that it is here associated with *brahma-hatya* and both have been put on a par with the anantaryas of the Buddhists shows that in the beginning of the fifth century A.D., it was raised to the category of *mahapatakas*. Thus go-hatya must have come to be considered a *mahapataka* at least one century earlier, i.e., about the commencement of the fourth century A.D.

The question is why should a Hindu king have come forward to make a law against cow-killing, that is to say, against the Laws of Manu? The answer is that the Brahmins had to suspend or abrogate a requirement of their Vedic religion in order to overcome the supremacy of the Buddhist Bhikshus.

If the analysis is correct then it is obvious that the worship of the cow is the result of the struggle between Buddhism and Brahmanism. It was a means adopted by the Brahmins to regain their lost position.

Why should beef-eating make Broken Men Untouchables?

The stoppage of beef-eating by the Brahmins and the non-Brahmins and the continued use thereof by the Broken Men had produced a situation which was different from the old. This difference lay in the fact that while in the old situation everybody ate beef, in the new situation one section did not and another did. The difference was a glaring difference. Everybody could see it. It divided society as nothing else did before. All the same, this difference need not have given rise to such extreme division of society as is marked by untouchability. It could have remained a social difference. There are many cases where different sections of the community differ in their foods. What one likes the other dislikes and yet this difference does not create a bar between the two.

There must therefore be some special reason why in India the difference between the Settled Community and the Broken Men in the matter of beef-eating created a bar between the two. What can that be? The answer is that if beef-eating had remained a secular affair – a mere matter of individual taste – such a bar between those who ate beef and those who did not would not have arisen. Unfortunately beef-eating, instead of being treated as a purely secular matter, was made a matter of religion. This happened because the Brahmins made the cow a sacred animal. This made beef-eating a sacrilege. The Broken Men being guilty of sacrilege necessarily became beyond the pale of society....

Once the cow became sacred and the Broken Men continued to eat beef, there was no other fate left for the Broken Men except to be treated unfit for association, i.e., as Untouchables.

Before closing the subject it may be desirable to dispose of possible objections to the thesis. Two such objections to the thesis appear obvious. One is what evidence is there that the Broken Men did eat the flesh of the dead cow. The second is why did they not give up beef-eating when the Brahmins and the non-Brahmins abandoned it. These questions have an important bearing upon the theory of the origin of untouchability advanced here and must therefore be dealt with.

The first question is relevant as well as crucial. If the Broken Men were eating beef from the very beginning, then obviously the theory cannot stand. For, if they were eating beef from the very beginning and nonetheless were not treated as Untouchables, to say that the Broken Men became Untouchables because of beef-eating would be illogical if not senseless. The second question is relevant, if not crucial. If the Brahmins gave up beef-eating and the non-Brahmins imitated them why did the Broken Men not do the same? If the law made the killing of the cow a capital sin because the cow became a sacred animal to the Brahmins and non-Brahmins, why were the Broken Men not stopped from eating beef? If they had been stopped from eating beef there would have been no untouchability.

The answer to the first question is that even during the period when beef-eating was common to both, the Settled Tribesmen and the Broken Men, a system had grown up whereby the Settled Community ate fresh beef, while the Broken Men ate the flesh of the dead cow. We have no positive evidence to show that members of the Settled Community never ate the flesh of the dead cow. But we have negative evidence which shows that the dead cow had become an exclusive possession and perquisite of the Broken Men. The evidence consists of facts which relate to the Mahars of the Maharashtra.... the Mahars of the Maharashtra claim the right to take the dead animal. This right they claim against every Hindu in the village. This means that no Hindu can eat the flesh of his own animal when it dies. He has to surrender it to the Mahar. This is merely another way of stating that when eating beef was a common practice the Mahars ate dead beef and the Hindus ate fresh beef. The only questions that arise are: Whether what is true of the present is true of the ancient past? Can this fact which is true of the Maharashtra be taken as typical of the arrangement between the Settled Tribes and the Broken Men throughout India.

In this connection reference may be made to the tradition current among the Mahars according to which they claim that they were given 52 rights against the Hindu villagers by the Muslim King of Bedar. Assuming that they were given by the King of Bedar, the King obviously did not create them for the first time. They must have been in existence from the ancient past. What the King did was merely to confirm them. This means that the practice of the Broken Men eating dead meat and the Settled Tribes eating fresh meat must have grown in the ancient past. That such an arrangement should grow up is certainly most natural. The Settled Community was a wealthy community with agriculture and cattle as means of livelihood. The Broken Men were a community of paupers with no means of livelihood and entirely dependent upon the Settled Community. The principal item of food for both was beef. It was possible for the Settled Community to kill an animal for food because it was possessed of cattle. The Broken Men could not for they had none. Would it be unnatural in these circumstances for the Settled Community to have agreed to give to the Broken Men its dead animals as part of their wages of watch and ward? Surely not. It can therefore be taken for granted that in the ancient past when both the Settled Community and Broken Men did eat beef the former ate fresh beef and the latter of the dead cow and that this system represented a universal state of affairs throughout India and was not confined to the Maharashtra alone.

This disposes of the first objection. To turn to the second objection. The law made by the Gupta Emperors was intended to prevent those who killed cows. It did not apply to the Broken Men. For they did not kill the cow. They only ate the dead cow. Their conduct did not contravene the law against cow-killing. The practice of eating the flesh of the dead cow therefore was allowed to continue. Nor did their conduct contravene the doctrine of Ahimsa assuming that it has anything to do with the abandonment of beef-eating by the Brahmins and the non-Brahmins. Killing the cow was Himsa. But eating the dead cow was not. The Broken Men had therefore no cause for feeling qualms of conscience in continuing to eat the dead cow. Neither the law nor the doctrine of Himsa could interdict what they were doing, for what they were doing was neither contrary to law nor to the doctrine.

As to why they did not imitate the Brahmins and the non-Brahmins the answer is two-fold. In the first place, imitation was too costly. They could not afford it. The flesh of the dead cow was their principal sustenance. Without it they would starve. In the second place, carrying the dead cow had become an obligation though originally it was a privilege. As they could not escape carrying the dead cow they did not mind using the flesh as food in the manner in which they were doing previously.

The objections therefore do not invalidate the thesis in any way.